THE GHOST
WHO WANTED REVENGE

HAUNTING DANIELLE

THE GHOST
WHO WANTED REVENGE

BOBBI HOLMES

The Ghost Who Wanted Revenge
(Haunting Danielle, Book 4)
A Novel
By Bobbi Holmes
Cover Design: Elizabeth Mackey

ISBN 978-1-949977-03-5

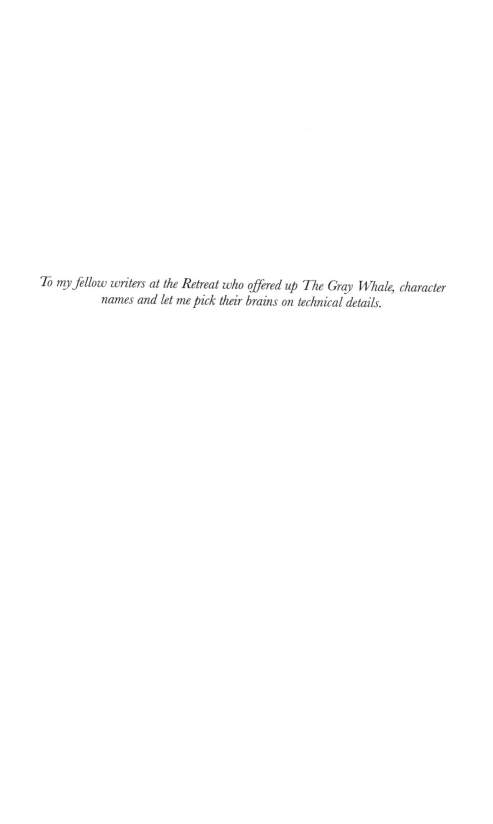

To my fellow writers at the Retreat who offered up The Gray Whale, *character names and let me pick their brains on technical details.*

ONE

Clasping his right hand over the bullet hole in his gut, Stoddard Gusarov couldn't stop the blood. It oozed out, slipping between his fingers, soaking the white living room carpet in a warm puddle of red.

It hadn't hurt when she first shot him. If asked, he would explain he was stunned, surprised to find her in his house, aiming a .38 in his direction. The first shot sounded like a car backfiring, and for an instant he thought the blast had come from outside. But then he looked down and saw the blood spilling from his belly.

He felt the second shot. That one hit his right knee and sent him tumbling to the floor. Helpless, he looked up. Unable to suppress his plea, he moaned, "Help me..."

She stood over him. "There's no way I'm going to let your high-priced attorney get you off. You're going to pay for what you did to my friend." Her pistol-wielding hand trembled.

"Please...help me..." Overwhelmed with pain, he felt the room spin. His vision blurry, he watched as her gloved hand slipped the pistol into the red purse hanging from her shoulder. When he and Darlene had seen her getting into her new car in the grocery store parking lot, Danielle had been carrying that same handbag. At the time, his wife had suggested to Stoddard that Danielle had probably bought the ugly red purse to match her car.

"I understand this is a slow and painful way to die." She tucked her braid up into the baseball cap atop her head.

"I never hurt your friend…" he managed to say.

"You didn't? You kidnapped her. Tattooed her arm, tried to frame me for your niece's murder, when you knew I had nothing to do with her death. Don't play innocent. You were going to kill Lily when she regained consciousness. Don't lie to me."

"Please…" Reaching out to her with one hand, he looked up pleadingly into her dark eyes. "You can't just leave me to die."

She patted her purse and said, "I could just finish you off. But what fun would that be?"

Stoddard watched as she walked across the room and picked his cellphone up from the coffee table. Going to the far side of the room, she set the cellphone atop the fireplace mantel. Even if he managed to crawl to that end of the room, there was no way he could stand up and retrieve his phone to call for help.

"Do you have a landline?" she asked, glancing around the room. He did, but there wasn't a telephone in the living room.

"No," he lied. There was no way he could reach the cellphone, but if he could manage to crawl to the other room, he might be able to get to the telephone there and call 911.

Now standing over him, she said, "Don't worry, you won't be alone for long. Your wife will be joining you shortly."

"No!" he groaned. Hit by a wave of nausea, he closed his eyes and pulled himself into a fetal position. Searing pain shot through his injured knee. Crying out in misery, he opened his eyes in time to see his attacker slip out the front door, closing it behind her. He was alone.

Licking his parched lips, his eyes watering, he looked around the room in a panic. He was going to die, alone and bloodied on his living room floor. But he couldn't die now; he had to protect Darlene. She was carrying his child. He'd waited so long to have a son—it had to be a son.

Taking a deep breath, he fought against the pain and stubbornly forced his body to crawl—inch by excruciating inch—from the living room toward the hallway leading to the study and the closest telephone.

Random images flashed through his head in rapid succession. There was his niece dead on her sofa. Calling Christiansen in a panic over Isabella's untimely death. Isabella being carried from her home in the middle of the night to be taken to the cemetery and hidden in the Marlow Crypt. Lily Miller comatose in the upstairs bedroom as the tattoo artist worked on her arm. Darlene telling him of the baby—the baby he had long been waiting for. He had to protect Darlene. He had to protect his child. If he'd only known Isabella had changed her will, none of this would be happening now.

Pain ripped through his right leg. Gasping for air, he grabbed his thigh and squeezed tightly. The fabric was wet. Looking down, he expected to find his pant leg covered in blood, yet there was no blood on his thigh. His crotch was soaked, as was the portion of pant leg above the knee. He'd wet himself.

Refusing to die in such a humiliating fashion and determined to save his wife, Stoddard dragged himself over the carpet, leaving behind a trail of blood. He made it to the entry hall when he heard what sounded like a disposal truck compacting garbage. It was trash day. If he could only make it to the door, maybe he could open it and get help from the garbage collector. Reaching for the door, he lost consciousness.

DARLENE GUSAROV once dreamed of becoming an actress. In high school, she was a member of the drama club, regularly landing the starring role in school performances. During her senior year in high school, someone told her that if she bleached and cut her hair, she could pass as Marilyn Monroe. Like Marilyn, she had blue eyes and was of a similar height and body type.

Darlene promptly made an appointment with the local beauty shop and transformed herself from a slightly overweight brunette into a curvy blonde partial to snug-fitting clothing and spiky high-heeled shoes. The new look garnered her more attention from the boys and her drama coach. After high school, she landed roles in community theater, yet found it impossible to secure a paying acting job.

Darlene met Stoddard Gusarov on her twenty-first birthday. She was visiting a friend in Portland, who had taken her to a local strip club to celebrate. At the time, Darlene was shocked to discover how many strip clubs were in the Portland area and almost refused to go when her friend made the suggestion. But after a couple shots of tequila at another bar, it started to seem like a good idea.

Stoddard had come to the club looking for a diversion from his failing marriage. He was much older than the men Darlene typically dated, but he obviously had money, and she was tired of waitressing while waiting for her elusive acting break. The fact that he was already married was a minor obstacle. She didn't intend to remain his mistress indefinitely. Within a year, she became the third Mrs. Gusarov.

Everything seemed to be working out for Darlene. But then, Isabella unexpectedly died, setting into motion a series of events jeopardizing her comfortable lifestyle.

Darlene sat in the passenger seat of the police car, looking out the window as Brian Henderson drove toward the Gusarov Estate. Nervously twisting a lock of blonde hair between her fingertips, she glanced over to Brian.

"I really appreciate this. Especially considering everything," she said.

"No problem." Brian shrugged.

"I tried calling Todd, but he wasn't answering his phone," she explained.

"Yes, you mentioned that."

"It will just take a minute to grab my extra set of keys."

"I said no problem." Brian glanced over at Darlene and smiled.

"It's been a nightmare. I can't believe Todd would do something like this." Darlene moved restlessly in the seat. "I still don't believe he did."

"And you had no idea it wasn't Isabella?" Brian asked.

"I really didn't know her that well. She rarely came around. It's not like we had any kind of relationship. After all, even Sergeant Morelli thought it was Isabella, and he's known her for longer than I have."

"Stoddard was emphatic that you weren't involved," Brian said.

"You don't sound like you believe that."

"I suppose it only matters what the DA thinks."

"I care about what people in Frederickport think. I have to live here."

"So you'll be staying?"

"Of course. It's my home. And we don't know if Todd will have to serve any time."

THE GHOST WHO WANTED REVENGE

Brian glanced over to Darlene and frowned, withholding comment. He pulled up in front of the Gusarov Estate and parked.

Darlene unbuckled her seatbelt. "It will just take a minute."

"How are you planning to get inside without a key?"

"Todd's here; he'll let me in."

Unless he's skipped town, Brian thought as he watched Darlene run up the walk to her front door.

Sitting in the police car, Brian's mind wandered as he absently watched Darlene. She stood on the front porch, ringing the doorbell. When no one answered, she pounded on the door. After a moment, she tried the doorknob. It wasn't locked. She went inside.

Her scream jolted him back to reality. Hastily unhooking his seatbelt, Brian bolted from the car and ran up the walkway toward the house. When he reached the front porch, he found the door wide open, with Darlene inside, cradling her husband's bloody body.

Holding Stoddard's head in her lap, she rocked back and forth, sobbing, "You can't leave me, Todd. I need you."

Kneeling down, Brian checked Stoddard's vitals. The injured man was still alive—but barely. Brian immediately called for medical assistance and backup while dashing to the nearby powder room to find a clean washcloth or hand towel. He returned with a washcloth and quickly pressed it against the belly wound.

"Wake up!" Darlene's arms tightened around her husband. A moment later Stoddard opened his eyes and looked up into Darlene's face.

"You're alive!" Darlene sobbed. "I love you so much! Who did this to you?"

"The ambulance is on the way," Brian said while holding the cloth against the wound, applying pressure. "Is anyone else in the house?"

Stoddard shook his head no and tried to speak. With effort, he managed to form words. "She's going to hurt Darlene. Keep her safe," he whispered.

"Who did this to you?" Darlene asked with a sob. "Who shot you?"

Weary, Stoddard turned his face toward Brian. "Please keep her safe. She wants to destroy me."

"Who did this to you, Stoddard?" Brian asked. "If you know

who it was, tell us so we can help you—so we can keep Darlene safe."

Stoddard nodded his head and whispered, "Danielle Boatman."

"Danielle Boatman?" Brian repeated, surprised to hear the name. "Are you saying it was Danielle Boatman who shot you?"

"Yes," Stoddard forced the words. "She wants to destroy me. My family. She told me she was going after Darlene next."

"Why would Danielle Boatman do this?" Brian didn't mean to ask the question, the words just popped out.

"She's afraid my lawyer will get me off. She wants me punished for what we did to Lily."

"Are you sure it was Danielle Boatman? Did you see her?" Brian asked. "Did she say anything?"

"Isn't that what he just said?" Darlene shrieked.

"It was her," Stoddard said. "I saw her. Heard her. She told me why she was doing this. You have to stop her."

A moment later, the paramedics and backup arrived. After gently prying Darlene from her husband, one of the officers led her outside while the medical team worked on Stoddard. But it was too late. Stoddard Gusarov, heir to the Gusarov fortune, died just moments after they placed him on the gurney.

While the team roped off the crime scene, Brian Henderson called in an arrest warrant for Danielle Boatman—wealthy heiress and the owner of Marlow House. Brian wondered how Danielle would try to explain her way out of this one.

TWO

W edging the binoculars between the slats of the window
blinds, he watched the woman next door. If she looked his
way, he doubted she would notice him.

As far as everyone knew, he had left town—gone away for the
week, seeking a little R and R. After all, he needed it, considering all
that he had been dealing with. But there wasn't anywhere he
wanted to go—at least, not alone. Which was why he decided to stay
in town, quietly renting a little beach house belonging to one of his
Portland friends. He imagined his co-workers would think him crazy
to rent a house just blocks from his own home. But his place wasn't
on the beach, and here—at the rental—no one would bother him.

It all seemed like a good idea until she showed up. What was she
doing here anyway, poking around at the house next door? No one
was there. He knew the people who owned the property, and they
had packed up and headed home weeks earlier. That was one
reason he had decided on the house he was renting. By the end of
September, its neighborhood was a virtual ghost town. Only the
house on the corner had a full-time occupant—Mrs. Beasley, who
was practically deaf and preferred staying indoors with her six cats.

When the woman had arrived, over an hour earlier, she had
gone first to the neighbor's front stoop, where she persistently
pounded on the door while hollering, "Hello, it's Danielle Boatman!" He had left his windows open to capture the morning breeze,

which was why he had heard her. Glancing at the wall clock, he had noticed it was just 7 a.m., which seemed early for such a noisy visit. That was assuming someone was actually home next door, which didn't seem to be the case.

He had grabbed the binoculars he found sitting on the kitchen counter and took a closer look. Yes, it was Danielle Boatman. Glancing toward the roadway, he noticed her new red Ford Flex parked in the street, between his mailbox and the neighbor's. She had purchased the car right after Lily came home from the hospital.

When he looked back to Danielle, she was no longer pounding on the door, but talking on her cellphone. At the end of her conversation, she slipped her phone in her back pocket and headed to the side yard, making her way to the back of the neighbor's house.

Curious, he continued to watch. Making herself at home, she took a seat on the neighbor's back porch swing and began pushing it to and fro with one foot while looking out to the ocean.

A movement from the street caught his eye. He looked in that direction. For a moment, he thought someone was driving off in Danielle's car, but then he realized it was a second vehicle, another red Ford Flex. It parked briefly behind her car. He couldn't see its driver, as trees partially obscured his view. He assumed whoever was driving the car was probably checking out Danielle's Flex, comparing it to his own. A moment later, the second car drove off.

Looking back toward Danielle, he found her still sitting in the porch swing, gently swaying back and forth. She had obviously made herself at home.

DANIELLE REPEATEDLY PRESSED the toe of her shoe against the grassy patch of ground, keeping the porch swing in steady motion. Yawning, she felt lazy, and if her eyes closed, she imagined she could easily fall asleep. Breathing in the early morning beach air, she smiled, content to be alive and living in such a beautiful area. For a brief moment, she wished Marlow House was on Ian's side of the street, looking over the ocean, but she quickly chided herself for being greedy. *I have much to be grateful for*, Danielle thought.

A moment later, her cellphone began to ring. Standing up briefly, she took it from her back pocket and looked to see who was calling. It was Lily. She had hoped it was Mrs. Anderson. Answering the phone, she sat back down on the swing.

"I thought you'd be home by now," Lily said. "Are you taking the piano?"

"I haven't seen it yet," Danielle said.

"You haven't? You left over an hour ago. Where are you?" Lily asked.

"I'm at the house. Mrs. Anderson isn't here yet. I guess she had some sort of emergency and didn't leave until early this morning. I'm waiting for her."

"Why didn't you just come home?"

"She called me. Said they were only twenty minutes away. Figured by the time I got home, I'd be turning around, coming back over here."

"But you've been gone for over an hour."

"I know." Danielle watched the waves breaking along the sandy shore. "She suggested I wait around back. They have this great swing looking out over the ocean. We need to get Ian one of these, and I'll go over to his house and use it," Danielle said with a laugh.

"I still don't understand why they haven't showed up if they said they were only twenty minutes away. When did they call?"

"The first time, about ten minutes after I got here. They called again about thirty minutes later. I guess they had some sort of car trouble, but promised to be here in twenty minutes. I told them not to worry. I'm enjoying their back view. It really is amazing, Lily."

"Okay, I was just getting worried about you."

"Are you alright? Walt taking care of you?"

"He brought me some coffee after I first got up—at least I assume he brought it. Watching a cup of coffee float through the air is a little unnerving. I keep wondering what Ian would say if he ever walked into the house and witnessed some of Walt's levitations."

"He would probably write a book about it." Danielle chuckled.

"I imagine you're right."

"Have you heard from Ian?"

"He's coming home in the morning. I'll sure be glad to see him."

"I tell you what, if Mrs. Anderson doesn't show up in the next fifteen minutes, I'll give her a call and arrange to see the piano another time."

"Don't hurry home because of me, I'm fine. I was just worried about you."

"But you haven't had breakfast yet. Walt didn't make your breakfast, did he?"

"Now that would be interesting to watch," Lily said with a hearty laugh. "Would love to capture that on video and post it on YouTube. Nothing like watching eggs and frying pans floating through the air."

"Don't get any ideas," Danielle teased.

"Don't worry. Anyway, Joanne's here now. She's making me breakfast."

"Wow, I have been here for a while, must be after eight."

"Almost 8:30."

"If Joanne's there, I suppose there's no reason to hurry back. Might as well enjoy the scenery while waiting for Mrs. Anderson. I can't imagine they'll be much longer."

LILY HAD JUST HOBBLED from her bedroom into the hallway when she heard someone ring the doorbell.

"I'll get it," Joanne called out, scurrying from the kitchen down the hall to the front door. "I have your breakfast almost ready."

Lily followed Joanne to the door, using a crutch to ease the pressure on her bad leg. When Joanne opened the door, it was Brian Henderson standing on the front porch, with two other officers.

"Is Danielle Boatman here?" Brian asked curtly.

"Morning, Brian," Joanne returned, frowning at his impersonal tone. "No, she's not."

"Where is she? When did she leave?" he asked.

"She went to look at a piano," Joanne told him. "I don't know when she left. She wasn't here when I arrived this morning."

"What's this about?" Lily asked, making her way to the door. She stood by Joanne. Glancing outside, she noticed there were several police cars parked in the street.

"Where is Danielle, Lily?" Brian asked.

"Like Joanne said, she went to look at a piano. What is this about?"

"What time did she leave?"

"Around seven, why? Has something happened?"

"Have you heard from her?" Brian asked.

"Yeah, I talked to her a little while ago."

"Where was she?"

"Waiting to look at the piano."

"What piano, where?" he asked.

"Over on the south side of town. What's going on?"

At Lily's mention of the south side of town, Brian exchanged knowing glances with the officers by his side.

"What's this about a piano?" Brian asked.

"Danielle wants to get a piano for Marlow House. She went to look at one this morning. Do you want me to call her?" Lily asked.

"Isn't it a little early in the morning to be shopping for pianos?" Brian asked.

"The lady who owns it is from Portland, and she's meeting Danielle over at her house to show her the piano. Should I call her?" Lily asked again.

"No, I don't want you to call her. Do you know where she's going after she looks at the piano?"

"Back here. What is going on, Officer Henderson? Why won't you answer my questions?" Lily asked impatiently.

"I'm not at liberty to say right now, Lily. Do you know when she plans to return here?"

"I imagine within the hour, maybe sooner. You're sort of freaking me out. What the hell is going on?"

"I agree with Lily." Joanne spoke up. "What's going on, Brian? Has something happened to Danielle?"

"No, that's impossible!" Lily shook her head in denial. "I just talked to Danielle ten minutes ago, there can't be anything wrong. Has there been an accident or something?"

"As far as I know, Danielle is in perfect health." Brian reached into his pocket and removed a piece of paper. "I have a warrant to search Marlow House."

Lily turned and began hobbling back to her room.

"Where are you going?" Brian asked sharply.

"To call Danielle and see what in the hell is going on," Lily called back.

Brian quickly stepped into the house and grabbed hold of Lily's forearm. She started to stumble, but was saved by the unseen hand of Walt Marlow.

"I'm afraid I can't let you do that," Brian said. "I want you ladies to wait in the library with one of my officers."

Lily looked down at her forearm, which Brian continued to clutch. "Let. Go. Of. My. Arm."

Before Brian could respond, he flew backwards, landing on his backside. Immediately his hand went to his chin. If he didn't know better, he'd swear someone had hit him. Yet that was impossible. The other officers rushed into the entry as he stumbled to his feet. They looked around, yet like Brian, they didn't see anyone other than Lily or Joanne, and it was clear neither of the women had hit Brian.

"Looks like I'm not the only one having a problem walking," Lily quipped.

"What the hell just happened?" Brian asked, rubbing his chin.

"Looked to me like you just fell backwards," Joanne said. "Are you alright?"

"I guess so…" Warily, Brian glanced around the entry hall. "But I will still need you ladies to go with an officer into the library."

"And if we refuse?" Lily asked.

"Then I'll have to put you under arrest for obstruction of justice."

"Come, Lily." Joanne reached out and took Lily's arm. "Let's just go into the library. I'm sure Danielle will be here any minute and sort this out."

"Sort what out?" Lily asked as she let Joanne lead her down the hall. Just as she and Joanne reached the library door, more officers swarmed into the house, some heading up the stairs.

"What in the hell is going on?" Lily muttered. Glancing around, she wondered where Walt was and what he might do to Brian and the other police officers now searching through Marlow House.

THREE

Danielle glanced at her cellphone. It was almost 9 a.m. "This is ridiculous," she muttered to herself. Taking a deep breath, she tried calling Mrs. Anderson again. The call went immediately to voice mail. It was a generic recording, not Mrs. Anderson's voice. Since Danielle had redialed the number that had called her earlier, she didn't doubt she had called the correct number.

"Hello, this is Danielle Boatman. I hope everything is okay. I have to get going. I've been here all morning and need to go home. When you get this, please call me."

When Danielle pulled up her street ten minutes later, she was surprised to find four Frederickport police cars parked near Marlow House. One blocked the entrance into her drive. Frowning, she parked her car on the street and got out. Just as she slammed the door shut, she found herself surrounded by police officers—each pointing a gun in her direction. Where they had magically come from, she had no idea. One minute she was alone on the street and in the next a half dozen armed officers, wearing what appeared to be SWAT gear, surrounded her.

Someone screamed for her to freeze and raise her hands. Later she would wonder how he expected her to do both. Eyes wide, she raised her hands above her head. The first officer she recognized was Brian Henderson, who immediately grabbed her hands and pulled them behind her back.

While putting her in handcuffs, Brian said, "Danielle Boatman, you are under arrest for the murder of Stoddard Gusarov." He then went on to recite her Miranda rights.

Stunned, she stood mute, unable to think of a single sassy zinger to hurl in Brian's direction. She heard someone yell, "I found it!" Dazed, she looked toward the voice and saw an officer pull a gun from the back of the Flex, clutching it with a glove-covered hand. He raised the gun over his head for all to see before dropping it in an evidence bag.

"Where did that come from?" Danielle muttered. She felt Brian give her a jerk, roughly pulling her toward his police car.

WALT STOOD helpless at the attic window, watching Officer Henderson load Danielle into the backseat of the police car. He didn't regret slugging Brian earlier. If he had it to do over, he would hit him again—but this time harder.

He had pieced together snippets from the officers who had searched the house that morning. From what he gathered, someone had murdered Stoddard Gusarov—the man being charged for Lily's abduction. He couldn't imagine why they thought Danielle would do such a thing—why would she? Gusarov had already confessed to most of the charges, and although he and his lawyer were doing some major backpedaling, no one thought he would be able to beat the charges. Gusarov's attorney had already offered Lily a substantial settlement, to which she had so far refused, insisting her first priority was seeing the man put behind bars.

What Walt found especially frustrating was that there was no one to talk with. He couldn't leave Marlow House, and neither Joanne nor Lily could see or hear him. If Danielle wasn't able to return to Marlow House, his only option was to jump into her dream or Lily's. Yet that would only give him information on what was happening. It wouldn't allow him to help Danielle. And from what he had just witnessed, she needed help.

DANIELLE PACED BACK and forth the length of the interrogation room, refusing to sit at the table or look in the two-way mirror, where she was certain members of the Frederickport Police Department watched her from the adjacent office.

"Has she called her attorney yet?" Chief MacDonald asked Brian Henderson when he walked into the office next to the interrogation room.

"She made her one call, but it wasn't to her attorney," Brian said. He and the chief stood side by side, watching Danielle.

"Do you know who she called?"

"I'm pretty sure it was Lily Miller."

"Has she waived her right to an attorney? Has she said anything?" the chief asked.

"To me?" Brian snorted. "She's only said one thing since I put her in the police car—that there was only one person at the Frederickport Police Department she'd talk to, but she wouldn't do it in the interrogation room."

"Because of the two-way mirror?" the chief asked.

"She didn't say, but that's what I assume."

"Who was it, Morelli? Did you tell her he's on vacation?"

"No, it wasn't Morelli." Brian turned to face the chief. "It's you. She said she'll only talk to you, but not in there."

"Okay, bring her to my office." The chief headed to the door.

Brian turned from the window to face his boss. "Are you sure?"

The chief paused a moment and looked at Brian. "If she's willing to talk to one of us—without her attorney present—then I want to hear what she has to say."

───

CHIEF MACDONALD SAT at his desk when Brian led Danielle into his office.

The moment Danielle entered the room she lifted her hands, now cuffed in front of her body, and asked the chief, "Is this really necessary?"

"Are they too tight?" he asked.

"They are insulting," Danielle grumbled, flashing a glare in Brian's direction.

"Let's leave them on for now. After all, you are under arrest, and I did agree to meet with you in my office—and not in the interrogation room." He pointed to a chair.

Danielle nodded toward Brian and said, "If he's staying, I'm not talking."

"You can leave now, Brian," MacDonald said, again pointing to the vacant chair. Brian flashed Danielle a harsh look before leaving her alone with the police chief.

"What is this all about?" Danielle asked as she sat down.

"I was under the impression Brian told you when he put you under arrest."

"He said I was under arrest for the murder of Stoddard Gusarov."

"Then you know why you're here." MacDonald leaned back in his chair and studied Danielle.

"If the man really was murdered, I certainly had nothing to do with it. Why would I kill him?"

"Revenge for what he did to Lily?" he suggested.

"That's ridiculous. He was going to jail for that."

"Then tell me where you were this morning."

"I was over on Sea Cliff Drive."

"Sea Cliff Drive? That's only a couple blocks from the Gusarov Estate."

"But I didn't go to the Gusarov Estate. I didn't even drive down their street. I was at a house over on Sea Cliff, trying to look at a piano."

"I suppose someone can verify this? How long were you there?"

"I arrived around seven. Left a couple hours later, came right home. Then Brian arrested me."

"Who can verify you were there? I need someone's name."

"Well…" Danielle squirmed nervously in the chair. "They never showed up. They had car trouble, but I talked to them on the phone a couple times. I also talked to Lily once."

"I don't understand. You say you went to look at a piano, but no one was there, yet you stayed two hours, and no one can corroborate your story?"

"I know that sounds bad…are you saying Gusarov was murdered today, at the estate?"

"Yes. Sometime between 7:15 and 8:30."

"Why do you think I did it?"

Chief MacDonald studied Danielle a moment before answering. "Because Stoddard said it was you. He said you shot him—twice.

And then when he was dying, you told him you'd be going after his wife next."

Danielle bolted up straight in her chair, her eyes wide. "Why would he say something like that?"

"I assume because you killed him."

"I didn't! I promise! I was at the house on Sea Cliff all morning! I don't even own a gun."

"That's another problem. We found the gun in your car after you returned to Marlow House."

Danielle slumped back in her seat, her head spinning. It was true; they had found a gun in her car. *But how did it get there?* she asked herself.

"I swear, Chief, I didn't do this. I don't even know how to use a gun. Did you check for fingerprints?"

"The gun had been wiped clean."

"Why would I do that and then keep it?"

"I assume you just hadn't gotten around to dumping it."

"I swear I didn't do this. I have no idea how that gun got into my car or why Gusarov said it was me. He's mistaken."

"The only problem is, he's dead now."

Tears filled Danielle's dark eyes. She felt sick.

"Okay, why don't you tell me about this piano?" the chief suggested.

Danielle took a deep breath and willed her tears not to fall. "I've been thinking about getting a piano for Marlow House, but I wanted an older one—something that would fit in with the décor of the house. So I started asking around, letting people know what I was interested in, in case they knew of one in the area. The other day, a Mrs. Anderson called me. Told me she had a summerhouse on Sea Cliff, with an old piano she'd been thinking of getting rid of. She told me she was planning to come in this morning and would be willing to meet me at the house, but only if I could be there at seven, because she had an appointment in Astoria. I agreed."

"I take it she didn't show up?"

"I got there around seven. No one was at the house. I was there for about ten minutes when she called, told me she got a late start but should be there within twenty minutes. She suggested I wait in the back—make myself comfortable on her swing—promised she was on her way. I couldn't see the point of going home and coming right back."

"So you just waited all that time?"

"About twenty minutes later, she called again. Said she had car trouble. Apologized. Said it would be another twenty minutes. It was a nice morning, so I just waited. But when she never showed up, I tried calling her, and when she didn't answer, I decided to come home."

"And you never saw anyone this morning?"

"No, just Lily at Marlow House."

"Did you tell anyone about meeting up with Mrs. Anderson to look at her piano?"

"A couple people, but I never mentioned where I was going or whose piano I was looking at—other than Lily. I told her."

"Was there a reason you didn't mention who had the piano you were considering?"

"Mrs. Anderson asked me not to say anything. Said she preferred people in town didn't know her business. I could understand that, so I didn't mention her name to anyone outside of Lily—and Lily didn't know who she was anyway."

"Did you say anything to Ian?"

"Ian? No. He's been out of town for the week. He left before Mrs. Anderson contacted me."

"Is there anything else you remember? Anyone who may have seen you? Maybe someone walking their dog, someone on the beach?"

Danielle considered the question a moment and then shook her head. "No. I didn't see anyone. But even if I had seen someone on the beach—which I didn't—you can't really see the swing from the beach because of the bushes."

"I'd like to check out a few things. I'm going to have Brian take you back to the interrogation room."

DANIELLE WAITED ALONE in the interrogation room for almost an hour before the chief joined her.

The moment he walked into the room, she stood up and asked, "Did you get ahold of Mrs. Anderson?"

"Yes, I did." MacDonald took a seat and motioned for Danielle to sit down.

"What did she say?" Danielle asked anxiously, returning to the chair.

"You were right. The address you gave me—it is owned by the Andersons. Unfortunately, Mrs. Anderson claims to have never heard of you. Says she doesn't own a piano and is currently in Florida, attending a funeral. She didn't recognize the phone number you gave me, and after doing some checking, that number seems to belong to one of those throwaway phones you pick up at the grocery store."

Danielle frowned. "I don't understand."

"There is another problem. Wednesday morning is trash day for that section of town. We got ahold of the men from the truck servicing Stoddard's street, to find out what they saw. They both described a red SUV with dealer plates. One thought it was a Flex. It was parked down the street from the Gusarov Estate."

"There are other red SUVs in town."

"One of the men claims he saw a young woman leaving the estate and getting into the car around 7:30 this morning. According to his identification, she was in her late twenties or early thirties, about five feet five inches tall, brunette, wearing a braid."

FOUR

D anielle sat alone in the dreary jail cell. During her last arrest, they had kept her in the interrogation room. Of course, that time, a murder victim hadn't been the witness against her.

She guessed it was close to 3 p.m., and she hadn't had anything to eat all day. Her head throbbed. It was 6:45 a.m. when she had left Marlow House that morning, planning to eat breakfast with Lily when she returned home. But she had missed breakfast and then lunch.

Motion from the corner of the jail cell caught her attention. Standing up, she narrowed her eyes and focused on the dark corner. A sphere of light appeared; it twisted and twirled, transforming into a blurred vision of a man. He walked toward her, his face staring down at the floor. She couldn't tell who he was.

Stepping backwards, she bumped against the barred walls of the cell, preventing her from putting more distance between her and the impending apparition. Trapped between the bars and the spirit, she held her breath a moment, waiting for him to show himself. When he was just a few feet away, he lifted his head and looked into her face. It was Stoddard Gusarov—and by his expression, he was furious.

Stoddard reached for Danielle, his hand moving through her wrist. He made a second grab, yet he was still unable to make physical contact. Screwing his face into an angry scowl, he yelled, "I will see you in hell for taking my life!" He then disappeared.

"Crap," Danielle muttered, glancing around the room.

A few minutes later the chief entered lockup, carrying a white paper sack.

"I brought you something to eat," he said, holding up the bag.

"How did you know I was starved?" Danielle asked as she reached through the bars to accept the food.

"I figured you've been here most of the day and hadn't eaten since breakfast."

"I didn't even have breakfast." Danielle opened the sack. Inside she found a soda, a wrapped burger, and fries. She reached in and pulled out the burger. Sitting on a bench, she folded down the paper wrapping. Pausing a moment, she looked up to the chief. He stared at her.

"I know now why Gusarov said I killed him," she said before taking a bite of the burger.

MacDonald stepped closer to the barred walls. "What do you mean?"

"He was here just a moment ago. You missed him." She took another bite of the burger.

"You saw Stoddard?"

Danielle nodded.

"Did he say anything?"

"Yes." Danielle wiped her mouth with a napkin and looked up into the chief's face. "He was pissed. Told me he would send me to hell for taking his life."

"What are you saying?" The chief frowned.

"For some reason, Stoddard Gusarov believes I killed him. That's why he told Brian I was the shooter. I'm not. I don't know who the trash men saw, but it wasn't me. I didn't drive down his street today. I didn't shoot him, and that gun they found in my car is not mine. Someone is trying to frame me. And they've done one hell of a job, considering they've even convinced the victim."

"Danielle, you know I like you, and I want to help you. But you're really not giving me anything to go with, other than confirming the fact our victim believes you're his killer."

"I was rather hoping that if I was to run into Stoddard, he'd be telling me the name of his killer and then explain why Brian misunderstood him." Danielle reached into the sack and pulled out a French fry. She popped it into her mouth.

"I always assumed the spirit of someone who died would instinctively know something like their killer." The chief leaned against the bars, looking down at Danielle.

"Unfortunately, it doesn't work that way. Look at Walt Marlow," Danielle said.

"What do you mean?" he asked.

"Walt Marlow didn't know how he died. Everyone thought he killed himself. He didn't. And while he had a good idea it wasn't a suicide, he really didn't know how he had died."

"What about Cheryl; did she know her killer?" he asked.

Danielle shook her head. "Not at first. With Cheryl, she couldn't remember everything that had happened to her—it came back in flashes. When she saw Renton talking to me, before his attack, she remembered."

"If you're right, why do you think someone is framing you for Stoddard's murder?"

"I've been wondering that myself." Danielle took another bite of the burger. A moment later she said, "I'll have to admit, until I saw Stoddard earlier, I wondered if Brian made up the story about Stoddard's dying words. According to what I overheard, his wife was hysterical, so it's possible she was too distraught to remember exactly what was said. I knew I wasn't the shooter, so the logical conclusion is that Brian lied."

"Brian Henderson would never frame an innocent woman!"

"Sorry." Danielle shrugged. "I know he's one of your men, your friend, and you trust him, but look at it from my perspective. Since Cheryl disappeared, he's been convinced I'm either psychotic or homicidal. Maybe both."

"It's just that he doesn't understand—that you—well, you know."

"It doesn't matter what Brian thinks about me. I know now he didn't lie about Gusarov. But why is someone trying to frame me?" Finished with her burger, she took out the soda and shoved her trash into the bag. Danielle pushed the straw into her soda cup's lid after removing its paper wrapper. She took a sip of the soda.

"The only person I can think of who might harbor a grudge against you is Stoddard. Without your intervention, Lily would probably be in Canada now, and he never would have faced jail time. But I don't see Stoddard sacrificing his life just to get back at you."

"Neither do I." Danielle considered the possibilities as she sipped the soda. "What about Darlene? She is just as guilty as Stoddard."

"Not according to Stoddard. He swore she didn't know anything about it."

"And do you believe him?" Danielle studied the chief's face.

"Not really, but we don't have anything to prove otherwise. But I don't see Darlene killing her husband just to get back at you—and from what Brian said, she was hysterical this morning."

"I suppose you're right. Plus, I imagine Stoddard would recognize his wife if she was the one who shot him." Danielle stood up and shoved her empty soda cup into the sack. She walked to the bars and handed the trash to MacDonald.

"I do have a favor to ask you," Danielle said.

"What's that?"

"Lily's arranging an attorney for me. If my attorney manages to get me out on bail, I'd like one of those ankle monitoring thingies. Even if a judge agrees to release me on bail without one, I still want it."

"Why?"

"Because someone is trying to frame me. And if they really told Stoddard that Darlene was next, I don't want to be out on bail if the killer is successful, and then get charged with two murders. My luck is not so terrific."

"You're serious." MacDonald frowned.

"Very. The more I think about it—I bet this is about money. Stoddard is worth a fortune, especially after inheriting Isabella's share of the estate. Who inherits if Darlene is gone?"

The door to lockup opened. It was Brian Henderson.

"Ms. Boatman's attorney is here," Brian said.

"Bring him in," the chief said, no longer leaning against the bars.

"It's a woman," Brian clarified.

"Then show her in."

"Thanks for the food," Danielle said.

"No problem. I'll see what I can find out about his estate. I sincerely hope we can figure this out," the chief said, giving her a brief nod. Danielle watched as he followed Brian out of the room.

Several minutes later, a person Danielle had never seen before entered the lockup area. Tall and slender, she was an attractive woman who appeared to be in her mid-forties. She wore a tailored linen business suit and her blonde hair cropped short. In her left hand, she carried a leather briefcase.

Behind her was a second person—Ian Bartley. Dressed casually, he wore denims, a red sweatshirt, jogging shoes, and his beloved Cub's baseball cap.

"Ian!" Danielle called out, her hands gripping the bars. "I thought you weren't coming back until tomorrow."

"Are you kidding? Lily called me this morning in a panic. Told me you'd been arrested. We figured you needed a good attorney. I want you to meet my old friend—Candice Holloway. She's one of the best criminal attorneys in the state. Candice, this is the woman I was telling you about, Danielle Boatman."

"Ms. Boatman," Candice greeted her, slipping her right hand through the bars to shake Danielle's hand.

Danielle accepted the gesture and said, "I really appreciate you coming." She glanced at Ian. "Both of you."

"Ian wanted me to start working on your bail, but I explained I needed to meet with you first—and if you agree to hire me—"

"If Ian says you're the best, then that's good enough for me. And I definitely need an attorney."

"Ian insists you're innocent, but I've looked at what they have, and it's going to be a challenge."

"I'm not guilty, Ms. Holloway. I didn't kill Stoddard Gusarov. I promise."

"I don't really care about that," Candice said. "My job is to give you the best legal defense possible, regardless of whether I believe you're innocent or guilty."

"If you don't believe me, how can you help me?" Danielle asked.

"Danielle, trust Candice. She really is the best," Ian urged.

"Ms. Boatman, what I personally believe won't impact the jury's decision."

"I suppose I can't blame you for thinking I did it." Danielle sat back down on the bench.

"All we need to do is present reasonable doubt."

"That's going to be impossible, considering the prosecution's prime witness is the victim," Danielle said.

"I believe we can show the jury how a man who has been critically wounded—suffering from incredible pain due to his injuries—could become delusional. He knew what he did to your friend, so it's only natural for him to start imagining you're the one who shot him. I suspect Mr. Gusarov was out of his head by the time the officer arrived on the scene."

"What about the gun they found in my car?"

"You've already admitted you were at a house only a block or so away from Mr. Gusarov's home. I assume you parked in the street."

"Yes."

"Did you lock your car?" the attorney asked.

"No."

"Was the car in your sight the entire time you were at the house?"

"No. I was on the back patio, watching the ocean for almost an hour."

"Then it's possible the killer left Mr. Gusarov's house and put the gun in your car."

"Wow, you're making me feel better already." Danielle smiled.

"Hopefully we can get the jury to see it our way. But for now, why don't I go see what I can do to get you home for the night."

"I'd really appreciate that." Danielle smiled.

When Candice left a few minutes later, Danielle looked at Ian and said, "You don't know how much this means to me."

"I don't believe for a minute you shot Gusarov," Ian declared.

"Thanks for coming. I was worried about Lily."

"She's fine, aside from being sick worrying over you. The nurse was at the house when I stopped by Marlow House, and Joanne is coming back over later to make her dinner."

"That makes me feel better." *And of course, Walt is there,* she thought.

"Have you seen Joe? I didn't see him upstairs," Ian asked.

"No. He wasn't there when they arrested me, and I haven't seen him all day."

"I don't suppose you asked where he was. I'm surprised he's not involved in the case."

"I didn't ask." Danielle shrugged. "Figured it was his day off or something. Anyway, I don't really need him around. Just someone else to insist I'm guilty."

25

FIVE

B rian Henderson wasn't happy Danielle managed to make bail. It didn't seem right she wouldn't be spending the night in jail, especially considering that—according to Stoddard—she threatened to kill Darlene. Chief MacDonald reminded him she would be wearing an ankle monitor, yet to Brian that was simply another example of how a spoiled little rich girl could get away with murder and then go home at night and sleep comfortably in her own bed. Electronic monitoring came with a fee for the accused—a fee Danielle Boatman could easily pay.

"IF LOOKS COULD KILL, we'd both be dead now," Ian said as he drove Danielle home that evening.

"What do you mean?" She sat in the passenger seat, looking out the side window.

"Brian—did you see him glaring at us when they were checking you out?"

"Yeah, I noticed that. Capital punishment is legal in this state. If they decide to fry me, Brian would probably be the first in line to volunteer to pull the kill switch."

"Damn, Danielle, don't even talk that way!" Ian cringed. "And whatever you do, don't say something like that to Lily!"

"Not up to gallows humor?"

"Anyway, I think kill switch implies you turn something off. In that case, Brian would be saving you."

"Like that would happen," she snorted.

"How can you be so flippant?" Ian asked.

"I don't know," Danielle murmured. With a shrug she added, "Defense mechanism, maybe?"

They were silent for a few moments, lost in their own thoughts. With a sigh, Danielle glanced over to Ian. To her horror, Stoddard's spirit sat in the driver's seat with him. The two men seemed to blend, with Stoddard's image a ghoulish film-like overlay covering Ian.

Eyes wide, she watched in morbid fascination as Ian drove toward Marlow House, unaware of the extra passenger sharing his seat—his lap. Stoddard's hands clutched the steering wheel with Ian's. The dead man turned to look at Danielle, his eyes wild, crazed. He smiled—an unnerving, malicious smile—and then, just as they were about to pass a truck, Stoddard's hands jerked to the left, toward the oncoming vehicle, in an attempt to steer them into disaster. Without thought, Danielle let out a startled yelp.

"What?" Ian looked over to Danielle, then back down the road, wondering what she'd seen.

"I'm sorry. I…I guess I'm a little unraveled." Danielle glanced around, wondering where Stoddard had gone.

"I understand, but don't do that again." Ian shook his head. "Don't want to get us killed. Lily would never forgive me."

When they pulled up to Marlow House a few minutes later, Danielle saw Stoddard again. He stood in the street, in the exact location where Ian intended to park his car. Danielle held her breath as Ian pulled alongside the curb, running the vehicle through Stoddard, who remained standing, stubbornly refusing to move. When Ian parked, the upper half of the ghost's body stuck up over the hood of the car. Stoddard reached for Danielle, his hand moving through the windshield. She leaned back in the seat and quickly unfastened her seatbelt.

Stoddard trailed alongside Danielle and Ian as they walked from the parked car up to the front door of Marlow House.

"I'll find some way to do it," Stoddard hissed. "You will die, and I'll send you to hell."

27

"Maybe I should grab us a pizza after we get you settled," Ian suggested.

"Uhh...huh..." Danielle glanced warily from Ian to Stoddard. "That would be nice."

"It should be slow. I want you to suffer like you made me suffer, but a hundred times worse," the ghost threatened.

When they reached the front door, it was already wide open, with Lily standing inside, Walt behind her, and Sadie sitting between the two, squirming excitedly, her tail wagging.

"Dani!" Lily squealed. "I was so worried about you!"

Sadie started to greet Ian and Danielle but stopped when she spied Stoddard. Sitting back down, she cocked her head from side to side and then let out a bark.

"Hey, girl, what are you barking at?" Ian laughed, giving his dog a pat.

"Who's that with you?" Walt asked, eyeing Stoddard.

"Lily!" Danielle stepped into the house and hugged her friend. Over Lily's shoulder, she looked at Walt and mouthed, *Stoddard's spirit.*

All of this was new territory for Danielle. She had no idea what would happen when Walt's ghost confronted Stoddard's or what sort of paranormal activity might be set in motion when the two collided. She would like an opportunity to have a quiet discussion with Stoddard—to try to explain to him he was mistaken. She was not his killer. But as long as Ian was around, that wouldn't be happening.

To her surprise, Stoddard did not follow her into the house. Yet it was not for his lack of trying. While Ian was preoccupied with hugging Lily, gently lifting her up and kissing her, Danielle turned to close the door.

Stoddard stood at the doorway, attempting to enter Marlow House, but it was as if an invisible shield prevented his entrance. Each time he made an unsuccessful attempt, his anger accelerated. After she closed the door, he moved to the window, pounding on the glass—yet there was no sound coming from the windowpane. From the way his lips moved, he was obviously shouting, yet she could not hear his words.

"Did you just say that's Stoddard Gusarov, the man who was murdered?" Walt asked.

Danielle nodded in response.

As it turned out, Ian didn't need to go for pizza. Joanne had made a batch of chili, which she had left warming in the crockpot in the kitchen. Twenty minutes after Ian and Danielle arrived at Marlow House, they sat with Lily in the kitchen, eating chili and discussing the day's events. Walt stood nearby, silently listening and smoking his cigar. Outside, Stoddard's frustrated spirit silently pounded on the kitchen window, wanting into the house, his presence a persistent distraction for Danielle and Walt.

They had been sitting at the kitchen table for over an hour when Danielle finally stood up. "I hope you guys don't mind, but I'm going to bed. I'm exhausted."

"Can we do anything for you?" Lily asked.

"No. You've already done so much. Thanks, both of you, for finding me an attorney." Danielle took her bowl to the sink and rinsed it out.

"If it wasn't for me, you wouldn't be in this mess," Lily said.

Danielle turned from the sink to face Lily. "None of this is your fault, Lily."

"I know, but if I hadn't pulled into that stupid rest stop, none of this would be happening."

"What is happening isn't the fault of anyone in this room," Ian said angrily. "If I wasn't out of town, I could just have easily been framed for killing Stoddard. Hell, I actually thought about it."

"Ian!" Lily gasped and then smiled. She reached over and patted his hand.

"Not me," Danielle said with a smile, looking over to Walt. "I don't really see death as the ultimate punishment—more like the next adventure. But I would like to have seen Stoddard spend some time in prison—let him experience a little of what he tried to do to Lily. But death, no. As far as I'm concerned, he's skirted justice."

"I suppose you're right," Ian said with a sigh. "Maybe not kill him, but I would have loved to have beaten the crap out of him. That might have brought a little satisfaction."

"Slugging Brian made me feel better," Walt noted. "Might even give it a second go if he comes back over here." Danielle flashed Walt a smile yet reserved comment, since she was the only one in the room who was able to hear him.

"So what's the plan for tomorrow?" Lily asked.

"I'm meeting with my attorney. After that, I'm not really sure."

"I'll be doing a little digging," Ian said.

"How so?" Lily asked.

"Find out who benefits financially with Stoddard dead," Ian said.

"Wouldn't that be Darlene?" Lily asked.

"Not necessarily. I'm curious to see what happens to the company with him out of the picture," Ian explained.

"Remember, whoever killed Stoddard also threatened Darlene. What happens with both of them out of the picture?" Danielle wondered.

"But was the threat for real?" Ian asked.

Lily looked at Ian. "What do you mean?"

"Maybe Stoddard's killer was just taunting him. It was obvious they wanted to make the man suffer. After all, they shot him twice, why not just shoot him a third time and end it for him?" Ian asked.

"That's sick." Lily cringed.

"No...it wasn't about making him suffer!" Danielle blurted out, a new thought coming to her.

"What do you mean?" Ian asked.

"Think about where they shot him. In his knee. Painful, yes, but it makes it difficult for him to move and is not something that will kill instantly. But a belly wound, aren't those known for being a slow and agonizing death?"

"Yes, they can be. But not always. I don't see your point." Ian frowned.

"Think about it. With his dying breath, Stoddard tells Brian I killed him. I didn't, but I'm certain Stoddard actually believed that. Someone made it a point to make him think I was the killer—and they wanted him to live long enough so he could share that information. Which he did."

"But that's pretty risky—I mean there's always a chance he'd die before someone reached him. And what are the chances it's a cop that witnesses his final words?" Ian asked.

"But it was a cop," Danielle reminded him.

"So was that planned or just a lucky coincidence for the killer?" Lily asked.

"If it was planned, then that would seem to point to Darlene as the killer. She's the one who brought the cop with her."

"If she was involved with the murder, then that means she had an accomplice," Danielle said.

"Why do you say that?" Lily asked.

"Come on, do you really believe Stoddard wouldn't recognize his own wife?" Danielle asked.

"Maybe they planned for Darlene to find the body, and Brian being there was an unexpected bonus," Ian suggested. "After all, they obviously didn't intend to rely solely on Stoddard's dying words. They planted the murder weapon in Danielle's car. I bet they knew when the trash truck would be coming down the street so they'd have reliable witnesses there to see a car like Danielle's."

"And according to the description of the other Flex's driver, she looked just like me," Danielle grumbled.

"If that's the scenario, then I don't see Darlene as the lone shooter, even if she was able to convince her husband she was someone else," Lily said.

"Why do you say that?" Ian asked.

"Because I don't think Darlene's that bright," Lily explained.

"You haven't really met her, have you?" Ian asked.

"No…" It wasn't entirely true. During her out-of-body experience, Lily had an opportunity to observe Stoddard and Darlene. Darlene was evil enough—she'd wanted her husband to smother Lily with a pillow. Yet could she plan and execute such an elaborate scheme? Lily didn't seem to think so. "It's just from what I've heard about her," Lily lied.

SIX

Walt appeared in Danielle's bedroom just as she started to crawl under her sheets. Instead of the pajama bottoms and T-shirt combos she typically wore to bed, tonight she had slipped on a pink floral cotton nightgown after her shower.

"I bet you're exhausted," he said.

"I was, but I think I got my second wind. I can't tell you how great that shower felt. Nothing like being put in a jail cell to make you feel grimy." Danielle pulled the covers to her waist and scooted over, making room for Walt to sit on the bed. He accepted her silent invitation. They lay side by side, leaning back against the headboard.

Glancing to the window, they startled at an unexpected sight. Stoddard peered into the second-floor window of Danielle's bedroom, his fists furiously pounding against the windowpane in a silent tantrum.

"What is that all about?" Walt nodded to the window.

"I think I'm being haunted."

"I thought that was my job." Walt chuckled.

"Yes, and I like your way a lot better. Dang, am I going to have to look at that all night?"

Walt waved his hand and the curtain closed. They could no longer see Stoddard.

"I'm just glad he can't get in here." Danielle grimaced.

"Why do you think that is?"

Danielle pondered the question a moment. "I don't know. I've been thinking about it all night. For some reason he seems unable to pass the threshold into Marlow House, in the same way you can't leave."

"Cheryl's spirit didn't have that problem."

"Thankfully, Stoddard's does. I'm just trying to figure out how it all works. You know, he tried to kill us tonight. Me and Ian."

"What?" Walt looked in horror at Danielle.

"We're driving back from the police station, and Stoddard appears in Ian's car—sitting in the driver's seat with him. We pass this truck, and Stoddard tries to take control of the steering wheel and send us careening into the truck."

"Good lord, how did you stop him?"

"I didn't. He's not able to harness his energy. If he was, I'd be in a lot of trouble."

"What happens if he figures it out?"

"I don't think it works that way…it's not possible…" Danielle stared at the curtain-covered window.

"Why do you say that?"

"Think about it. Imagine if all murdered spirits—or any spirit with a grudge—was able to wander around freely with harnessed energy. The universe knows what it's doing. It's not going to allow that. Chaos would ensue."

"What about me? I've harnessed my energy. I even hit Brian Henderson this morning, not to mention I smashed Renton with the bronze statue, pelted Adam and his sidekick with the croquet set, oh, and I even smacked Cheryl."

Danielle turned to Walt. "Yes, we need to address your violent tendencies." She grinned and then added in a serious tone, "Remember, you're trapped in Marlow House—confined to this area until you choose to move on to another level. It's not unusual to hear about paranormal activities in specific—limited—locations. Old haunted inns, houses, even graveyards. But I suspect those spirits—the ones who've harnessed their energy—are limited in their abilities. Like I said, the universe knows what it's doing."

"What about Isabella? She hit the dognapper over the head with a rock."

"Yes, but until she needed to help someone, she hadn't been able to do anything like that. I suspect if she'd tried to hit an innocent

33

with a rock—let's say some child just walking by—she wouldn't have been able to move it. And look at your wife."

"Let's not," Walt grumbled.

"Angela apparently has some limited abilities. I believe she was responsible for my car stalling and the cellphone not working when she got me to stop at the cemetery the first time. But she obviously can't move objects like Isabella did when she saved us."

"So you aren't afraid of Stoddard's ghost?"

"There you go again, using the G-word."

"I told you, I don't like it when it's applied to me. But considering Stoddard's behavior, the term ghost seems fitting."

"Do you think he's still out there?" Danielle asked.

Walt waved his hand, and the curtain opened. They had their answer. Stoddard hovered persistently at the window, his fists furiously pounding against the glass.

"I'd like to talk to Stoddard. See if I can make him understand that I didn't kill him. Maybe even figure out who did."

"I don't like the idea of you going out there."

"I can't stay in this house indefinitely. And while I don't think he can actually do anything to me, if I have to look at *that* for the rest of my life, he just might drive me insane."

"I would feel better if I could go outside with you."

"Well, you can't. But I'll be okay. Remember, he isn't the first snarky ghost I've encountered. When I was much younger, I had an especially nasty ghost try to invade my space."

"I suppose you don't have a choice." Walt sighed.

"Do you know if Ian is still here?"

"He went home when you were in the shower," Walt told her.

"Is Lily in bed?"

"Yes. But I'm not sure if she's asleep. Why?"

Danielle started to get out of bed. "Because I'm going to go downstairs and see if I can reason with that ghost."

———

DANIELLE STOOD on the back porch outside the kitchen door. She hadn't slipped on a robe, and she was barefoot. Her dark hair, still damp from the recent shampooing, fell past her shoulders. The cotton nightgown fluttered in the evening's breeze, and overhead a crescent moon provided a glimmer of light to the dark night sky.

Glancing around, she didn't see Stoddard. She wondered if he was still hovering overhead by her bedroom window, making those ridiculous faces. With a sigh, she walked out into the yard and sat down on the bench, waiting.

"I'm going to kill you!" Stoddard shouted when he appeared a moment later, sitting next to her on the bench.

Turning to face him, Danielle said calmly, "Good evening, Stoddard."

Her greeting startled Stoddard, who jumped up and stared down at her. "You really can see me!"

"I can hear you too." Danielle smiled sweetly. "And it's getting awful annoying, if you ask me."

"If you hurt Darlene—"

"I didn't shoot you, and I have no intention of hurting your wife, in spite of what you two did to Lily."

"Darlene had nothing to do with that!" he shouted in outrage.

"Oh no?" Cocking her head slightly, she lifted her brows and stared into Stoddard's face, challenging him to disagree.

"She knew nothing about it. She was innocent. She thought that was Isabella."

"So you're saying it was Isabella she wanted to smother with a pillow? Nice wife you have there."

"What...what are you talking about?" Stoddard shifted nervously from one foot to another.

"Oh, sit down, and talk to me like a respectable ghost. Your wiggling all over the place is almost as annoying as the way you keep peeking in my window. Charming, you die only to spend your eternity as a peeping tom."

"I don't know what you're talking about. Darlene would never hurt anyone," Stoddard grumbled as he sat back down on the bench.

"Oh, stop lying. This isn't the end of the road for you. You've another place to go. Maybe you can temporarily avoid going, but eventually you'll have to move on. If you want to settle into a cooler climate, I suggest you stop your lies.

"Lily overheard you and your wife talking. When she was in her coma, her spirit was free—in the same way yours is now. She heard Darlene tell you to smother her with a pillow to get rid of her. Of course, at the time she thought you were talking about Isabella. She didn't realize you both knew it was Lily in that room, not your niece."

"Is that why you killed me?"

"I didn't kill you. Hey, when it's my time to check out, I really don't want to settle in Flame Flats. Or wherever those who've made the naughty list end up. If I was you, I'd be a little more concerned about your hereafter."

"I don't believe you. I saw you. You shot me—you even laughed about it. You, woman, will be going to hell. Maybe I can't send you there, but you will get there."

"Are you saying you saw my face?"

"Of course not, you wore that ski mask."

"A ski mask? The person who shot you was wearing a ski mask? Then why assume it was me?"

"She carried a purse just like your red one."

"You noticed my purse?" Danielle frowned.

"She also wore her brown hair in a braid like yours."

"You remember my purse?"

"So? I have an excellent memory."

"Maybe Darlene shot you. She and I are about the same size. I bet she's the one who stands to inherit your money. She could have easily been wearing a wig."

"Don't be ridiculous. I would recognize my own wife. I looked into your brown eyes when you shot me. My wife has blue eyes."

"Well, whoever the shooter was, it wasn't me. I don't go around killing people—especially when I think that person is going to jail to pay for his crimes."

"That's just it; you believed my attorneys would get me off."

"In your dreams," Danielle snorted. "There is no way you wouldn't have had to serve some time. And considering your former lifestyle, even six months would have been torturous for you."

"You're just saying all this because you want me to go away. But I'm not going. If I have to stay by your side every minute for the rest of your life just to repay you for what you took from me, I will."

"Did the woman who shot you say she was me?"

"You didn't come out and say your name, but you did tell me you were repaying me for what I did to your friend and for trying to frame you for Isabella's murder."

"Which were especially nasty things for you to do; however, not me. Think about it a moment. Don't you find it a trifle odd that I'm having this conversation with you? Wouldn't you expect a normal woman to—well—let's say—run away hysterically if she thought a dead man—especially one she supposedly killed—started popping up in unexpected places like jail cells, cars, and at the window of her bedroom? Not to mention the fact you tried to get Ian and me into a car accident. And trust me, had that little move worked and you killed us both, you'd be checking into Hades already."

"I don't know what to make of that. No one else seems to be able to see or hear me."

"That's just it. I can see ghosts. I've been able to since I was a child. That's how I happened to find out what you did to Lily. By the way, I met your niece—after she died. My point being, since I'm rather familiar with how all this afterlife stuff works—well, kinda sorta—I would be the last person to risk going to jail to plot anyone's murder. Especially yours."

"Why do you say especially mine?" He frowned.

"Because you, Stoddard Gusarov, simply are not worth the trouble. What you did to Lily—what you did to your niece—was inexcusable."

"I didn't hurt my niece," he argued.

"You don't think hiding her body, letting her friends think she just took off, wasn't hurtful?"

Stoddard abruptly stood up. "This only proves you're the killer."

"How do you figure that?" Danielle frowned.

"Because you must have known about the baby. You knew how important it was to me—to finally be a father. But now I will never be able to hold my son."

"Darlene is pregnant?" Danielle remembered Adam had once mentioned something about Stoddard's wife being pregnant, yet later heard that wasn't true. Or had it been? "And it's a boy?"

"I don't know if it's a son. It may be a daughter, which is another way you hurt me. I no longer have the opportunity to try for a second child if the baby is a girl. Then not only do I never get to hold my child, I never get my son. Maybe you win now, but mark my words, you will pay for what you did to me! You might think you've won, but you haven't!"

Stoddard disappeared, leaving Danielle alone in the backyard of Marlow House.

SEVEN

Morning's sea breeze sent the bedroom curtains fluttering inward. Before going to bed the night before, Joe Morelli had opened the windows to take full advantage of the beachfront rental. He enjoyed the soothing serenade of the ocean breakers. Awake for almost thirty minutes, only the promise of morning coffee could coax him from bed.

Rolling off the mattress, he tossed the sheets aside. Standing up, he stretched lazily, walked to the window, and looked outside. There was no one on the beach—at least not that he could see.

Wearing just his boxers, he turned from the window and made his way to the kitchen to make a pot of coffee. When he got there, he flipped on the radio to listen to some music. As he filled the glass pot with water, the newsbreak began. Joe half listened to the news, yet froze when the newscaster mentioned a familiar name.

"Marlow House Bed and Breakfast owner, Danielle Boatman, has been released on bail after her arrest for the murder of longtime Frederickport resident, Stoddard Gusarov..."

Joe turned abruptly, shut off the water, and faced the radio.

"According to an unidentified source, Stoddard Gusarov named Boatman as his killer just moments before his death..."

"WHAT ARE YOU DOING HERE?" Chief MacDonald asked Joe Morelli when the young sergeant walked into the break room at the police station thirty minutes later. "I thought you were on vacation for the rest of the week."

"I imagine he heard about Boatman," Brian said, following Joe into the break room.

"I didn't go out of town," Joe said as he grabbed a mug from the cupboard and filled it with coffee. "I rented a beach house on the south side."

"And this is exactly why you need to leave town for vacation," MacDonald said.

Brian grabbed himself a cup of coffee. He and Joe took a seat at the table with the chief.

"What's going on with Danielle?" Joe asked. "I turned on the radio this morning and heard she'd been arrested for Stoddard's murder. Stoddard is dead?"

"As a doornail," Brian said, taking a sip of his coffee.

"They said he identified Danielle as his killer—according to an unidentified source. But that can't be true." Joe shook his head.

"Yes, it can," Brian said. "Not sure who the unidentified source is, although I suspect it's Darlene."

"Darlene? You're not telling me you've arrested Danielle because of Darlene's account. She'd be my top suspect, considering what she's likely to inherit."

"I said Darlene was probably the unidentified source, not that she was the only one to hear Stoddard say Danielle Boatman shot him," Brian explained.

"Who else heard?" Joe asked.

The chief tipped his cup toward Brian and said, "He did."

"Stoddard told you Danielle shot him?" Joe asked incredulously.

"I'm not sure I believe it either—oh, not that Brian didn't hear Stoddard accuse Boatman, but I'm not sure Stoddard knew what he was talking about," the chief said.

"You're just like Joe; you have a soft spot for that girl." Brian shook his head. "I keep telling you both, she's nothing but trouble."

The chief shrugged and took another sip of coffee.

"But you arrested her?" Joe asked the chief.

"I didn't have a choice. Not only did Stoddard tell Brian she was the shooter, we found the murder weapon in her car. Doesn't look good for her," MacDonald explained.

"Were her fingerprints on it?" Joe asked.

"No, the gun had been wiped clean. But I suspect she was getting ready to dump it," Brian explained. "The serial numbers had been removed. Of course, she insists she doesn't own a gun, claims she doesn't even know how to shoot one."

"I don't think she does," Joe said.

"Why do you say that?" the chief asked.

"Once, when we went out, we got on the topic of guns. She told me she had never shot one and was a little afraid of them."

"She obviously got over her fear," Brian snorted.

"Did she have gunshot residue on her hands?" Joe asked.

"No, but we figured she wore gloves," Brian said.

"Did you find any gloves?"

"No."

"Tell me what happened. Start at the beginning," Joe urged.

Brian set his mug on the table. "Yesterday morning I stopped in the diner to have breakfast, and I ran into Darlene Gusarov in the parking lot, cursing up a storm. She's driving Stoddard's little T-Bird and had just locked the keys in the car. I figured I could probably get the key out for her—not too hard on those old cars. Of course, I needed a piece of wire. But Darlene's paranoid about scratching the car, says Stoddard will kill her. Tells me she already tried calling him to see if he'd bring down the extra set of keys, but he wasn't answering the phone. One thing leads to another, and I end up driving her home to pick up her extra set of car keys."

"And you found Stoddard?" Joe asked.

"Technically, Darlene found him first. I was waiting in the car while she ran up to the house to get her extra set of keys. The minute she went in the door, she started screaming bloody murder. When I got up to the house, he was barely hanging on, been shot twice—once in the gut and once in the kneecap."

"I can't believe Danielle would do something like that." Joe shook his head in denial.

"While waiting for the paramedics to arrive, I asked Stoddard who had shot him. He said Danielle Boatman. I admit, at first I thought he was confused. According to Stoddard, he saw her—heard her. In fact, she threatened to kill Darlene too for what they'd done to Lily and for trying to convince us she had murdered Isabella."

"I find this impossible to believe." Joe felt ill.

40

"I'm having a hard time believing it too," the chief said. "Danielle says someone is trying to frame her."

"Right," Brian scoffed. "Pretty good frame-up when you get the victim to play along."

"Wait a minute...you said this happened yesterday morning?" Joe frowned.

"Yes. Stoddard was shot sometime between 7:15 and 8:30 yesterday morning," the chief explained.

"I got there a little after 8:30, and Chuck Christiansen—Stoddard's right-hand man—claims to have talked to Stoddard on the telephone at seven that morning—the call lasted about fifteen minutes, when Stoddard said he had to go because someone was there. The phone records check out."

"But that's impossible. Danielle couldn't have killed Stoddard!" Joe said excitedly.

"Why is that?" Brian frowned.

"Because I saw Danielle yesterday morning!" Joe jumped to his feet and started pacing the small room. "Chief, she's right, someone is trying to frame her!"

"What are you talking about?" Brian asked.

"I've been staying at a beach house on the south side of town. Yesterday morning I heard someone pounding on the neighbor's door. I looked out the window. It was Danielle. It was 7:00 a.m. I know because I looked at the clock."

"Was the rental on Sea Cliff Drive?" the chief asked.

"Yeah, how did you know that?" Joe asked.

"Because Danielle claims to have been on Sea Cliff Drive the time of the murder. Said she was there to look at a piano someone was selling."

"She was there for about an hour. I got the feeling she was waiting for someone. She made a couple calls and finally went to the back of the house and sat on the porch swing. I thought the whole thing was a little odd."

"Danielle didn't mention seeing you," Brian said.

"No, she wouldn't have. I stayed in the house."

"How can you be sure it was her?" Brian asked.

"Well...I..." Joe shuffled his feet in embarrassment. "I was watching her through binoculars."

The chief raised his brows. "Binoculars?"

"But what about the guy who works for the disposal company

saying they saw someone matching Danielle's description leaving the house—in the same model car she drives?" Brian asked.

"The car!" Joe combed his fingers through his hair. "There was a red car that went down the street when Danielle was sitting on the back swing. She wouldn't have seen it. It looked like hers; in fact, I wondered for a moment if someone had taken off in her new car. It stopped a moment by hers before taking off again."

"Did you see who was driving the other car?" the chief asked.

"No." Joe shook his head.

"Did you see them put anything in Boatman's car?" Brian asked.

"You mean like the murder weapon? No. But they could have."

The chief stood up. "Are you positive this was yesterday?"

"Of course. Just because I decided to spend a few days alone doesn't mean I'm drinking alone and getting my days confused!"

"Joe, I think we need to have a little talk with the DA and judge. See about getting the charges dropped against Danielle."

"I wonder if that will be possible," Brian murmured.

"What do you mean? I saw her. If he was killed during that timeframe, then she's innocent."

"And considering your history with Danielle, you don't think the DA or judge might question your motives for coming forward?"

"Are you suggesting I'm not telling the truth?" Joe asked angrily.

"Of course not," Brian insisted. "But if I was the DA and the victim claimed to know the killer—and then the ex-boyfriend of the killer came forward with a story—"

"I was never Danielle's boyfriend. We only went out a couple times."

"No, but we all know you wanted to be," Brian retorted.

"And we all know the reason Danielle is no longer interested—I helped arrest her for Cheryl's murder."

"And what a perfect way to ingratiate yourself to her. Be the star witness to exonerate her in what appears to be a slam dunk case," Brian said.

"Enough!" the chief interrupted. "If Joe had come into this office yesterday morning before we filed charges on Danielle, then we wouldn't be having this conversation. Brian, I can't believe you'd doubt Joe's word."

"I never said I doubted him."

"It didn't sound like that to me," Joe grumbled.

"I was just playing the devil's advocate," Brian insisted.

"One thing I'm fairly confident about," the chief said. "Danielle Boatman is innocent, and someone is trying to frame her for Stoddard's murder. Whoever did this went to a lot of trouble to implicate Danielle. Darlene is looking like a prime suspect."

"She seemed sincerely upset at Stoddard's death," Brian said. "And you don't think Stoddard would recognize his own wife?"

"I would suspect she had an accomplice," the chief said.

"Why do you think she's involved at all?" Joe asked.

"For one reason, she's the one who brought Brian to the house when she found her husband," the chief said.

"But how would she have known..." Joe paused a moment, considering his question. He turned to Brian and said, "That's right. You said you were having breakfast at the diner—which you do every morning. Darlene knew right where to find you."

EIGHT

E arthbound Spirits headquarters perched high atop a rocky
ridge overlooking a section of Frederickport's northern beach.
The Hilton family—no relation to the hotel chain—built the house
in 1935. The property remained in the family until the passing of
Helen Hilton, who died at the age of ninety-eight. She bequeathed
her entire estate to Earthbound Spirits, much to the displeasure of
her four grandchildren.

Even Helen's great-nieces and nephews took umbrage over the
bequest, arguing Helen was only a Hilton by virtue of marriage to
her late husband and the property should remain within the Hilton
family.

Had Helen been around to argue her decision, she would
remind her unhappy family that since none of them made an effort
to visit her during her final years, none of them was entitled to the
property. The grandchildren contested the will, but their attorneys
were no match for the legal team employed by the secretive and
wealthy organization.

Peter Morris, founder of Earthbound Spirits, sat at his desk,
examining the two documents just handed to him by his protégé,
Cleve Monchique. The two men sat alone in the office, the
doors shut.

Morris, who had recently turned sixty, looked more like a man
in his late forties. Standing just under six feet, with a tennis player's

physique, his regular manner of dress reflected what a wealthy and cultured CEO might wear at the golf course. He concealed his gray hair under Nice'n Easy's Natural Black—though Natural Light Carmel Brown would have been a more flattering shade for his complexion.

"You got both wills..." Peter murmured. "Impressive."

"It answers the question, did Isabella put Earthbound Spirits in her will as she said—or was she just telling us what we wanted to hear while trying to annoy her uncle. I much prefer doing it this way instead of creating our own forgery."

While comparing the two documents, Peter sighed. "Earth-bound Spirits was obviously the beneficiary, if only for a brief time. I was rather hoping Stoddard's will was a forgery."

"None of that matters as long as we have this one!" Cleve said excitedly. "This is the original. We know Stoddard's is nothing but a photocopy—which we can easily argue was forged."

"I suppose this is my fault, having to do it this way." Peter wearily shook his head. "I should have realized I was pushing her too hard."

"It wasn't as if you asked more of Isabella than any other member," Cleve argued.

"But the pressure alienated her from us, and that didn't have to happen. Had I only known she was telling the truth, I could have eased off. Then maybe she would have never changed her will back, leaving everything to her uncle."

"I disagree. You didn't do anything wrong. Isabella was always more difficult than the others. Treating her differently would have set a bad example."

"True, Cleve. But at one time, she was one of the more dedicated members."

"It really doesn't matter now. Isabella is gone, we have both wills, and Stoddard is dead."

"And with him gone, easier for us to cry forgery when we hand over Isabella's will leaving us her estate. And considering what Stoddard did to that woman, trying to pass her off as Isabella, shouldn't be too hard to convince the court this was just another one of his cons."

"This is going to work." Cleve smiled with satisfaction. "If Isabella knew what her uncle was capable of doing, she'd thank us for setting this right."

45

"I feel better about it now, now that you have both originals. And you're sure all other copies have been destroyed?" Peter asked.

"Positive." Cleve sat in a chair facing Peter.

"Clarence won't be a problem." Peter set the documents on the desk and looked at Cleve. "But what about that woman who worked for him—Gloria Comings—wasn't that her name?"

"Yes, but she moved from the area. Considering what we have, there's no reason for anyone to track her down."

"All I have left to do is finalize things with Darlene." Peter leaned across the desk and pushed one of the wills toward Cleve. "Shred it. I don't want anyone coming across this."

With a nod, Cleve stood up and took the document. He glanced at it briefly, making sure it was the newer will, the one leaving Isabella's estate to her uncle. He smiled and then walked over to the paper shredder.

"I'd like you to put it in probate tomorrow," Peter said. "But wait until you hear from me and we know everything is set with Darlene."

"Sure."

Peter studied the will leaving Isabella's estate to Earthbound Spirits as Cleve fed the other document through the paper shredder. "There is one thing that's still bothering me. We all know Stoddard assumed Earthbound Spirits stood to inherit Isabella's fortune—that's why he took that woman. I can't believe he just stumbled across Isabella's current will in his files. Someone had to have told him where to find it."

"I suppose we need to be prepared for that possibility—one of Isabella's friends coming forward with a story about how Isabella told her—or him—that she'd changed her will back and put a copy of the revised document in her uncle's file cabinet."

"One way to handle it, we'll show there was a bribe—a payoff," Peter suggested. "If someone comes forward. There is a lot of money at stake."

"I suppose it wouldn't be too hard to discredit one of Isabella's friends—if one does come forward. But from what I understand, she lost touch with most of her old friends when she got involved with Earthbound Spirits. I kept a close eye on her when she pulled away from the group. No one stands out as a special confidant."

"What about that guy she used to date—Adam Nichols? The one who owns Frederickport Vacation Properties," Peter asked.

"Well, she did see him after he was arrested and released for that woman's murder from Marlow House back in July."

Peter nodded with approval. "You really were keeping an eye on her."

"A lot of money at stake." Cleve shrugged.

"I don't know what we'd do without you, Cleve."

"I hope getting rid of Christiansen won't be too much of a problem."

"I've been rethinking that. I know we want to bring in our own man—and I'm certain I can convince Darlene to vote with us to get rid of Christiansen, but maybe that's not the smartest thing to do."

"You don't seriously think we'll be able to work with Christiansen?" Cleve asked incredulously. "He's going to be a problem, you know it."

"But he also knows the company inside out. I don't want to take over a multimillion-dollar business and watch its value plummet. Maybe we'd be smarter to offer Christiansen a financial incentive—something to make him want to stay with the company and continue making us money."

Cleve shook his head. "I don't know. Christiansen thinks of the company as his own."

"Even better, nothing like an employee who takes a personal interest in the company he works for." Peter grinned.

"While you aren't worried about Darlene contesting our claim, I am a little concerned about Christiansen."

"I understand what you're saying. I'm sure Christiansen is counting on taking the helm with Stoddard gone. After all, Darlene isn't capable, and from what I understand, Christiansen's been virtually running the company for the last few years anyway," Peter said. "If he feels we plan to push him out, he'll undoubtedly jump in and try to contest our will in favor of Stoddard's. After all, Darlene will be much easier to control. But if we let Christiansen know we want him on our team—that we don't want to get involved with the management of the company—we could get him on our side. Everything would go much smoother with Christiansen on board."

"I suppose you might be right," Cleve said reluctantly. "Perhaps offer him a pay increase."

"That's pretty much what I'm thinking. From what I understand, Christiansen has some sort of profit share in the company. Increasing his share would probably seal the deal. I understand

Stoddard wasn't the easiest man to work with. If Christiansen feels we'll be a silent owner—agreeable to letting him run the business as he sees fit, then why wouldn't he stay? Why would he care if it's Darlene who owns the company or Darlene and Earthbound Spirits?"

"Just as long as we keep a close eye on the company. Regular audits."

"You don't trust Christiansen?" Peter asked with a laugh.

"I'd trust him more if he was a member of Earthbound Spirits," Cleve grumbled.

"Well, maybe we need to work on that conversion—after we get this settled."

"I've met Christiansen. I don't think he's a likely candidate."

"If Christiansen doesn't work out, we can get rid of him later," Peter said.

"But if he continues managing the company after we take over and he doesn't work out, he might not be so easy to get rid of," Cleve said.

"We thought Stoddard Gusarov was going to be a problem," Peter reminded him with a laugh. "But look how nicely that worked out."

NINE

Joe sat in the passenger seat of the squad car. He glanced over at Brian, who drove the vehicle toward Marlow House.

"I'm surprised the chief's not going with me instead of you—considering how Danielle feels about you." Still wearing his street clothes, dressed casually in new denims and a golf shirt, Joe leaned back in the seat.

"The feeling's mutual," Brian grumbled.

"I don't know why you have such a problem with Danielle. And she didn't kill Stoddard."

"Maybe not, but this used to be a nice, quiet, law-abiding town. Since Danielle Boatman arrived, we've been stumbling over dead bodies, and she seems to always be in the center of the drama."

"I understand you took quite a tumble when you went to arrest her yesterday. Fell on your butt?" Joe studied Brian's reaction.

Frowning, Brian turned to Joe and then looked back down the road. "Who said that?"

"Doesn't matter. Did you really fall in Marlow House after grabbing hold of Lily?"

"I didn't grab her exactly," Brian snapped. "I barely touched her."

"But one of the guys said you practically flew off your feet, landing on your back. Said the way you got up rubbing your chin, one would think someone had slugged you."

"Nobody hit me. I just slipped and fell."

"They didn't say anyone hit you. In fact, the way they saw it, you pretty much flew backwards without anyone's help."

"So? You've never fallen before?"

"I just was wondering; why did you get up rubbing your chin when it was your backside you landed on?"

"Why do you care?"

"When they told me..." Instead of finishing his sentence, Joe thought back to another fall he'd witnessed at Marlow House.

"They or he? Or she? Who's the chatty gossip we work with?"

"Doesn't matter." Joe shrugged. He leaned back in the seat and looked ahead. "But when they described it, it reminded me of Cheryl."

"Cheryl?" Brian frowned. "Boatman's cousin?"

"Yeah. I remember the day of the open house, before people started arriving. Cheryl fell in the hallway of Marlow House. No one saw her fall, but she landed on her backside—like you. Her face was bruised. She insisted Danielle shoved her, but Danielle swore she hadn't touched her cousin. At the time, Cheryl was grabbing at Danielle—like you were grabbing at Lily."

"Lily didn't shove me. No one touched me. I just fell," Brian insisted.

"But isn't it interesting—you both fell backwards in the hallway at Marlow House, and in both cases you felt as if someone hit your face."

"I never said anyone hit my face. Anyway, it wasn't in the hallway exactly. More like the entry."

"Close enough. Why were you rubbing your chin?" Joe asked.

"What's the big deal?" Brian snapped. "Fact is, Boatman probably did smack her cousin. You even saw the bruises. I just slipped. It happens. I don't know why you think one has anything to do with the other."

"I don't know." Joe shrugged. "I'm just trying to understand Danielle—make sense of things I've seen, or thought I've seen."

"I wonder what you would be thinking right now if you'd gone somewhere else for your vacation and hadn't seen Boatman yesterday morning. Then maybe you wouldn't be in such a hurry to find an excuse for all her past behaviors."

"You're right..." Joe murmured, looking out the side window.

"I'd probably be helping you lock her up...and that realization scares the crap out of me."

WHEN JOE and Brian arrived at Marlow House a few minutes later, Ian Bartley answered the front door.

"Joe, Brian, I'm surprised to see you two here," Ian coolly greeted, not inviting them inside.

"We'd like to talk to Danielle," Joe explained.

Ian raised his brow curiously, eyeing each officer. He noticed Joe was dressed in street clothes while Brian wore a uniform.

"Without her attorney present, really?" Ian asked.

"We understood her attorney was here," Joe explained.

Ian didn't respond, but silently studied both men a few moments while holding the edge of the front door. Finally, he opened the door wider, letting the officers inside the house.

"Wait here," Ian instructed after closing the front door. Silently, Joe and Brian waited in the foyer while Ian walked down the hallway to the library, where Danielle was meeting with her attorney, Candice Holloway.

"How did you two make it past the front door?" Walt asked when Ian left for the library. Neither man could see or hear Walt, yet that did not stop Walt from trying to make his presence known.

With his hands behind his back, Walt—dressed in his favorite pinstripe suit and leather shoes—circled the men while critically looking them up and down.

"I never understood what she saw in you," he told Joe. "Lily says you're good looking, but I don't see it at all. And you..." He turned his attention to Brian and paused a moment. "I want you to stay away from Danielle." Walt reached out and jabbed Brian on his right forearm.

"Ouch!" Brian called out, grabbing his now bruised forearm.

"Crybaby," Walt snorted. "That didn't even hurt."

"What was that for?" Brian asked Joe.

"What are you talking about?"

"You poked me," Brian accused.

"I didn't poke you."

Before Brian could respond, Candice Holloway exited the library and made her way down the hall toward the waiting officers.

She looked just as Brian remembered from their brief meeting the day before. Yet today, she wore a pink linen suit.

"Gentlemen, I understand you wish to speak to my client," Candice said primly, holding out her hand in greeting. Joe briefly shook her hand as he introduced himself. She had already met Brian.

"We were hoping to speak to both of you," Joe explained.

"I suppose we can listen to what you have to say, but at this time, my client really has nothing to say." Candice smiled sweetly.

"I'm sure your client will be thrilled with what we have to say," Brian said dryly.

"We'll see." Candice turned and headed toward the library, leaving the officers to trail after her.

"I wasn't thrilled over the fact Danielle's lawyer is a woman," Walt said as he walked toward the library with the two silent police officers. "But she doesn't seem particularly intimidated by you two palookas." Walt chuckled. "Maybe she'll work out after all."

In the library, they found Lily and Danielle sitting on the sofa together, talking to Ian, who sat in a chair across from them. When the attorney reentered the library, followed by Joe and Brian, the three turned toward the doorway. Ian stood, yet Danielle and Lily remained seated.

"The officers have something they wish to tell us. But I've already informed them that Ms. Boatman has nothing to say at this time," Candice explained as she walked into the library and headed to the seat next to Ian. Both she and Ian sat down and looked up at the officers, who remained standing.

Walt followed them into the room and sat on the edge of the desk, observing the unfolding scene. With a wave of his hand, a thin cigar appeared between two of his fingers. He took a puff and looked over at Danielle, who warily eyed Brian and Joe.

"We knew it was only a matter of time until Joe got in on the act," Walt told Danielle. "I don't know why Ian let the clowns in my house."

Danielle glanced over to Walt, prepared to send him a scolding glance. She hated when he rambled on when other people were present—it made it too difficult for her to focus—but then motion from the library window beyond Walt caught her eye. It was Stoddard's ghost. He stood outside the window, his fists silently pounding against the pane as he wailed pitifully. Or at least, she assumed he was wailing pitifully, considering how his mouth was moving. Fortunately for her, she couldn't actually hear his caterwauling, at least not with the window closed.

"Chief MacDonald did try calling you," Joe told the attorney. "Your phone went to voice mail."

Danielle turned her back to Walt and the window, trying to focus her attention on what Joe and Brian had to say.

"So you decided to just come over here?" Candice said.

"We thought you'd want to know immediately. Charges against your client have been dropped," Brian explained, his tone void of any emotion.

"They have?" Danielle exclaimed, sitting up straighter.

Silently Candice motioned for Danielle to remain silent, wanting to hear everything the officers had to say.

"It seems a witness has come forward and claims to have seen Ms. Boatman during the time Stoddard was murdered. His story corroborates Ms. Boatman's account."

"And who is this witness?" Candice asked.

"I am," Joe said softly, looking over at Danielle.

Walt shot off the desk, bolting upright. Now standing, he looked from Joe to Danielle.

"He better not be making this up just to get back in your good graces," Walt said angrily. "His so-called help could end up backfiring and cause you more harm."

Danielle glanced to Walt and back to Joe. She wanted to ask questions, but continued to follow her attorney's instructions and remained silent.

"I don't understand; Joe is the witness?" Lily asked. All eyes turned to Joe, waiting for him to explain. He and Brian remained standing.

"I've been on vacation. Instead of going out of town, I rented a beach house on Sea Cliff Drive." As Joe talked, his eyes remained on Danielle. "Yesterday morning I heard someone knocking at the house next door. I looked out the window—it was Danielle. I noticed the time; it was 7 a.m. This morning when I got up, I turned on the radio and heard a news report about Danielle being arrested. At the time, I didn't know when the crime had been committed. It wasn't until I went into the station that I learned the details of the case—and I realized it couldn't have been Danielle."

"And if you hadn't seen me with your own eyes, you would've

believed I murdered Gusarov?" Danielle asked angrily, unable to contain her comment.

"I'm sorry, Danielle," Joe said. "I didn't know what to think when I heard the news report. I couldn't imagine you would have done something like that."

Candice stood up and walked to Danielle. Keeping her eyes on Joe and Brian, she gently placed her hand on Danielle's shoulder.

"Thank you for coming over here and telling us," Candice said. "Have there been any new leads in the case?"

"If what Joe says is true, then I guess this means someone has gone through a great deal of trouble to frame your client, considering the eyewitnesses who claim to have seen Danielle driving by Stoddard's house during the morning of the shooting," Brian said.

"And is there some reason you doubt Sergeant Morelli's account of the events?" Candice asked.

"No…" Brian said, glancing over to Joe, who was now glaring in his direction.

"I'd like to hear exactly what you saw yesterday," Candice asked Joe. She walked over to the desk and picked up a pad of paper and pen.

Joe gave Candice a nod and then proceeded to tell her what he'd seen and heard yesterday morning, beginning when he first heard Danielle pounding on the neighbor's door. He explained how he heard Danielle introduce herself when knocking on the door, how he'd been watching her with the binoculars, and about the car that had driven down the street when Danielle was sitting at the back of the house on the porch swing. The car, as Joe explained, appeared to be the same make and model as Danielle's, and it was entirely possible, Joe said, that whoever was driving the second car might have put the murder weapon in Danielle's vehicle.

Candice took notes as Joe told his story, and she asked several questions during the telling. When he was done, she thanked him, but she didn't allow Danielle to ask any additional questions.

"THAT'S GOOD NEWS, isn't it?" Ian asked after Joe and Brian departed.

"I feel as if a tremendous weight has been lifted," Danielle said with a sigh, slumping against the back of the sofa.

Lily reached over and patted Danielle's knee. With a smile she said, "I knew this would all work out."

Candice tucked the notepad inside her briefcase. "I'd like to say this is all over."

"What do you mean?" Danielle asked warily.

"I'm just saying this is still an open investigation, and the victim did name you as his killer," Candice explained.

"But Joe said he saw Danielle at the time of the murder," Lily said.

"I understand that," Candice said. "And hopefully, this will be the end of it. But if the DA decides he can make a case against Danielle and believes Joe has perjured himself because of his past relationship with Danielle, then they could possibly refile charges. We have no idea what else the police might uncover."

TEN

"Stop being annoying, you miserable excuse for a spirit!" Lily shouted from the open kitchen door, into the side yard of Marlow House. "Why don't you get your scrawny ghost butt moving onto the next level and face the music, you coward! Go haunt your own house, you loser!"

"Umm, Lily, he isn't there anymore," Danielle said when she walked into the kitchen.

Lily turned from the open doorway and looked at Danielle. "He isn't?"

"Nope. He's up by the attic window, making ugly faces at Walt."

"What's Walt doing?" Lily closed the door, hobbled over to the kitchen table, and sat down.

"Silently staring at him while smoking a cigar. I'm not sure what they would be doing if they could actually be in the same room together." Danielle took a seat at the table and glanced up at the clock. It had been almost twenty-four hours since she learned the local authorities had dropped the murder charges.

"I find it exceedingly annoying Gusarov has the audacity to hang around here throwing his ghost fits after what he did to me! I wish I could see the dead old goat; then I would be able to tell him off properly!" Lily said angrily.

"Consider yourself lucky you can't see him. Because trust me, it's getting old having him hang out in the yard. I don't even want to go outside anymore."

"That's what makes me so darn angry. All of this is his fault, but he's making it something you did."

"He's obviously pissed to be dead. Not sitting well with him. I just hope…" Danielle glanced toward the window.

"Hope what?"

"That he doesn't figure out how to harness his energy."

"I thought you said that wasn't possible."

"I'm only guessing." Danielle sighed. "It's like with you and your reflection in the mirror—nothing more than an assumption on my part."

"But you were right," Lily reminded her.

"True. But I could have been wrong. And when it comes to harnessed energy, we know it's possible, look at Walt."

"But you said spirits who are able to harness energy usually have a limited space to do it in—like with Walt."

"Yes, that's my experience. There are some haunted places where disruptive paranormal activity has been reported—instances where a spirit might be capable of harming a living person. Things like scratches and moving objects, which could result in injury. The pattern seems to indicate those destructive powers are limited to a small area. The ghost can't just wander at will causing havoc."

"So what is the problem?" Lily frowned.

Danielle looked at Lily. "What happens if Stoddard is able to cultivate a sphere of power here…around my house. Since I first moved in, I knew this was a haunted house—but Walt, well, you know Walt. Not exactly a spirit that sends my guests running and screaming from the premises."

"Can't say the same for those who break in—or try to arrest you." Lily giggled.

"True." Danielle smiled.

"I see what you're saying though. If Stoddard sticks around long enough, he might learn to harness his power and be a menace to Marlow House."

"Exactly." Danielle let out another sigh. "I tried talking to him last night. When I told him the charges against me had been dropped, I hoped he'd take that to mean I was innocent and he was wrong. But he just got angrier."

"About those charges being dropped. I hope your attorney is

wrong. I don't want to even consider the possibility the DA could still bring new charges against you."

"I think she was just being brutally honest. Her job is to consider all the possibilities. And what she said didn't really come as a big surprise to me. I understand that charges can always be refiled if for some reason they feel Joe isn't telling the truth or if something else comes up during their investigation."

"Oh, Dani, how can you say that and sound so calm?" Lily asked.

Danielle shrugged. "I guess I have to have faith that eventually everything will work out."

Before Lily could respond, the doorbell rang.

"That wouldn't be your nurse, would it?" Danielle asked as she stood up.

"No. She was already here this afternoon. You were upstairs. I think in the attic."

"Wow, she was quick." Danielle started for the door.

"Takes less than forty minutes," Lily said. "I don't think it's Ian. He had that meeting over in Astoria this afternoon."

"Just as long as," Danielle called out from the doorway leading to the hallway, "it isn't the police again!"

When Danielle answered the front door a few moments later, it wasn't anyone from the Frederickport Police Department. Nor was it anyone she knew—although he did look somewhat familiar.

A tall lanky man wearing pressed denims, a crisp white long-sleeved shirt, bolo tie, and cowboy boots and hat stood on the front porch. She guessed he was about the same age as Lily's parents.

"Hello, can I help you?" Danielle greeted him cheerfully, trying to place the man.

"Are you the proprietor?" he asked.

"Yes, I am. What can I do for you?"

"I was hoping you had a vacancy. I would have called, but I'm afraid I don't own a cellphone, and no one seems to have pay phones anymore."

"Oh, I'm sorry. I'm not taking reservations at this time," Danielle apologized.

"I was afraid of that. All full up, huh?"

"Well, actually…" Danielle paused and took a closer look at the man. "You're Billy Bob Wayne, aren't you?"

The man laughed. "Goodness, little lady, I certainly never imagined I would be recognized up in these parts!"

"You never hear them complain when they buy a car from Billy Bob Wayne!" Danielle sang.

"You really do know who I am!" He laughed again.

"I used to visit a friend of mine who lived in Phoenix, and I remember your commercials. You are something of a celebrity."

"Ahh yes, I have to fight off the lovely ladies." He grinned.

"Would you like to come in? Maybe I can help you find someplace to stay. I'm Danielle Boatman, by the way. I own Marlow House."

Billy Bob Wayne accepted Danielle's invitation and followed her into the parlor. When he was standing on the front porch, she hadn't noticed his cane. It wasn't until they were in the parlor and he was preparing to sit down that she noticed it. That, and the fact he walked with a limp.

"I'm really sorry to hear you're full up. I picked up one of your brochures when I got into town. This place sure looks more interesting than the local hotels."

"I assume you're traveling alone—or did you leave someone sitting in your car?" Danielle asked.

"Oh no, just me." Billy Bob smiled.

"The Seahorse Motel is nice, and it's right on the ocean," Danielle said. "I could call them for you; see if they have any vacancies."

"I really didn't come here to look at the ocean." He removed his cowboy hat and set it on his lap.

"You aren't here on vacation?" Danielle asked.

"I suppose I am," Billy Bob said with a sigh. "I recently retired. Finally getting around to doing some traveling."

"You don't have the car dealership anymore?"

"No. Sold it a few months ago. Figured I'd been doing it long enough."

"Is this your first time in Frederickport?"

"Actually, I used to live here," he said.

"Oh, so you're in town visiting friends…family perhaps?"

"Never really kept in contact with anyone. Been years since I lived here. But my wife and daughter are still here. That's why I decided to come. Should have come earlier. But there are no do-overs in life."

59

"Your wife and daughter live in Frederickport? Maybe I know them."

"I doubt it. They don't live here exactly. Their graves are at the Frederickport Cemetery."

"Oh...I'm so sorry."

"It's been a long time. But I figured I wanted to make it here—at least one more time before I cash in my ticket."

"How long were you planning to stay in town?" Danielle asked.

"Just a week. Rented a car in Portland. Flying home next Friday."

"The thing is..." Danielle glanced briefly at his cane. "I have a friend staying with me—she is convalescing. She has an infection in her leg, which requires IV treatments three times a day. I thought it best not to take any guests while she's recovering."

"Oh..." Billy Bob sat up straighter in his chair. "I wouldn't be any problem, I promise. I'd stay out of her way, wouldn't disrupt her sleep."

"The only problem, she's using the only downstairs bedroom. While I wouldn't mind letting you stay—especially considering the circumstances—the only available rooms are upstairs, and we don't have an elevator."

"Oh, this?" Billy Bob gave his lame leg a light smack with his cane. "Slows me down a bit, but I can manage stairs. At the dealership, my office was upstairs. Walked them every day."

"If you're sure." Danielle smiled.

"I'd really appreciate it, Ms. Boatman."

"Please, call me Danielle." She stood up. "I think we can fit you in."

"And please call me Will."

"Will?" Danielle frowned.

"I only used Billy Bob for advertising purposes. I was born in California. You really think my folks named me Billy Bob?" He laughed.

"William Robert?" she asked.

"Yep." He grinned.

"And the boots and hat? Please don't tell me you aren't a real cowboy," she teased.

"Strictly drugstore. Never been on a horse in my life."

Danielle laughed and then said, "Let me go check the Red Room. I believe Joanne has it already made up."

"Joanne?"

"She's our housekeeper, sometimes cook. You'll meet her later."

Will stood up. "While you check on the room, I'll go out to the car and grab my suitcase."

A few moments later Walt appeared in the entry hall just as Will walked outside and shut the door behind him.

"Who's that?" Walt asked, peering out the window.

"Our new guest," Danielle said brightly.

"I thought you weren't taking any new guests until Lily got better," Walt asked while following Danielle down the hallway.

"Oh, Lily, I better tell her before she wonders about the strange man walking around the house!"

Instead of continuing to the staircase, Danielle turned into the kitchen. Lily was still sitting at the table.

"Lily, we have a houseguest!" Danielle announced.

"Fine, ignore me," Walt grumbled.

"What do you mean?" Lily asked.

"The person who was at the door—he was looking for a place to stay."

"I thought you weren't going to take any new guests for a while," Lily said.

"That's what I asked," Walt said, knowing only Danielle could hear him.

ELEVEN

"Are you insane?" Chuck Christiansen shouted as he paced the floor in the home office at the Gusarov Estate. He'd just driven in from Portland and wasn't happy with what Darlene was telling him.

Clutching her hands in her lap, Darlene cringed and looked up at Chuck. "Don't yell at me. Someone is going to hear." She sat primly on the chair next to Chuck's desk.

"The door is closed," he snapped. "Not to mention, your house-keeping staff doesn't speak English."

"They can still hear you screaming at me—and I am your boss," she squeaked.

"Right," Chuck snorted. He stopped pacing and looked down at Darlene, his hands on his hips. "You and that group of fruit loops are my new bosses. Thanks to you."

"Well, what does it matter?" Darlene shrugged. "Me or them. I understand they want to keep you on."

"That makes me feel just peachy keen," he snapped.

"It's not my fault. You didn't expect me to lie, did you?" She looked up into his angry face.

"I certainly didn't expect you to tell the probate court Stoddard forged Isabella's will!"

"Don't yell at me! I didn't know the will was forged until Tuesday night."

"And you didn't think to tell me all this—why?"

"Todd assured me there was no other will. I just figured he worked something out with Renton. Everything happened so fast. I was afraid."

"You should have just played dumb instead of handing over half of the estate to that group of nuts. We have attorneys; we could have fought them."

"They caught me by surprise." Darlene looked down at her hands fidgeting nervously on her lap. "With everything going on, I just didn't want to deal with this. I told them the truth—that I learned about the fake will the night before Todd was killed, and I didn't know what to do—and then he was murdered." Darlene looked up at Chuck. "They can't blame me for something Todd did —something I just found out about."

"So just like that, you hand over half of the estate?"

"What do you care? What does it matter if I'm a sole owner or not—it doesn't change your position with the company. I told you, they want you to stay on."

"Does this mean you've talked to them?"

Darlene nodded. "Yes, this morning."

"Before or after you talked to the court?"

"What does it matter?"

"What does it matter?" Chuck shouted. He stomped over to the chair behind Stoddard's desk and sat down. "I haven't worked my butt off—put my entire life and soul into this company, risked every-thing—just to end up working for some wacky cult like Earthbound Spirits. I didn't sign up for this!"

"I didn't know what else to do," Darlene whispered.

After a few moments of silence, Chuck sighed and said, "I suppose I always knew the will was a fake."

"Why do you say that?"

"Stoddard told me someone called him anonymously—said he assumed it was a friend of Isabella's—letting him know where to find the will. I should have known he'd done something like this."

"I'm not happy about this either." Darlene rubbed her temples.

"I guess you aren't. But I wonder, does this mean Isabella's share of the estate is protected from Lily Miller's lawsuit?"

Darlene stopped rubbing her temples and looked over at Chuck. "What do you mean?"

"Think about it. If Isabella's estate goes directly to Earthbound

Spirits and not to Stoddard, then I don't see how she can touch it. But the share you get from Stoddard—his half of the company— her attorneys might be able to wrestle a portion of that from you."

"But it's mine. Before Todd died, he told authorities I had nothing to do with taking Lily Miller."

"Yeah, right."

"My point is, if she can't touch Isabella's estate because Isabella had nothing to do with the abduction, then Lily shouldn't be able to touch my share either! As far as the authorities know, I knew nothing about it!"

"It doesn't work that way. I already explained that to you. Technically, it doesn't belong to you yet—it still belongs to Stoddard."

"He's dead."

"Obviously. Don't be obtuse, Darlene; you know very well you may have to pay off a chunk of the estate to Miller."

"Well, I didn't think it would all come from my half." Darlene stood up and rubbed her forehead. Agitated, she paced the room.

"I see it just sank in." Chuck leaned back in the chair and watched Darlene pace. "Whatever Miller gets in way of a settlement, it wouldn't hurt as much if your estate was twice the size— which it was this morning until you so foolishly opened your big mouth."

"I didn't even consider that." Darlene paced faster.

"Sit back down. You're making me dizzy." Chuck pointed to the chair.

Darlene stopped pacing, looked at Chuck, and then quietly sat back down.

Chuck studied Darlene for a moment. Her fair complexion appeared paler than normal, with no hint of blush on her cheeks or discernable makeup enhancing her clear blue eyes. While he hadn't seen her cry, her long dark eyelashes seemed to glisten with unshed tears. The way she pulled her blonde hair back in a silk scarf reminded him of a Russian peasant. The designer pantsuit and Christian Louboutin shoes offset the peasant look.

"Of course, that is the sunny version," Chuck said. "There is another, darker scenario."

"What are you talking about?" Darlene frowned. "I'd say that version is anything but sunny."

"I spoke to our attorneys last night, and it seems that because corporate resources were involved—such as paying for the medical staff to care for Miller—the corporation, as well as your private estate, may be held liable. Which I'm sure won't please your new business partner—Earthbound Spirits."

"But I thought we took care of all that? I thought that's what this was all about?" Darlene whined.

"Only where it touches us personally—it won't protect the company or Stoddard's interests."

"This just keeps getting worse and worse." Darlene closed her eyes for a moment and took a deep breath.

"But we have other things we need to discuss," Chuck announced.

"What else could there be? This is more than enough for us to deal with."

"I talked to Chief MacDonald this morning. Seems they dropped the charges against Danielle Boatman."

"What do you mean they dropped the charges? I was there when Todd told Brian Henderson Boatman was the shooter. He heard him!" Darlene jumped to her feet and slammed her fist on Stoddard's desk.

Chuck shook his head. "Apparently there was a witness who saw Boatman somewhere else during the time Todd was murdered."

"That's impossible! Who saw her, where?" Darlene sat back down.

"I don't know. MacDonald wouldn't say who it was. But obviously, he believes the witness."

"That's ridiculous. With Todd's dying breath, he named his killer. Do you know when this so-called witness saw Boatman?"

"Apparently between 7 a.m. and when you and Henderson found your husband." Chuck removed a cigarette from an ivory box on Stoddard's desk and lit it with a lighter he'd fished from one of the desk drawers.

Darlene stubbornly folded her arms across her chest and leaned back in the chair. "Well, that doesn't mean anything. She could have killed him before seven."

"Unfortunately, there's another witness that proves Stoddard was still alive at seven—so if the police believe this anonymous person saw Boatman after seven, she won't be charged and they will start looking at other suspects."

Darlene narrowed her eyes and glared at Chuck. "Who is this other witness?"

"I am. Did you forget I talked to Stoddard on the phone that morning?"

"Maybe you were wrong about the time. Maybe you talked to Todd fifteen minutes earlier, which would mean Boatman had time to shoot him before the witness saw her."

"They have my phone records, remember?"

"What about the men from the disposal company who saw Boatman in the neighborhood during that time frame? They saw her car! We know they're telling the truth! Who is to say Boatman isn't paying off someone to give her an alibi! She has the money!"

"I mentioned that to the chief." Chuck flicked an ash into a silver bowl on the desktop.

"What did he say?"

"He claimed his mystery witness is unimpeachable."

"Bull. Anyone can be bought."

"Very true. And Danielle Boatman has unlimited resources. She could easily find someone to come forward as a witness."

"Exactly," Darlene said with a nod.

"I think you need to go down to the police station and raise hell."

"Me? What do you mean?" Darlene frowned.

"You're Stoddard's widow. You were there when your husband died in your arms—when he told you and Officer Henderson the name of his murderer. You have every right to be outraged—you should be outraged—knowing his killer is getting away with murder. For you not to be furious wouldn't be natural, considering the circumstances."

Darlene stood up. "Of course, you're right. After all, Todd himself told us who shot him. When Brian asked him pointed questions, he clearly identified Danielle Boatman as his assassin. If Todd was still alive, they wouldn't be pulling this." Darlene walked to the window and looked outside.

"If he was alive, then we wouldn't be discussing the fate of his killer," Chuck scoffed.

"I know that," Darlene snapped, looking at Chuck briefly before turning back to the window. "I just meant people listened to Todd; they respected him. He wouldn't let the police just ignore something like this."

"And Stoddard also got himself—and others—into one hell of a mess by hiding Isabella's body and then taking Lily Miller."

Darlene looked over her shoulder at Chuck. "And he's paid dearly for his crime, hasn't he?"

Chuck was silent for a moment and then said with a sigh, "I suppose he has."

Darlene walked back to the chair and sat down. "I loved my husband. I would have been happy to spend the rest of my life with him."

"Yes, I understand that," Chuck said wearily. "But it just didn't work out like that. Things happen in our lives that we can't control."

"I wish I could have given him a baby while he was still alive." Darlene looked down and touched her belly. "He always wanted children," she said dramatically.

"I wonder..." Chuck leaned back in his chair, contemplating a thought.

"What?"

"I wonder if Danielle Boatman plans to go to Stoddard's funeral tomorrow."

"Why would she do that?" Darlene frowned.

"She went to Isabella's funeral," Chuck reminded her.

"Which I thought was ridiculous. She didn't even know Isabella."

"But some people feel compelled to attend funerals, even if they barely knew the deceased."

"Danielle Boatman didn't know Isabella. They never even met."

"But Danielle found the body."

"What's your point, Chuck?"

"Just that I wouldn't be surprised to see Danielle Boatman at Stoddard's funeral—and just in case she's there, you should be prepared."

"Prepared how?"

"Think about it. The woman who murdered your husband, do you really want her at his funeral?"

Darlene silently considered Chuck's words. After a few minutes, she screwed up her face in a frown and said, "You're right! That woman—that cold-blooded killer has no business coming to my husband's funeral! Why is she there...to gloat? To make sure the poor man is actually dead? What kind of woman does that? Just because she fooled the police—paid off some witness with all her money—doesn't make her any more innocent!"

TWELVE

"I'm just surprised you took in someone from off the street," Lily said before taking a bite of chocolate cake. She sat with Danielle and Walt in the parlor. While she couldn't see or hear Walt, she knew he was there. She and Danielle had finished dinner an hour earlier, which they had shared with William Robert Wayne. He was now upstairs in the Red Room.

"This is a bed and breakfast. Taking people off the street is what we do." Danielle sat on the sofa with a plate of chocolate cake. She took her first bite and closed her eyes briefly while savoring the taste. "This is darn good cake, if I do say so myself." Danielle took a second bite.

"You should consider opening a bakery," Lily teased.

"I'm already baking too much—and eating what I bake!" Danielle grinned and licked off a smudge of chocolate frosting from the corner of her mouth.

"I suppose I'll have to take you dancing and work off those calories," Walt teased.

Danielle flashed him a grin. "I'd love that. Even though it doesn't work on calories."

"What are you talking about?" Lily frowned, looking to where she assumed Walt stood.

"Oh, nothing, a private joke," Danielle said with a dreamy smile.

"Geez, please, I feel left out enough around you two." Lily speared a bite of chocolate cake.

"Sorry, Lily, I guess that was rude." Danielle flashed Walt another smile, which he returned.

"Back to this new guest of yours. Why exactly did you decide to take him in? It's not that I really care. I mean, I never thought you needed to stop taking guests because of me, anyhow. I'm just curious. Why him?" Lily took another bite of her dessert.

"I suppose I felt sorry for him." Danielle shrugged. "He's here to visit the graves of his wife and daughter. Just seemed so sad. And I knew who he was."

"Yeah, Billy Bob Wayne. I'd never heard of him myself," Lily said.

"He's really only famous in the Phoenix area. Or was. He told me he sold his dealership a few months ago, so I imagine there's some new Billy Bob to take his place."

"Do you know what happened to his wife and daughter?" Lily asked.

"I didn't want to pry. I imagine he'll go over to the cemetery tomorrow."

"Aren't they having Stoddard's funeral tomorrow?"

"Yes. Marie called me up this afternoon and quizzed me about the arrest. I guess she heard all about it. While we were on the phone, she mentioned his funeral, told me if I wanted to go, I could go with her and Adam."

"You aren't going, are you?" Lily asked.

"Heck no! You know how I feel about cemeteries in the first place. And why would I want to go to that man's funeral? Not with his annoying ghost haunting my yard." Danielle shuddered at the thought.

She picked up her empty cake plate—now just littered with crumbs—and placed it atop Lily's. Danielle started to carry them to the kitchen when the doorbell rang. Setting the plates on the desk, she went to answer the front door.

A few minutes later, she returned to the parlor with Chief MacDonald. Instead of his police uniform, he wore street clothes—denims and a button-down shirt.

"Evening, Chief, you didn't come to arrest my friend again, did you?" Lily asked, only half teasing.

"Not today, Lily. But I imagine she'll get herself into some mischief in the future, and I'll have to lock her up—for the safety of Frederickport." He grinned and took a seat.

"The chief says he needs to talk to me about something, and I told him you already know all my secrets, so no reason to leave the room." Danielle sat back down on the sofa.

In the corner, Walt summoned a lit cigar. A moment later, he exhaled and watched as the smoke drifted up to the ceiling.

Catching a whiff of the spicy scent—which wasn't there when he walked into the room—MacDonald took a deep breath. "Cigar smoke. Does that mean Walt Marlow is in the room?"

"Wow, you catch on quickly," Lily said with a chuckle. "When Danielle told me you understood, I didn't quite believe her."

"I don't understand exactly," the chief clarified. "But I do believe she has a gift. My grandmother taught me that."

"As for the cigar smoke," Lily went on. "It only means he is smoking. Walt might be in the room when there's no hint of cigar because he doesn't smoke all the time."

"Fascinating. I'm intrigued that I can smell it. I would expect it would only be something Danielle could smell," the chief said.

"I believe everyone has some degree of psychic powers," Danielle explained.

"Should I really wow him?" Walt asked mischievously.

Danielle flashed Walt a rebuking frown. He ignored her less than friendly expression and waved his hand. The cigar vanished. He then walked to the curio shelf on the wall and removed a small figurine.

Chief MacDonald sat speechless, his eyes wide as he watched a small porcelain horse float through the air in his direction.

It took Danielle a moment to realize what had captured the chief's attention. She frowned and said, "Stop showing off, Walt!" The porcelain horse fell into the chief's lap.

"Holy crap," the chief muttered, picking up the figurine and looking at it. Warily, he glanced around the room.

"Ignore Walt," Danielle said as she stood up and snatched the porcelain horse from his grasp and then placed it back on the shelf.

"Yeah, like that's possible," the chief said nervously, glancing around.

"You never let me have any fun," Walt said with an exaggerated pout. "See if I take you dancing."

THE GHOST WHO WANTED REVENGE

"So what did you want to talk about?" Danielle asked, ignoring Walt.

The chief shook his head and then continued. "I had an interesting call this afternoon from someone I know over in the probate court. Apparently, Earthbound Spirits has filed a will with the court —Isabella's will—which leaves them her entire estate."

Danielle had been the one who told Chief MacDonald about Isabelle's most current will, which Isabella had hidden at the Gusarov Estate months before her death. Danielle had acquired that information from Isabella's spirit—something the chief knew. According to Isabella's spirit, she had changed her will back, leaving her estate to her uncle and not to Earthbound Spirits. Since MacDonald couldn't very well call Stoddard and tell him where to find his niece's will, he had made an anonymous call to Stoddard, pretending to be one of Isabella's friends.

"It's a fake," Danielle said. "We know Stoddard has Isabella's most current will. Not that I care who inherits her estate, but it's a fake."

"That's what's interesting," the chief said as he leaned back in the chair. "According to Darlene Gusarov, the night before Stoddard was murdered, he admitted to forging the will and planting it in his house. Darlene's not contesting Earthbound Spirit's claim on Isabella's estate, which should be going to her now, but won't."

"While I'm thrilled to know that woman ends up with less money, she's lying," Lily said. "Isabella told Danielle about the new will. Stoddard didn't forge it."

The chief nodded. "Exactly. And yet, Darlene is telling the court it's a fake, handing over half of the company to Earthbound Spirits, and why?"

"It doesn't make any sense." Danielle frowned.

"Is it possible Stoddard told her that for some reason?" Lily asked.

"I don't know why he would," MacDonald said.

Danielle stood up. "There is one way to find out. I'll ask him."

"Don't tell me…he's here?" MacDonald asked.

Danielle marched from the room to confront Stoddard's spirit, leaving Lily to explain about the unwelcome haunting. As Lily chattered away, Walt turned his attention to MacDonald. Narrowing his eyes, he silently studied the man. Since adjusting to life—or death— as a spirit, Walt realized he was no longer adept at judging a person's age. Everyone seemed so much younger than how he remembered from his life in the 1920s. When first seeing Danielle, he guessed she was in her early twenties—never imagining she was thirty.

The chief was obviously older than Joe and Ian, yet younger than Brian Henderson. Danielle mentioned he had several small boys. How young they actually were, he didn't know. He supposed a woman might consider the tall, stocky man handsome, yet Walt thought he looked rather ordinary, with graying brown hair and blue-gray eyes. He gave the chief points for having faith in Danielle, and perhaps he might actually like the man if they were to meet in another time or place—yet he didn't particularly want to like him.

THE MOMENT DANIELLE stepped from the kitchen to the side yard, Stoddard swooped down from above and shoved his face just inches from hers as he let out an angry howl and waved his arms, reminding her of a wounded bird trying to take flight.

"Would you please stop that for a moment. I have a question for you," Danielle asked in a bored tone as she did her best to ignore his facial contortions. He didn't stop immediately. When he couldn't get her to show fear or anger, he settled down on his feet.

Crossing his arms across his chest, he faced Danielle. "What?"

"Did you, by any chance, tell your wife Isabella's will—the one you found in your house—was fake? That you forged it?"

In response, Stoddard started shouting again, telling her the will wasn't fake and asking her what she was pulling. "If you're trying to hurt my wife by—"

"Quiet, please, and listen!" Danielle shouted. Miraculously, he did. "I know the will isn't fake. I know it was not forged. Just who do you think is responsible for you finding it in the first place?"

"What are you talking about?" Stoddard frowned.

"Your niece's spirit told me about the will. She explained she changed it months ago—taking Earthbound Spirits out of it and putting you back in. She then told me where to find it. That's why you received the anonymous phone call."

"Then why did you ask me that question?"

"Because your wife has told the court you forged Isabella's will

—the one you found—and Earthbound Spirits has filed a second will with the courts, leaving them your niece's estate instead of you."

"Why would Darlene say something like that?"

"I have no idea. I was hoping you knew."

Stoddard was silent for a moment and then narrowed his eyes and glared at Danielle. "All this is your fault, if you hadn't killed me!"

Disgusted with his new outburst, Danielle turned and headed back to the house, leaving Stoddard hurling insults in her direction.

"HE SAYS he never told Darlene that," Danielle said when she walked back into the parlor. "And I believe him."

"Why would she tell a lie like that?" Lily asked.

"That's what I'd like to know. As far as a motive for murder, Darlene is at the top of my list, primarily because she had the most to gain financially. But now this. Why would she tell the courts her husband forged the will and just give away half of the company?" Danielle asked.

"I can only think of one reason. Some sort of payoff." MacDonald suggested. "Maybe she and Earthbound Spirits were in this together. With Stoddard gone, they divide the company. Although, from everything we've uncovered so far, there doesn't seem to be any connection between Darlene and Earthbound Spirits —no phone calls, no meetings, nothing."

"But the investigation has only been going on a few days; it's entirely possible there's a connection you've missed," Danielle suggested.

"Let's say we do find something—phone calls, meetings—why would Darlene give up such a large share of the estate to get rid of her husband? Isabella's share was a fortune—why wouldn't Darlene just wait and find someone she could pay to do the job for far less money?" MacDonald asked.

"I don't know, maybe hit men are simply hard to find?" Danielle shrugged.

They were silent for a few moments. Finally, the chief asked, "Are you going to Stoddard's funeral?"

"I wasn't planning on it. Why?" Danielle frowned.

"It might give you a chance to get a closer look at all the players. Maybe you'll pick up something useful," he said.

"I told you I just see spirits. I don't read minds or have ESP or anything like that."

"I understand. But would you consider going? You're the only ones I can discuss this with. I need someone I trust who I can bounce ideas off, and if you go tomorrow, maybe you'll pick up something I missed. Not because you have any special psychic powers. I can't very well announce Darlene is lying, that she's giving away half of her estate for some reason, or even suggest that possibility. I have nothing to back it up aside from the fact Isabella's ghost told you where to find her will."

Danielle let out a deep sigh and said, "Okay, I'll go."

THIRTEEN

Lily and Will sat in the dining room of Marlow House while Danielle served them a breakfast of homemade blueberry muffins, scrambled eggs, bacon, and fresh fruit. She had set three places at the table and intended to join them once all the food was brought out from the kitchen.

"We could have eaten at the kitchen table, like we did last night. I feel bad making you go to all this trouble," Will said.

"Don't be silly." Danielle refilled each of their coffee cups before sitting down at the table. "Eating in the dining room is more civilized. And I can't have people saying Marlow House is anything but civilized!"

Lily looked down the long dining room table with all the empty seats. "Yeah, right. And it's real cozy too."

"Oh hush, Lily!" Danielle laughed.

"So what are you ladies doing today?" Will asked.

"I'll be doing the same thing I do every day—lay around the house and wait for the nurse to arrive and hook me up to the IV," Lily grumbled. Danielle reached over and patted Lily's hand.

"Does it hurt when she hooks you up?" Will asked.

"Nahh, I'm just being a big ol' baby." Lily flashed Will a guilty grin and took a bite of her muffin.

"I'm going to a funeral this morning. Perhaps I'll see you at the cemetery?" Danielle asked.

"Funeral?" Will frowned. "I'm sorry. Was it a close friend?"

"Close friend? No. Definitely not." Danielle shook her head and grabbed some bacon.

"Doesn't sound like you were fond of the departed," Will observed.

"Stoddard Gusarov, I mentioned him last night. The one who was murdered earlier this week."

"The one who held Lily?" Will glanced from Danielle to Lily. During dinner on Friday night, they had told Will the story of Lily and the Gusarov family and of Danielle's brief arrest for Stoddard's murder.

"Yes. The SOB who is responsible for this lovely tattoo." Lily looked at her arm and cringed.

"I don't know if it makes you feel any better, but that's really a beautiful tattoo. Although, I don't imagine you can see the beauty, since it was forced on you," Will said.

Lily looked at her arm again. "You really think so?"

"I do. While the tattoo artist totally lacked character and ethics, he's not without talent. The colors, the details are brilliant. And it's not that big."

Danielle noticed Billy Bob—or Will as he wanted to be called —didn't sound as countrified in speech as he had been when they first met, although he still dressed the part of the drugstore cowboy.

"I guess. I might as well get used to it." Lily sighed and went back to eating her breakfast.

"I never thought to ask, but when you lived in Frederickport, did you know Stoddard Gusarov?"

"I knew who he was—the family had money." Will shrugged. "I didn't know him well. Yet from what I did know about him, his actions toward Lily don't really surprise me."

"Will I be seeing you at the cemetery this morning?" Danielle asked.

"When is the funeral?" he asked.

"Ten thirty. They're having a reception at the Gusarov Estate afterwards, which I'll definitely be missing." *I don't care if MacDonald wants me to go to that too, not happening.*

"I'll probably be going over there this afternoon when it's quieter." Will looked up at Danielle. "I am a little surprised you're going to the man's funeral, considering what he's done."

"I suppose I'm going more to check out the possible suspects," Danielle confessed.

"Really?" Will raised his brows.

"I did get arrested for the murder. Someone obviously went to a lot of trouble to frame me."

"You be careful, young lady. If someone is trying to frame you, remember, they've already killed one man. These are obviously dangerous people."

DANIELLE CALLED Marie and told her she would be going to Stoddard's funeral after all. She didn't want to show up after turning down Marie's offer for a ride without telling her she had changed her mind. Marie immediately reissued an invitation to pick Danielle up for the funeral. In truth, Marie was offering the services of her grandson, Adam, as Marie, at age ninety, no longer drove. Danielle declined the offer, explaining she didn't plan to attend the wake after the services at the Gusarov Estate. Marie wouldn't take no for an answer and said Adam would be happy to drop Danielle off at Marlow House after the funeral and before the wake.

"I'M sorry you had to do this," Danielle told Adam as she climbed into his car later that morning. "But your grandmother wouldn't take no for an answer." She shut the car door and buckled her seatbelt.

"Hey, no need to explain. Trust me. I know Grandma." Adam put his car in drive, heading towards Marie's house to pick her up.

"Yeah, your grandma can be pretty stubborn." Danielle leaned back in the car's seat and looked out the window.

"Speaking of Grandma, she's been pretty worried about you. What is this about you getting arrested again? I heard something on the radio, but just got the tail end of it. What in the world is going on with you?"

Danielle gave Adam a quick recap of her arrest and subsequent release.

"Sounds like someone is going to a lot of effort to frame you."

"Why did they have to pick on me?" Danielle grumbled.

"That's pretty obvious." Adam glanced over to Danielle, who was now looking at him. He looked back down the road. "I doubt it's anything personal."

"It feels pretty darn personal!"

"They obviously want someone to take the rap for Stoddard's murder so the cops will stop investigating. You have a good reason to be pissed at the guy, so you make a good target."

"Unfortunately for them, they didn't figure a witness would come forward as my alibi."

"You didn't say who that witness was." He glanced briefly at Danielle again.

"The chief would prefer I not say right now." Danielle shifted uncomfortably in the seat.

"Let's just hope whoever killed Stoddard doesn't come after your witness—or do something to discredit his testimony."

"I figure the best thing I can do is try to figure out who killed Stoddard."

"Is that why you're going to his funeral? I wouldn't be going if it wasn't for Grandma."

"You never liked him much, did you?" Danielle asked.

"Not much. But I didn't dislike him enough to kill him."

"Oh, I never even thought…"

Adam laughed. "I didn't think you did. Just thought I'd put it out there anyhow. Truth is, it wasn't as much about me disliking Stoddard. It's that he never cared for me. Figured I was out to marry his niece and then get my hands on his precious company."

"Your grandmother wanted you to marry Isabella, didn't she?"

"Grandma would be thrilled if I'd settle down with any halfway respectable woman and start giving her great-grandchildren." He glanced over at Danielle and chuckled. "After all, why do you think I'm driving you today?"

"Yeah, well, that's not happening," Danielle snorted.

"I guess I should be insulted." Adam didn't sound insulted.

"Maybe I'll find you a nice young lady you can't resist and then Marie will stop trying to play matchmaker."

"Gee, thanks, what did I ever do to you?" Adam frowned.

Danielle considered giving him a list—beginning with the time he broke into Marlow House looking for the Missing Thorndike. Instead, she decided to change the subject.

"So who do you think are the likely candidates for Stoddard's murder?" she asked. "You've lived in Frederickport all your life."

"I suppose wife number three would be on the top of the suspect list. From what I understand, Darlene will be inheriting Stoddard's estate. Now, had Isabella not died and if Stoddard had known Isabella changed her will back, I imagine Isabella would be inheriting the bulk of the estate. Stoddard was big on keeping the family business in the family. Of course, if Darlene had children—then a different story."

"I understand Darlene is pregnant."

Adam briefly glanced over at Danielle. "Where did you hear that?"

"I can't recall," Danielle lied. She couldn't very well tell Adam that Stoddard's ghost had told her.

"I find that hard to believe," Adam said.

"Why do you say that?"

"I saw Darlene last night at The Gray Whale. She was pounding them down pretty heavy. I'm just surprised she'd be drinking like that if she were pregnant. She was smoking too, now that I think about it."

"Unfortunately, some people keep drinking and smoking through a pregnancy."

"I guess. Just thought she was smarter than that." Adam shook his head.

"So Darlene would be at the top of your list?"

"Yes, but if she's pregnant like you say, I'd be tempted to take her off the suspect list. Does a woman really knock off the father of her unborn child? And considering the pregnancy, it insures her place in Stoddard's pocketbook—if not his heart."

"I know a woman's risk of being killed by a lover or spouse increases when pregnant, yet have never heard about the reverse situation." Danielle paused a moment and glanced over at Adam. "Adam, how did you know about Isabella changing her will back to leave everything to Stoddard?"

"Grandma told me."

"How did your grandmother find out?" Danielle didn't believe it was common knowledge.

"Grandma knows everyone in town. She may be ninety, but she probably knows more about what goes on in this town than most."

"I guess she doesn't know the latest."

79

"Latest?" Adam asked.

"From what I understand, Earthbound Spirits produced another will—leaving Isabella's estate to them."

"I imagine it's the old will." Adam shrugged. "Probably will be tossed out."

"According to Darlene, Stoddard never found Isabella's new will. According to Darlene, there was no new will—Stoddard confessed to forging it. So now Isabella's estate is going to Earthbound Spirts, not Stoddard's heir."

Adam let out a low whistle. "Not saying that surprises me. When Grandma told me about the new will Stoddard supposedly found, the thought went through my head that Stoddard forged it. But that doesn't make sense; why didn't Darlene just play dumb and let the courts sort it out? Could have gone her way. There's a lot of money at stake."

FOURTEEN

It was late September in Frederickport, and the remnants of summer gave way to autumn. With temperatures in the low seventies, there was a nip in the air, and a beach breeze rustled the skirts of the women attending Stoddard's funeral, those who chose to wear dresses instead of something more casual. One of those women was Marie Hemming Nichols, who had added a floppy straw hat to her morning ensemble.

"I don't think I've ever seen this place so crowded," Danielle noted as they made their way from the parking lot to the chapel, Marie on her arm.

"Looks like the whole town's here," Marie observed.

"Stoddard must have had a lot of friends," Danielle said.

Marie laughed. "Hardly. I've known Stoddard since his family moved to Frederickport, and he was always an annoying little twerp. Only reason for all these people, morbid curiosity and the fact he's been a member of this community for eons."

"Plus, he was a prominent local businessman," Danielle added.

"Oh pish!" Marie spat. "If Stoddard's parents hadn't left him the family business, he'd be pumping gas right now."

"As you can see, my grandmother doesn't have the highest opinion of the dearly departed," Adam said with a chuckle.

"I assume he must have some business savvy considering his company is supposedly worth a small fortune," Danielle suggested.

"Chuck Christiansen," Marie said.

"Chuck Christiansen? Isn't that the one they say is…or was, Stoddard's right-hand man?" Danielle asked.

"He pretty much runs the company," Adam explained. "Although, most people don't know that. Stoddard did a good job making everyone think he was at the helm all these years. I imagine the company will continue doing well if Darlene and Earthbound Spirits keep Christiansen on."

"Earthbound Spirits, what do they have to do with it?" Marie glanced over to her grandson, who walked next to her.

"According to Danielle, they've produced another will—the one leaving Isabella's estate to them, and apparently Darlene admitted the will Stoddard found was forged."

Marie glanced from Adam to Danielle. "You didn't tell me that."

"I was just telling Adam this morning on the way over to your house. Both of us find it odd Darlene didn't just play dumb and see if the court bought Stoddard's story. There's a lot of money at stake, and considering what she was willing to do to Lily, Darlene Gusarov obviously doesn't have the highest moral character."

"There she is now," Marie hissed under her breath, pointing toward the chapel, where an intimate group of people gathered around a woman in black.

"How can you tell?" Adam asked.

Danielle thought he had a point, considering the woman in question was covered in black—from the stocking feet clad in Louboutin black pumps to the ebony lace dress and veiled black hat obscuring the woman's face, revealing just a hint of blonde hair.

"Who else but the widow would dress like that," Marie said.

"True," Danielle agreed. "I didn't know widows still dressed like that."

"One thing you can say about Darlene, she always had a dramatic flair." Adam snickered.

They were about to step up on the sidewalk when Stoddard's apparition appeared less than a foot from Danielle, causing her to stumble to a sudden stop. Marie, still on Danielle's arm, found herself jerked back as she too came to an abrupt halt.

"How dare you show yourself here!" Stoddard screamed at the top of his lungs. That was, if he had lungs, which he no longer did.

"Something wrong, dear?" Marie asked as she steadied herself.

"Umm…" Danielle blinked and glanced from Stoddard to Marie and Adam, who eyed her curiously, and then back to Stoddard, who stubbornly blocked her way as he continued to hurl verbal insults. Frantically waving his arms, Stoddard grabbed at Danielle, yet his hands moved through her arms, which only made him more frustrated. He tried again, and this time she felt something. Glancing down, Danielle's eyes widened when she noticed a small scratch on her arm. It began to turn red. In the next instant, Stoddard vanished.

"Danielle, are you alright?" Adam asked when Danielle failed to respond to Marie's question.

Blinking her eyes again, Danielle looked over to Adam and Marie. "I'm sorry. I guess I sort of zoned out."

Marie patted her arm. "That's okay, dear, these situations can be a little unsettling. And considering all Stoddard has done to you and Lily…well…you're a very good person to even come today."

"Yeah, if it was me, I would have stayed home," Adam said as he eyed his grandmother—the only reason he was attending Stoddard's service.

As Danielle started to step up on the curb, she spied Chief MacDonald across the way, beyond Darlene and her little group. He was checking out the crowd. She wondered, was Stoddard's killer in the group? Was the person—or persons—who tried to frame her for Stoddard's murder among the people around her?

When MacDonald saw her coming in his direction, he waved. Momentarily distracted by the police chief, Danielle failed to notice the small crowd around Darlene had parted and now looked at her. Marie noticed and gave Danielle's arm a little tug. Danielle stopped walking and glanced at Marie. The elderly woman nodded toward Darlene. Danielle saw Darlene staring in her direction—at least she assumed Darlene was staring, considering the black lace veil covered the widow's face.

Darlene took a step towards Danielle. "How dare you show yourself here!"

Danielle paused again, shocked not so much at the outburst, but the fact Darlene parroted the same exact words her dead husband had used just moments earlier.

"Don't make a scene, Darlene," Marie snapped as she clung protectively to Danielle's arm.

"Don't make a scene? Don't make a scene?" With each

sentence Darlene's shrill voice increased several octaves. "This woman murdered my Todd! She is a cold-blooded killer!" Everyone within hearing distance turned their heads to watch the unfolding drama.

Chief MacDonald stepped forward and placed a hand on Darlene's shoulder. Danielle hadn't noticed before, but Officer Brian Henderson was with the chief. She didn't see Joe anywhere in sight.

"I understand you're upset, but Danielle had nothing to do with Stoddard's death," the chief said, intentionally speaking loudly and clearly so everyone who'd heard the widow's accusations could hear what he had to say.

"How can you say that?" Darlene sobbed. "I heard Todd with my own ears—just before he died. He named his killer!" She turned to Brian. "Didn't he, Brian? You were there, you heard him! Todd didn't deserve to die like that. He was in so much pain!" She began to sob uncontrollably.

Brian looked over at the chief, who nodded. Tucking his hand under Darlene's arm, Brian led her away from the crowd and into the chapel.

"HOW CAN you let that woman get away with murder?" Darlene asked Brian after he led her into a private room in the chapel, intended for grieving family members.

Closing the door behind them, he said, "You need to pull yourself together, Darlene. Making a scene won't help Stoddard."

With a wave of her right hand, Darlene swept the veil from her face and threw it over her hat, revealing her face to Brian.

Glaring at him, she hissed, "I don't understand you, Brian. Are you taking her side? I didn't even think you liked her."

Brian looked down into Darlene's angry eyes. If he expected to find tears, he was surprised to see there were none.

"This isn't about taking sides. But if Boatman didn't kill Stoddard, there really is nothing I can do."

"You heard Todd—that woman—that monster—killed my husband in cold blood. With his dying breath, he told us all we needed to know to lock up his killer. But you haven't done that—have you, Brian? You dropped the charges, and now here she is, flaunting herself, attending the funeral of the man she murdered."

Brian shook his head. "I don't know why Stoddard said what he did. But he was wrong. Danielle didn't kill him."

Darlene was silent for a moment, staring up into Brian's eyes. Taking a deep breath, she lifted her right hand and caressed his cheek. The gesture startled him, and he stepped back.

"Please, Brian, don't shut me out," Darlene whispered, taking a step toward him. She reached up again and touched his face. Before he could respond, she stood on her tiptoes and brushed a kiss over his lips.

"What are you doing, Darlene?" Brian snapped, pushing her away.

"We were good once, Brian. We could be again."

"You made your choice when you decided to stay with Stoddard. Taking second place doesn't appeal to me."

"Second place? I always wanted you, Brian! I thought you knew that! I had to stay with Todd. I didn't have a choice. But it was you I wanted. You I always wanted."

"What you really wanted was Stoddard's money. That's what you chose over us—not him. And now you have it all; I imagine you're happy now."

"I admit I didn't want to give up the security of Todd's money. But it was you I loved—you I always loved."

"Why is it so important to see Danielle Boatman go to jail for Stoddard's murder?"

Darlene just stared at Brian for a moment before answering. Tilting her head to one side, she said calmly, "Because she killed him. Maybe I was never in love with Todd—but I did love him. He was good to me. I wanted to make him happy. Seeing him die like that—it devastated me. And you—you saw it too. You watched him practically die in my arms as he named his killer—Danielle Boatman."

"And he was wrong."

"I don't know how you can say that. You heard him. Help me, Brian. See to it that Danielle Boatman is punished for what she did to my husband. The witness who claims to have seen her during the time Todd was murdered clearly lied. I bet anything Danielle paid the witness to give her an alibi. She can easily afford it. And then, after Danielle Boatman is sent away, we can be together. You and me. Like we should have been all along."

Brian stared at Darlene. He couldn't find the words to express what he felt. When she reached out to him again, her gloved hands gently cradled his face. He didn't move away, not even when she went up on her tiptoes. Closing his eyes, Brian surrendered to the kiss. Without thought, his arms wrapped tightly around Darlene and pulled her closer.

When the kiss ended, their breathing ragged, Darlene went down off her tiptoes, and Brian continued to hold her in his arms. After several moments, Darlene pulled away and looked up into Brian's eyes, her expression pleading.

"Will you help me, Brian?" she asked in a whisper. "Will you see that Danielle Boatman is punished for what she did to Todd?"

"And then what?" Brian asked, his expression unreadable.

"Then we can be together, like we always wanted." Once again, she reached up and stroked his face.

Grabbing Darlene's hand in his, Brian held it for a moment, giving it a squeeze. Their gazes locked. Pulling her captured hand to his lips, he kissed it. "I'll make sure Stoddard's killer is brought to justice," Brian vowed in a raspy voice.

Darlene narrowed her eyes and studied Brian. After a moment, she smiled and said, "I knew I could count on you, Brian." Taking back her hand, she flipped her veil back over her face and straightened her dress.

FIFTEEN

In the chapel, Danielle sat between Chief MacDonald and Marie. Adam sat on the other side of his grandmother. Moments after sitting down, a couple took the two empty spots next to Adam. Marie turned to the new arrivals and immediately recognized them. She and Adam greeted the couple and began making small talk while Danielle sat silently, contemplating what had just happened outside the chapel.

Danielle turned to Chief MacDonald and muttered, "Well, that was embarrassing."

"She definitely wanted everyone to know you murdered her husband," the chief whispered.

Taken aback by his comment, Danielle frowned. "What is that supposed to mean?"

"What I meant—it's obvious she still believes you killed Stoddard, and she wants the world to know."

"You honestly think she believes that?"

"Don't you? Her response seemed genuine. She reacted just as I'd imagine a grief-stricken woman might in this situation, attending her husband's funeral and faced with the person who she believes murdered him."

"Is this what this was all about? You were testing Darlene, trying to decide if you should keep her on the suspect list or not? Is that why you wanted me to come today?"

"The spouse is always the prime suspect. And considering the size of the estate, there is motive. Judging by her reaction to you, I think we need to look in another direction."

"Or she's just covering her butt," Danielle grumbled.

"You think she had something to do with Stoddard's murder?"

"We already know she isn't the nicest person, considering what she intended to do with Lily."

"I understand, but that doesn't mean she wanted Stoddard dead. Her grief seems sincere." MacDonald glanced to the front of the chapel and watched as Brian helped Darlene to a seat in the front row, next to Chuck Christiansen.

Danielle followed the chief's gaze and spied Darlene and Brian. "Who's that Darlene is sitting next to?"

"Chuck Christiansen. He was Stoddard's right-hand man."

Ahh, the man Adam mentioned. The one who is really in charge at Stoddard's company.

After Brian helped Darlene to her seat, he looked around the chapel. When he spied the chief, he gave a nod and started walking toward MacDonald and Danielle.

"Don't tell me he's sitting with us," Danielle groaned, glancing over to the empty seat next to the chief.

"Brian did come with me. He's a good man, Danielle. I wish you two could work out your differences."

Danielle and MacDonald continued to watch Brian. En route to the empty seat next to the chief, Brian paused a moment to speak to a man sitting several rows up.

"He hates me."

"He doesn't hate you."

"Maybe he doesn't hate me, but he does seem to delight in seeing me locked up. If you listened to Henderson, you'd assume I'm the cause of all the problems in Frederickport. I don't know, maybe he just has an issue with women."

"Well, you may have something there," MacDonald murmured.

"What do you mean?"

"About women. I admit his attitude toward women is—well, cynical. I guess that's the best way to describe it."

"What, did he hate his mother? Get dumped by some woman?"

"His wife left him about five years ago. I'm not gossiping, by the way—this is common knowledge."

"Oh, of course not," Danielle smirked. "Men never gossip."

"He was pretty broken up about it."

"Were there any kids?" Danielle asked.

"No. It was Brian's second marriage. They were married for quite a while. If I'm not mistaken, it wasn't long after their twenty-fifth anniversary that she left him. I remember they had this big party, and not six months later they were filing for divorce."

"So she left him?" Danielle asked.

"That was my understanding."

"You said it was his second marriage. What happened to the first one?"

"I never met his first wife. Not sure what happened there. They didn't have any kids either."

"So he has a lousy track record with women; why take it out on me?"

"I never noticed the cynicism back then, after his last divorce. It wasn't until a little over a year ago that I noticed it."

"What happened back then?" Danielle asked.

"Not really sure. I know he started seeing someone. Wouldn't say who she was, but he seemed a lot happier. And then he just changed. He never mentioned who he'd been seeing, but when one of the guys asked about his girlfriend, he snapped that there wasn't any girlfriend. From then on, I noticed the change in his attitude. It's not that he dislikes women exactly. Let's just say he doesn't seem to trust them. Figures they all have some angle."

"And you think that's a good trait for a cop?" Danielle asked.

"I never felt it affected his work—or how he treated women during the line of duty."

"What about me?" Danielle asked.

"In all fairness, Danielle, your behavior since coming to town has been suspect. Can you really blame Brian?"

"Sheesh..." Danielle slumped down in her seat and looked ahead. "With friends like you, who needs enemies?"

The chief chuckled. "Trust me; I'm probably the best friend you could have right now."

Danielle glanced over to the chief and sighed. "I suppose you have a point."

A few moments later Brian Henderson took a seat next to the chief. As he sat down, he flashed Danielle a less than friendly look. In return, Danielle looked away from Brian and the chief and stared toward the front of the chapel.

Marie noticed Brian's arrival. Leaning forward in her seat, she turned in his direction. "Did you get Darlene to settle down and get control of herself?" Marie asked Brian in a not so quiet voice.

"Grandma," Adam scolded under his breath.

"Oh, don't hush me, Adam. I'm not the one that was carrying on like a fool out there in front of everyone!"

Brian leaned forward and looked down the row to Marie. "She's fine, Mrs. Nichols," he said in a loud whisper. "She's just been through a lot, losing Stoddard so unexpectedly—so violently." He glanced over at Danielle.

"Don't look at Danielle like that," Marie ordered. "She had nothing to do with Stoddard's unfortunate death."

"Yes, I understand that, Mrs. Nichols."

"Grandma, maybe we could discuss this later. People are starting to stare," Adam said under his breath.

Marie glanced around. Sure enough, those sitting near her were staring. "What are you all gawking at?" she snapped. They quickly diverted their attention back to the front of the chapel.

A few moments later, Brian and Marie each settled back in their seats. Music began playing through the chapel speakers. The memorial service was about to begin.

Danielle was preparing to daydream once the minister began his portion of the service, when Stoddard appeared in the row ahead of her. He sat backwards in the seat, facing Danielle. The sudden sight caught her by surprise, and she jumped slightly. Worried someone had noticed her reaction, she glanced around. Those around her did not seem to have noticed. Brian, MacDonald, Marie, Adam, and even the couple next to Adam were looking to the front of the chapel, where the minister stood.

What Danielle found especially troubling was the fact there was already a man sitting where Stoddard perched. The man and spirit appeared to dissolve into a single two-headed form—the man head looking toward the pulpit, the ghost head staring at Danielle.

"You have no right being here!" Stoddard shouted. "Murderer!"

Danielle wanted to stick her fingers in her ears and block out the noise. He was a loud and persistent ghost, who continued chanting in a high-pitched tone: *Murderer, murderer, murderer, murderer!*

With each chant, Stoddard's frustration accelerated. Danielle tried to ignore his presence, but it was difficult, considering the sound of his voice rang in her ears, blocking out all other noise. If someone spoke to her now, she doubted she would be able to hear.

Stoddard's hand moved through the back of the pew and through the hymnal holder. Mesmerized, Danielle watched as Stoddard's ghostly hand repeatedly punched through the back of the pew, moving through the hymnal holder and the book held there. Each time his hand moved in her direction, he spread wide his fingers and tried snatching hold of her skirt's hem. She scooted back in her seat, adding distance between herself and the angry spirit.

MacDonald heard Danielle rustling in her seat. He glanced toward her and noticed her attention was not focused at the front of the chapel, where the minister stood, but at the back of the man's head sitting in the next row, directly in front of her. Frowning, he looked at her face and noted her peculiar expression.

"Are you okay?" he asked in a whisper. She didn't respond, so he leaned forward and asked again. When she still did not answer, he reached over and touched her shoulder. Danielle lurched back from the unexpected touch and then looked over to MacDonald, her eyes wide.

"Are you alright?" he asked again.

Danielle couldn't hear his words, yet she had no problem reading his lips. Shaking her head, she whispered, "It's Stoddard."

"Where?" he asked, looking around.

Danielle nodded toward the unruly spirit. MacDonald saw nothing out of the ordinary, just the church pew and the back of a man's head.

"This is why you aren't in jail!" Stoddard shouted. "You've tricked the police chief, haven't you? You've spun your lies! You've tricked him! I should have known it was something like this. I told Henderson it was you."

Stoddard spied Brian Henderson sitting next to the chief. "Do something, Henderson! Do your job! I told you what you needed to know!" When Brian failed to notice Stoddard's antics, Stoddard refocused his attention on Danielle.

"If they won't do anything, I will!" he said angrily.

Without conscious thought, Danielle glanced down at her arm, which Stoddard had scratched earlier. The visible mark was angry and bright red. Stoddard noticed where she was looking and glanced down at her arm. He smiled when he spied the red scratch mark.

"I did that, didn't I?" Stoddard began to laugh.

Danielle took a deep calming breath. *Don't give him power*, she told herself.

With renewed vigor, Stoddard reached through the pew again, this time knocking the hymnal book up and out of its holder. It landed on the floor with a loud thud. Those around Danielle looked in her direction. Their gazes dropped to the floor where the hymnal landed. MacDonald had witnessed the book's apparent launch from its holder.

Marie, now looking down at the book on the floor, frowned, confused at how it got there, since Danielle had been leaning back in her seat. While Marie tried to figure it all out, MacDonald leaned down and calmly picked up the book. Instead of placing it back in the rack, he set it on his lap and looked over at Danielle, whose complexion had lost all color.

Those around Danielle who had looked her way were now turning their attention back to the minister. Marie did as well, although she did so with a look of confusion on her face. Only MacDonald continued to study Danielle.

Gleeful over his accomplishment, Stoddard laughed wildly. The menacing sound filled Danielle's head. He continued to laugh—louder and louder.

Taking a deep breath, Danielle closed her eyes. *Dear Lord, thank you for my many blessings. Protect me from this troubled spirit. Keep me and those around me safe. Help Stoddard find his way home.*

The laughter stopped. The only sound came from the minister standing at the pulpit. Danielle opened her eyes. Stoddard was gone.

SIXTEEN

D anielle didn't see Stoddard again until she returned to Marlow House after the funeral service. She found him waiting for her on the front porch. Instead of hurling insults, he silently glared at her as she made her way up the front walk.

Inwardly seething, his arms by his sides, he balled his hands into tight fists. "How did you do that?" he demanded.

"Do what?" Danielle asked, trying her best to maintain an appearance of calm. She glanced back at the road and watched Adam and Marie drive away, en route to the Gusarov Estate for Stoddard's wake.

"You did something at the chapel. I could hear your voice in my head. It got louder and louder, and then I was back here."

"Back here..." Danielle grumbled, and then added under her breath, "You would have to end up here." Annoyed, she continued on her way to the front door, walking past Stoddard. When she reached the door, she turned and faced him. "I would think you'd have gone home for your wake."

"You'd like that, wouldn't you? You aren't getting rid of me, Danielle Boatman!"

"But don't you want to see your wife, all your friends?" Danielle forced a smile. "It might be the last time you see them all together."
I suppose you could have seen them at the funeral service if you hadn't been obsessing on me.

93

"Don't try to act like you care. You're the one who did this to me!"

I don't really care. I just want you gone. "I told you. I was not the one who shot you. You admit you didn't see the face of your killer."

"It was you. I heard your voice!"

With a sigh, Danielle opened the front door and walked inside Marlow House, leaving Stoddard alone on the front porch.

"How was the funeral?" Walt greeted her.

Closing the door behind her, Danielle flashed Walt a weary smile. "I should have stayed home. It was horrible."

"Horrible how?" Walt asked.

"First"—Danielle glanced around—"where is everyone?" She walked over to the entry table and set her purse on the tabletop.

"Your guest left about an hour after you did. Lily's nurse is here."

Danielle glanced over at Lily's closed bedroom door. "Ahh, IV time. Let's take this up to my room. I really don't want the nurse overhearing me talking to myself," Danielle whispered.

She picked her purse back up off the table and walked over to Lily's door. Opening it, she peeked inside. Lily sat up on the bed, the IV tube hooked up to the PICC line in her arm, as the nurse sat in the corner, jotting down notes in a journal.

"Hi. I'm back," Danielle greeted her.

Lily waved her in. "Come tell me about the funeral."

The nurse glanced up from the journal and smiled at Danielle.

"I'll talk to you later. I'm going to run upstairs and change my clothes."

"Yeah, sure." Lily sighed. "Say hi to Walt for me."

Once in her bedroom, Danielle tossed her purse on the bed and kicked off her shoes.

Taking a seat by the fireplace, Walt leaned back and studied Danielle. "So what was so horrible?"

Raising her brows, she asked, "Aside from the fact it was a funeral?"

"It's not like it was a funeral of someone you even liked."

Danielle pointed to the bedroom window. "It was horrible because of that!"

Walt glanced over to the window, where Stoddard hovered outside, silently beating against the glass pane.

"He's getting annoying." With a wave of Walt's hand, the

curtains closed, blocking Stoddard's ghost from view.

"I can't live my life with the windows always covered. Plus, I'm afraid he's learning to harness his energy."

Walt frowned. "How so?"

Danielle walked over to Walt and showed him the scratch on her arm. "This."

Narrowing his eyes, Walt studied the red mark. "Are you saying Stoddard did this?"

Danielle noted the abrupt change in Walt's demeanor. If he had been a cartoon character, she imagined there would be smoke coming out of his ears about now.

"Yes, at the funeral. He was grabbing at me. He wasn't making contact—his hands just moved through me. And then I felt something. When I looked down, I saw the scratch. For just an instant he managed to harness his energy enough that he scratched my skin."

"Did he do anything else?" Walt glanced over to the closed window. He imagined Stoddard was still outside, trying to get into Marlow House.

"This happened at the cemetery while we were still outside. When we were in the chapel, he planted himself in front of me during the service and did his best to harness his energy."

"Did he…touch you again?"

"No. But he did manage to fling a hymnal out of the rack and onto the floor."

"I don't like this, Danielle."

"You don't like it? How do you think I feel?" Danielle sat down on the bed and looked at Walt.

"So what happened? Did he just follow you home?"

"I was afraid he was going to do more than just toss a book on the floor, so I started to pray."

"You prayed?" Walt smiled.

"We were in a chapel. God's house, so to speak."

"True." Walt grinned. "I take it there were no lightning bolts?"

"Well, not for me."

Walt frowned and glanced briefly to the window. "For Stoddard?"

"In a way, I suppose. He vanished. One minute he was there, being incredibly annoying, yelling at me, drowning out the service, and the next I'm silently praying and, poof, he's gone. Just like that."

"But he's still here."

"True. He is still here. However, the prayer did work—at least I believe it did. Unfortunately, it didn't work exactly as I hoped it would. Didn't banish him completely, just from the chapel. He was waiting for me on the front porch when I got home."

———

LILY WATCHED as the nurse flushed her IV line. Mentally she counted the days left in her treatment; she was halfway there. She still didn't know the origin of the infection that had settled in her knee. According to her doctors, it might have come from either arm —the one with the recent tattoo done under questionable conditions or the one scraped and scratched after she was dumped on the rocky and harsh desert floor, left to die. Or perhaps neither arm was the culprit.

"How did physical therapy go today?" the nurse asked as she removed her gloves and tossed them into the trash can by the IV stand.

"I guess okay." Lily shrugged. "But I think he might be a sadist." She watched the nurse move the IV stand slightly while tidying the room. Lily guessed the nurse was a few years younger than herself— late twenties, perhaps.

"It's important to do all the exercises he gives you. It might hurt now, but it'll mean a faster recovery." The nurse turned to Lily as she picked up her purse and keys.

"Are you coming back tonight or the other nurse?" Lily searched her memory, trying to recall this woman's name. The first two nurses the hospital sent were Carol and Barbara. What their last names were, Lily couldn't recall. Carol took care of the morning treatment, while Barbara came in the evenings. The two nurses took turns giving the midday treatment. Last week this new nurse replaced Barbara—why exactly, Lily didn't know. She just assumed Barbara took another nursing job or was on vacation. Since making the change, Carol only came in the mornings, and this new nurse— what was her name?—came in afternoons and evenings.

Administering the IV medication wasn't as difficult as Lily had first imagined. If necessary, she could probably handle it herself, yet it wasn't something she felt comfortable doing. Lily's medical insurance, along with financial help from Danielle, covered her medical and living expenses, but according to her attorney, a settlement from

Stoddard's estate was inevitable, and that would allow her to repay Danielle.

"I'll be here this evening," the nurse told her.

"I'm really sorry, but I don't remember your name," Lily confessed.

"Samantha. But you can call me Sam," she told her.

"Sam. Cute name." Lily leaned back on her pillows. "I feel horrible you having to drag yourself over here every night at eleven."

"It's my job. You mentioned yesterday you might have an outing sometime this next week."

"Yes, Monday. I so need to get out of here and do something!"

"Don't overdo it. Where are you planning to go?"

"Ian—you met him—he's taking me to lunch in Astoria. We're planning to leave after you give me my afternoon IV treatment."

"It will probably be good for you to get out."

"You have no idea how much I'm looking forward to it."

"By the way, when I was here last night, I noticed another car parked in front of the house. Are there guests staying at Marlow House?"

"Yes. He checked in yesterday."

"He? Just one guest?" Samantha asked.

"Yes. An older gentleman."

"That surprises me. I thought you mentioned Ms. Boatman wasn't planning to take guests while you're recuperating."

"I guess she changed her mind." Lily shrugged.

"Will he be staying long?"

"I think he's leaving at the end of the week. Why?"

"Oh…" Samantha blushed. "I was just being nosey."

Before Lily could respond, the doorbell rang.

"Let me get that for you," Samantha said as she hastily grabbed her purse, exited the room, and went to open the front door. When she did, Ian and Sadie were standing on the front porch.

Instead of bounding into the house the minute the door opened, Sadie stood next to Ian, growling. The moment Samantha heard the golden retriever's threatening growl, she froze. Yet the dog was not looking in her direction, but slightly to the right, at the window adjacent to the front door.

"Sadie, what has gotten into you?" Ian demanded.

Sadie continued to growl. Crouching down, her rear end in the air, the fur on her back bristled as she focused on some unseen enemy.

"Sadie, heel!" Ian ordered. The dog ignored his command.

"Is something wrong with her?" Samantha asked warily, glancing around, trying to figure out why the dog was growling. She'd met Sadie during a previous visit and the dog was friendly—but now the canine seemed prepared to attack. Attack what exactly, Samantha had no idea.

"I'm beginning to think so," Ian grumbled when Sadie ignored him. He reached down and took Sadie by the collar, giving it a firm jerk. Samantha took that opportunity to scoot out of the house, slipping quickly around the growling dog.

"Lily is in her room," Samantha said as she rushed down the walkway toward the street.

Ian dragged Sadie into Marlow House and closed the door behind them. When he released hold of Sadie, she dashed to the window, leapt up on the window seat and began barking.

"Sadie, down!" Ian ordered.

"What's going on out here?" Lily asked as she hobbled out from her bedroom.

"The only thing I can think of, she's seen a mouse or something. I've never seen her act like this, but the last couple days, she's been acting strange."

"Stop barking, girl," Walt said when he appeared a moment later. Sadie did as he suggested and sat down by the window. She looked over to Walt.

"We need to figure out some way to get rid of him," Walt said. "But barking like that isn't going to do it, and it's just making Ian think there's something wrong with you."

Looking at Walt, Sadie cocked her head from side to side.

"At least she stopped barking." Ian looked down at Sadie and frowned. "But what is she looking at now?"

"She's just being a dawg," Lily said as she took Ian by the arm, using him for support. "Help me to the kitchen, would you? I'd love a sandwich."

Ian glanced down at a now calm Sadie. Shaking his head in confusion, Ian helped Lily make her way to the kitchen.

Glancing over her shoulder, Lily wondered what Walt had said to make Sadie stop barking. She didn't doubt the cause of Sadie's agitation—*Stoddard Gusarov.*

SEVENTEEN

By his manner of dress and the beach towel tossed casually over his shoulder, an observer would assume he was a tourist. Strolling along the stretch of beach adjacent to the houses on Sea Cliff Drive, a camera in hand, the man seemed more interested in capturing photographs of waves breaking on the shore than what was happening in the nearby houses.

JOE PARKED his car in the street in front of the Sea Cliff Drive beach house. He had rented the property through the weekend, but he had moved back home after hearing about Danielle's arrest on the radio and going down to the station. He was no longer in the mood for a vacation. *Next time*, he told himself, *I'll get out of town on my two weeks off.*

While he had packed up most of his belongings the day he had heard about Danielle's arrest, he had left a few things behind, and he still needed to clean up the place. There were linens to wash, a refrigerator to empty, and a barbecue to clean.

Joe was in the beach rental for fifteen minutes before he headed to the back patio. He didn't notice the tourist with the camera in his hand and a beach towel slung casually over one shoulder.

THE MAN PAUSED in front of the house next to Joe's rental. Hanging the camera by its strap over one shoulder, he spread the towel out on the beach. Glancing around, he brought the camera to his face and looked through the eyepiece, staring in the direction of the ocean. After a few moments of snapping pictures, he turned slightly, pointing the telephoto lens at the man cleaning the barbeque.

A moment later, he turned his attention back toward the ocean and then sat down on the towel. Setting the camera on the towel next to him, he glanced back at Joe's rental one more time before removing a cellphone from his pocket and placing a call.

On his third call, he told the other party, "I think we have our answer."

"You know who the witness is?" the voice on the other end asked.

"Joe Morelli. Apparently he was staying in the house next door."

"Sergeant Joe Morelli? The cop?" the person asked with disbelief.

"None other." He stared out to the ocean.

"That doesn't make sense. Why would he rent a house? He already has a house in town. Maybe he's there because of the witness. Someone else is in the house."

"No. I made a few calls. Seems he rented the place for his vacation."

"Who are you calling? You're going to screw this up if you aren't careful!"

Stretching out on the towel, he said, "Hey, I'm not the one who screwed this up! I thought you'd taken care of this possibility— made sure there were no neighbors around."

"There wasn't supposed to be anyone staying at the houses on either side. And they're never rented out."

He glanced over to the beach house. Joe was still outside. "One was this time. And to a cop no less."

"Are you sure he's the witness?"

"According to my sources, he was staying at the house alone. No one at the department had a clue he was still in town. By the looks of things, he's cleaning up the place."

"Crap. This really screws up the works. I thought everything was working out perfectly."

"You know, I was never sold on this plan. It was too risky, banking on Stoddard surviving the shooting just long enough to name his killer to a reliable witness."

"It obviously wasn't that crazy. The plan would have worked had Morelli had the good sense to go to Florida for his vacation."

"Well, he didn't." He glanced back over at Joe, who was still outside.

"There's always plan B."

Staring out to the ocean, he asked, "Plan B?"

"Set up Darlene for Stoddard's murder."

"At this point? You think that would be a good idea?"

"Maybe not. Let me think about this and I'll get back to you."

"Fine. I'll hang out here for a while and see if anyone else shows up. Maybe my sources were wrong and there was another witness."

After disconnecting the call, he tossed the phone on the towel. Picking up the camera, he stood up and pretended to take more pictures of the ocean. Glancing over to the beach house, he watched as Morelli walked back into the house. It looked as if he was locking the sliding door.

Fifteen minutes later, the cellphone rang.

"Yeah. What do you want to do?" he asked when he answered the call.

"At this point, I think there is only one thing we can do. Go with our original plan and make it work."

"How do you intend to do that?" He sat back down on the towel.

"We need to get rid of Morelli. He's the only witness that alibis Boatman."

"This is getting out of hand. We can't kill a cop." He glanced over to the rental.

"Do we have a choice? How do we turn back now? We're in too deep."

"It'll just make the police more suspicious. Morelli is one of their own. If he suddenly dies—especially from unnatural causes—they're going to be even more convinced Boatman is being framed and start looking in other places. And you know what that means. We did this to draw attention away from us. Killing Morelli only brings the spotlight back in our direction."

"Did you know Boatman and Morelli have a history?" the person on the phone asked.

"What do you mean?"

"They dated briefly when she first moved to town."

"So what does that mean?"

"It means he had a motive to lie for her."

"We know he didn't lie," the man on the beach reminded them.

"We know that, but no one else does. He was one of the arresting officers when that all came down with Renton."

"Must have cut their dating short," he snorted.

"Rumor has it he still has a sweet spot for Boatman. He's been trying to get back in her good graces."

"Everyone knows Morelli is a straight arrow. If you're trying to pitch the angle he fabricated an alibi for the woman just to get close to her again—"

"Men do all sorts of stupid things for women," the person on the phone insisted.

"True. But how does killing Morelli convince the cops he lied?"

"If it looks like Boatman is the one who killed Morelli."

"And why would Boatman kill her alibi?" Standing back up, he picked up the camera and hooked its strap over his shoulder. "What are you thinking?" Reaching down, he grabbed the beach towel and gave it a shake. Slinging the towel around his neck, he started walking back down the beach to where he had parked his car.

"If we just get rid of the witness, you're right. That'll only reinforce the cops' belief Morelli was telling the truth and someone wanted to shut him up. But if they think Boatman killed him because he was going to come forward and admit he never saw her, then that changes everything."

Walking down the beach, he glanced back at the rental house. "I don't see how you're going to get rid of Morelli and frame Boatman for it—at least not how you're going to make it believable. How do you plan to do that?"

"We need a professional to handle this one. Someone who can do the job at Marlow House."

He readjusted the camera strap hanging over his shoulder. "Stoddard didn't leave us any choice; we had to kill him. It was his own fault. I'm not thrilled about killing a cop, but if it has to be done, then I guess we do it. Not sure how killing him at Marlow House will convince the cops Boatman did it."

"Boatman's going to have to be sacrificed too."

The man on the beach stopped walking. "Wait a minute, now you're talking about killing Boatman too?"

"Hey, you didn't seem to have a problem when we decided to frame her for Stoddard's murder."

He started walking again. "Yeah, but that isn't the same thing as killing her. She's got money. I figured her attorneys would get her off with a light sentence—or off altogether. It wasn't about sending her to prison, just convincing the authorities she was guilty even if the jury disagreed."

"Well, that isn't going to work now. We need to set it up to look like she panicked and killed Morelli when she thought he was going to retract his story and then broke her neck while falling down the stairs."

He stepped from the beach onto the boardwalk leading to his parked car. "What about the other people at Marlow House? Too many people around."

"Don't worry about them. We'll make sure everyone is out of the house but Boatman when we take care of Morelli."

He reached his car and unlocked the passenger door. "I don't like this. I don't like this at all." He tossed the towel in the backseat and set the camera on the passenger seat before closing the door and walking to the driver's side of the vehicle.

"Do you want to go to jail for Stoddard's murder?"

"No. But I didn't kill him." He opened the driver's door and got into the car.

"You're an accessory to murder—we all are. None of us likes this, but we don't have a choice. Are you with us?"

"We really don't have a choice, do we?" he asked with a heavy sigh.

"Unfortunately, we don't."

"I suppose I can deal with Boatman and Morelli being collateral damage, but it has to stop there."

"Don't worry. This won't work if anyone else at Marlow House gets hurt. It will just be Boatman and Morelli."

"Then you better make sure everyone is out of the house before it's done."

"Don't worry. We'll make sure there aren't any witnesses like there was the last time."

A few minutes later, the call ended. Tossing the cellphone on the seat with the camera, he closed his eyes and leaned back. Sitting quietly in the car, his hands holding onto the steering wheel, he asked himself how everything had spun so wildly out of control. Yet it was too late to turn back now. The only way to salvage his life—all of their lives—was to give the authorities Stoddard's killer. Once they had that, no one would be looking into Stoddard's life—or the lives of those around him.

Taking a deep breath, he opened his eyes and put the key into the ignition. *Hopefully this will all be over soon*, he thought.

EIGHTEEN

D anielle found Lily staring into the hall mirror on Monday morning. The petite redhead was already dressed for her lunch date with Ian. She wore a green cotton dress her mother had purchased for her when replacing her wardrobe.

"I hate my hair," Lily announced when she heard Danielle walk into the hallway. She continued to stare at her reflection.

"I think you look cute with short hair. Shows off your green eyes." Danielle stepped up to the mirror and looked at Lily's reflection.

"Makes me look like a boy," Lily grumbled.

"You don't look like a boy." Danielle wasn't saying it just to make Lily feel better. With Lily's delicate features and natural rusty curls, there was no way anyone would mistake her for a boy, despite the shortness of the cut.

"I wish there was some way I could punch Stoddard's ghost in the face." Lily glanced to the front door. "Is he still hanging around?"

"Unfortunately, yes. He seems to spend most of his time hovering outside my bedroom window."

"Pervert. How can you even sleep knowing he's out there?" Lily fussed with her hair, fluffing up her short curls as she stared into the mirror, Danielle still by her side.

"I keep the curtains shut and try to ignore him." Danielle

shrugged. "I'm not sure what else to do until I can figure out some way to convince him it wasn't me. Hopefully the police will catch the real killer—or killers—and then he'll believe me and move on."

Danielle studied Lily's reflection for a moment and then said, "At least you have a clear reflection."

"There is that." Lily sighed. "A misty reflection is better than no reflection—but a clear reflection is way better than a misty one."

"Are you telling Lily to count her blessings?" Walt asked when he appeared in the hallway.

"Walt's here, Lily," Danielle said.

"Good morning, Walt," Lily chirped, sounding more cheerful than she had been when Danielle first joined her by the mirror. "Thanks for teaching me how to play cribbage."

Danielle glanced from Lily to Walt. "Cribbage?"

"Lily was a little restless last night, so I did a—"

"Walt visited me in my dream last night."

Raising her brows, Danielle asked, "And you played cribbage?"

"Just one game," Lily said. "I'd never played before. It was fun. I should get a cribbage board and teach Ian."

"Ask Lily when she's leaving for her lunch date with Ian."

"Walt wants to know when you're going on your lunch date."

"He's picking me up after I finish my afternoon IV treatment."

"Will he be leaving Sadie here?" Walt asked.

"Walt wants to know if Sadie will be staying here."

"No." Lily turned from the mirror and faced Danielle. "He made an appointment to have her groomed. We're dropping her off at the groomer's on our way out of town."

"I don't imagine Sadie will be thrilled with that." Walt chuckled.

"Hey, did you know Samantha has a date with Will this afternoon?" Lily asked.

"Samantha?" Danielle frowned.

"My nurse—the afternoon and evening one," Lily explained.

"What do you mean a date? Isn't she young enough to be his daughter?" Danielle asked.

"Men often find that the ideal age. More trainable," Walt teased.

Danielle flashed Walt a dirty look then turned her attention back to Lily.

"Some men find that the perfect age. Easier for them to train," Lily said. Walt began to laugh.

"Oh, hush," Danielle told Walt as she tried not to smile.

"What did I miss?" Lily asked.

"Oh, nothing...other than the fact you and Walt may be spending too much time together."

"What do you mean? I can't even see or hear him!"

"At least not when you're awake," Danielle reminded her. "So tell me, how did this date come about?"

"I'm not sure. But last night after my IV treatment, I went to the kitchen to get something to drink and Samantha was still here. She was sitting at the table with Will, having a glass of wine."

"When was that, about midnight?" Danielle asked.

"At least. I thought it was odd. But I feel a little bad about her having to come over here so late each night, so I didn't say anything. And I got the impression Will asked her to join him for a glass of wine. It didn't look like your wine, but something he picked up."

"Oh, I don't care about that. Just seems like an unlikely pair. So they told you they were going on a date?"

"No. After I got my water, I just left them in the kitchen together. This morning when I saw Will, he told me Samantha was taking him sightseeing this afternoon after my IV treatment."

"Sightseeing?" Danielle frowned. "Will used to live in Frederickport. Can't imagine he needs someone to take him sightseeing."

Walt laughed.

"I don't imagine Will really cares about seeing the sights—at least not of the town," Lily said.

"I suppose you're right," Danielle muttered, looking from Walt to Lily.

"Looks like this afternoon, it's just me and you, kid," Walt told Danielle with a grin.

LATER THAT AFTERNOON, Walt found Danielle in the parlor, dialing a number on the landline.

"Who are you calling?" Walt took a seat on the small sofa, cigar in hand.

"Myself." Danielle glanced around the room, holding the landline's receiver in one hand.

"Yourself?" Walt frowned.

"Dang. It isn't in here." Danielle hung up the phone and looked at Walt. "Have you seen my cellphone?"

"Did you check the charger in the kitchen?" Walt asked.

"Yes. But it's not there. I must have taken it off the charger without thinking about it. I hate when I do that!" Danielle stomped a foot in frustration.

"I'll help you look for it." Walt stood up.

"Let me try calling it again. Just listen for the ringer."

JOE MORELLI SAT ALONE in his office, eating a pastrami sandwich while reviewing the files on the Gusarov case, when his cellphone began to ring. Picking up the phone from his desk, he looked to see who was calling: Danielle Boatman.

Setting his sandwich on a napkin, he answered the call. "Dani, hello."

"Joe, are you alone?"

"Alone? Yeah, I'm in my office. What's wrong? Why are you whispering?"

"Is your door closed? I don't want anyone to hear you talking to me. You're the only one I trust."

"Is someone there?" Joe asked.

"No. I'm alone. I'm okay for now. But I need to talk to you—can anyone hear you?"

"No. My office door's shut. What's wrong?"

"Can you come over to Marlow House right now? Alone. But you can't tell anyone. I don't trust anyone."

"Are you in danger?"

"I'm safe right now—but I won't be for long if you don't help me. I'll explain everything when you get here. But please, I beg you, come alone, and don't tell anyone you're coming over here. Someone at the police department is part of this."

"Are you saying someone I work with was involved in Stoddard's murder?"

"Please, Joe. Come over here now. I'll explain everything when you get here. But hurry."

"Okay, Dani. Calm down. I'll be right there."

"DID YOU FIND IT?" Danielle asked Walt when he returned from the second floor.

"No. I take it you didn't either."

"Maybe I forgot to charge it—but I could have sworn I put it on the charger this morning. Yet that would explain why it isn't ringing."

"Maybe Lily grabbed it by mistake," Walt suggested.

"I can't believe she'd do that. Her phone's cover is a different color than mine."

"She was also excited to get out of the house. Maybe she grabbed it without thinking," Walt suggested.

"I suppose it's possible…hey…I know, I bet it's in the attic!"

"The attic?" Walt frowned.

"Yeah. I was in the kitchen this morning, straightening things up after breakfast, and came across that box with the extra linens that I shoved in the pantry. I've been meaning to take them up to the attic but kept forgetting. I bet I grabbed my phone without thinking and stuck it in the box when I was taking the linens up to the attic. I bet anything my cellphone is in that box."

Danielle started to head up the stairs when the doorbell rang.

"You answer that. I'll go up to the attic and see if I can find your cellphone."

"Thanks, Walt. And if it's not in the box, look around the attic. I put the linens in the cherry wood cabinet up there, and who knows where I might have dropped my phone. Dang, I hate when I do stuff like that!"

Danielle was surprised to find Joe Morelli standing on her front porch when she answered the door a few moments later. She wasn't particularly surprised to find Stoddard standing next to him, shouting angry threats in her direction. Not wanting to listen to Stoddard, she hurriedly ushered Joe into the house without asking why he was there. She was in no mood to listen to another one of Stoddard's tantrums.

"What can I do for you, Joe?" Danielle asked when she shut the front door, leaving Stoddard on the porch.

"What can I do for you?" Joe frowned. "You're the one who wanted to see me."

"What are you talking about?"

"Is this some kind of joke?" Joe asked angrily.

"Joke?" Danielle frowned.

"Danielle, you called me up not fifteen minutes ago, demanding I come right over here—that you had something you had to tell me. Made it sound like life or death."

"I'm sorry, Joe, it wasn't me. Someone's punking you."

"I know it was you. It was your cellphone."

"My cellphone? What do you mean?"

"Caller ID. The call came from your cellphone," Joe explained.

"Wait a minute—you said this was fifteen minutes ago?"

"Fifteen, maybe less. I came right over."

"Joe, I've been looking for my cellphone all morning," Danielle explained. "I can't find it. That call didn't come from me."

Before Joe could respond, the front door flew open. Danielle and Joe turned around simultaneously and found themselves face-to-face with a man neither had ever seen before—a man pointing a .38 in their direction.

With chilling calm, the man shut the door behind him, locked it and said, "Put your hands up above your head, and don't do anything stupid." Without hesitation, Joe and Danielle raised their hands into the air.

The man pointed his gun at Danielle and told Joe, "I want you to—very slowly—with your left hand, remove your gun and slide it on the floor to me. If you do anything stupid, she gets it straight between her eyes. And trust me, I won't miss, and I won't hesitate to shoot her."

"What's this about?" Danielle asked, silently wondering what was taking Walt so long.

The man leaned down, his gun still pointed at Danielle, and picked up the firearm Joe had just slid across the wood floor in his direction.

"I'll explain everything. Just don't do anything stupid and you'll both be able to walk out of here in one piece." He checked Joe's gun and then tucked his own firearm in his belt and pointed Joe's gun at Danielle and Joe. "Right now, I want you two to keep your hands up in the air and very slowly walk toward the library." He nodded down the hall. "I believe it's in that direction."

NINETEEN

A s they made their way down the hall toward the library, Joe started to say something, but the man immediately shut him up, telling him if he said another word—asked a single question—he would put a bullet through Danielle's head. Silently, the three entered the library.

The intruder pulled a piece of rope from his pocket and tossed it toward Joe. "I want you to tie her hands behind her back. Do a good job or—"

"You'll put a bullet through my head," Danielle finished for him.

The man looked at her and laughed. "Smart girl. Now sit your butt down on that chair and put your hands behind your back so your cop friend can do a good job."

Obediently, Danielle sat on the chair and put her hands behind her back, making it easier for Joe to tie her hands together—and then to the back of the chair—as per their kidnapper's instructions. As Joe silently tied her hands, Danielle kept glancing to the doorway, looking for Walt. She was tempted to call out his name, but was afraid the man with the gun might then make good his threat and put the bullet through her head.

When Joe was finished tying Danielle's hands to the chair, the man ordered him to sit on the floor a few feet away.

After Joe sat down, the man said, "Put your hands on your

head." Joe complied. The man walked over to Danielle and checked the ties.

"Good job," he told Joe. "Ropes are all nice and snug. Will keep her out of my way while I finish what I came here for."

"What did you come here for?" Danielle asked.

The man pointed the gun at Joe. "To begin with, kill your friend here."

"Wait a minute!" Danielle cried out. "You said if we did what you told us to, we'd both get out of here alive."

"I lied." The man laughed.

"You don't have to do this," Joe said from his place on the floor.

"Sure I do," the man said cheerfully, sitting on the edge of the desk. "Of course, no one will know I killed you—both—" The man laughed again.

"The least you can do," Danielle said, desperate to stall him until Walt showed up, "is tell us why you're doing this."

"Technically speaking I'm not doing this. You are," he told Danielle.

"Me?" Danielle frowned.

The man pulled something out of his pocket and tossed it on the floor in front of Danielle. She glanced down. It was her cellphone.

"You see, this poor chump"—he pointed the gun at Joe—"he was so crazy over you that he lied about seeing you when you killed Gusarov. Gave you an alibi. But being the basically honest and upstanding guy he is, you were starting to worry that he might recant his story, so you called him up and begged him to come over here so you two could talk."

"How did you get my phone?" Danielle asked numbly.

"Does it really matter?" The man laughed. "Do you want to hear the rest of the story, or should I just finish up so I can get out of here?"

"You aren't going to get away with this," Joe said.

Danielle glanced over to Joe, who looked as if he was preparing to do something stupid—like make a sudden jump for the armed man, which could get them both killed. The way Joe was sitting on the ground, there was no way he could stand up and successfully disarm the intruder. They needed to wait for Walt. *Where is Walt?*

"I want to know why you intend to kill us. Tell us the rest of the story," Danielle said calmly. "But what I'd really like to know—who killed Stoddard?"

"Who killed Stoddard? I really don't know or care." The man laughed. "But I can tell you the rest of the story. Now, where was I? Oh, I know. When your cop friend shows up, you realize you're losing your alibi. He lets his guard down, you get upset, and you manage to shoot the poor schmuck with his own gun. Then you panic and run up the stairs and tragically fall down the stairs—breaking your neck."

"What happened to originality?" Walt asked with disgust when he appeared to Danielle the next moment. "First, my brother-in-law gets the bright idea to toss me down a flight of stairs—which didn't work out too well, for me or him. And Renton decides to toss you down the stairs—which didn't work out too well for Renton. Now this guy, he wants to pick up where Renton left off." Walt paused a moment and looked at Danielle. "Who is this guy, anyway?"

"I have no idea," Danielle said.

"You have no idea about what?" the man with the gun asked.

"Walt wanted to know who you were. I told him I had no idea," Danielle said with a smile.

"Who's Walt? You trying to make me think you're crazy or something? Because I don't really care if you have a roomful of imaginary friends." He stood up, no longer leaning against the desk. "Time to get this wrapped up. Enough chitchat."

Turning to Joe, preparing to take aim, the man was startled when the gun in his hand flew from his grasp and sailed across the library, landing on the top bookshelf. Before he could react, the second gun, the one tucked in his belt, flew across the room, joining Joe's firearm.

Joe didn't pause to question how the guns seemingly moved across the room on their own volition. All he knew was that the man was now unarmed, and he needed to move swiftly. Leaping to his feet, Joe attacked the intruder, knocking him to the floor. The man was slightly larger than Joe, but a few years older. The two rolled around on the library floor like wrestlers determined to win the match while breaking all rules of sportsmanlike conduct.

"Are you going to do something?" Danielle asked Walt, who now sat on the desk, smoking a cigar while watching the spectacle rolling around on the floor.

"Joe seems to be handling it."

"Would you at least untie me!" Danielle snapped.

"Oh, sorry," Walt said sheepishly.

The ropes securing Danielle fell to the ground. Now free, she stood up and rubbed her wrists.

"Well, if you aren't going to do anything..." Danielle said with disgust as she picked up the landline off the desk, preparing to dial 911. On the floor, their would-be killer caught a glimpse of her reaching for the desk phone, and he managed to roll over with Joe in a death grip while kicking out his right leg, jerking the phone line from the wall.

Danielle let out a curse and dropped the telephone, redirecting her attention to the cellphone on the floor, now under the two men. They were blocking the exit, so she couldn't run from the library without going around them, which at this point looked risky. She glanced to Walt. He seemed amused and unwilling to help.

"I know you don't like Joe, but please help him!" Danielle pleaded.

"I never said I didn't like him." Walt sounded insulted.

"Then do something! Now! Before he gets hurt!"

"The man has his pride, Danielle. Look at him. He thinks he's protecting you."

"He's fighting for his life!" Danielle was tempted to grab something heavy to hit their would-be killer over the head, but the way he and Joe were rolling around on the floor, she was afraid her aim would miss and she would end up knocking out Joe.

Preparing to issue another plea to Walt, Danielle paused when a cracking sound caught her attention. It sounded like a head making unpleasant contact with the wood floor. Looking down at the two men, a sickening sensation washed over her. The sound had come from Joe's head. To her horror, he lay sprawled unconscious across the floor as the stranger started to pull himself up.

"Ouch." Walt winced. "I bet that hurt."

The would-be killer looked at Danielle, his eyes dark and menacing. "Not exactly how we planned it." He stood up and assessed the situation. By his stance, he was prepared to grab Danielle should she decide to take this opportunity to make her escape.

"Is he going to be okay?" Danielle looked down at Joe. There was slight movement—at least he was alive.

"Okay?" The man started to laugh. "Not after I kill him he won't be."

"That is a really annoying habit you have," Danielle said, no longer afraid. Maybe Walt had let Joe roll around with the man, but she had no doubt he would intervene before the stranger touched her.

"What are you talking about?" The man scowled.

"I love how fearless you are." Walt smiled.

"You laugh at the most inappropriate times." Danielle glanced at Joe. "This is going to get you locked away for a long time, attacking a police officer like that. Threatening to kill us both. Maybe if you tell us who you're working with, why you're trying to frame me, and who killed Stoddard, just maybe you won't have to spend the remaining years of your miserable life behind bars."

"Listen, lady. Just because I'm no longer armed, don't for a moment think you're getting away from me. There is no way you're getting out of here alive."

"Umm, about that…aren't you just a teeny bit curious as to how the guns just—well, flew across the room on their own? Or how I got untied?" Danielle waved her free hands at him and smiled. "After all, you did check the ropes after Joe tied me up."

The man frowned. He had forgotten all about the guns until she mentioned them—or about her being bound just minutes earlier. Narrowing his eyes, he looked across the room at the book-shelves where the guns had landed. He stared at them a moment and then looked back at Danielle, who smiled smugly in his direction.

Confused, yet prepared to finish what he had started, he lunged in Danielle's direction. He hit what felt like an unseen wall, causing him to stumble backwards. Dazed, he shook his head and stared at Danielle, who appeared unfazed over his attempt. She continued to smile, which spiked his anger.

Joe moaned and moved ever so slightly, his eyes still closed. The intruder looked down, preparing to finish the job, when something picked him up and sent him crashing into the far wall, headfirst. He crumpled to the floor. Danielle figured he was either unconscious— or dead—considering the severity of the impact.

"Why didn't you do that earlier, before he hurt Joe?" Danielle leaned by Joe's side and gently touched his forehead.

With a sigh, Walt picked up the rope from the floor and walked over to the unconscious intruder.

Kneeling next to Joe, cradling his head in her lap, Danielle asked, "Joe? Joe? Can you hear me?"

Groggily moving his head from side to side, Joe's eyes fluttered open and he looked up into Danielle's face.

"Danielle, are you okay?" he asked with a raspy voice.

"I'm fine, Joe. But I'm concerned about you. You hit your head pretty hard."

"Where is he...the man?" Joe tried to look around, but he winced from the pain.

"It's okay, Joe." Danielle glanced up at Walt, who had just finished tying up the intruder.

"The man isn't going anywhere."

TWENTY

The paramedics carried Joe and the intruder out of Marlow House on stretchers. Danielle had called 911 after checking on Joe and making sure the intruder was no longer a threat. He was still unconscious, which concerned Danielle—but he was alive. Joe was awake, yet disoriented and confused.

Brian had been one of the responders on the call. She told him what had happened and he asked, "And Joe will be able to confirm this?"

"If you would have just done something in the beginning," Danielle hissed under her breath to Walt when Brian walked back into the hallway to talk to the departing paramedics. "Then it would have made all of this much easier!"

"I'm sorry. You're right; I should have stopped Joe from trying to play hero."

"He wasn't playing hero. He was fighting for his life—our lives. But then, I already mentioned that."

"It's not like you were ever in any real danger."

"He didn't know that!" Danielle fumed. She and Walt sat together on the library sofa. Brian had given her firm instructions to sit down, stay out of their way, and wait quietly.

"I suppose that's true." Walt flicked an ash off his cigar. It disappeared before it reached the floor.

Chief MacDonald walked into the library a moment later.

"Hi, Chief," Danielle greeted him. "I'm surprised to see you here."

"When I heard a 911 call came in from Marlow House—and that one of my officers had been injured—how could I not come?" he asked, walking to the sofa.

"How's Joe?" Danielle asked. "The minute Brian and the others showed up, he made me sit down and would barely listen to me."

"Joe's a little out of it. Looks like he took a good knock to the head."

Danielle flashed Walt a reproving frown.

"What about the other guy? Do you know who he is?" Danielle asked.

"I've never seen him before. He didn't have an ID on him, and if he arrived by car, someone must have dropped him off."

"Did he say anything?" Danielle asked.

"He's still out. I'm a little concerned about that. I'd really like the guy to wake up so we can question him. What happened? Brian said you told him the man was planning on killing you both and framing you for Joe's murder to make it look like Joe had lied about seeing you on the day of Stoddard's murder and now regretted giving you an alibi."

"That pretty much sums it up."

"Who is he working with?" the chief asked.

"I don't know. He never said. And when I asked him who murdered Stoddard, he said he didn't know or care. And I believe him."

"Something else went on in here," Brian announced when he walked back into the library. The chief and Danielle turned and looked in his direction.

"What do you mean?" the chief asked.

"First off, where is Joe's gun? Danielle claims the man was armed, but where is it?" Brian asked.

"Up there." Danielle pointed to the top bookshelf. Both officers looked in the direction she pointed and frowned.

Brian walked over to the bookshelf and looked up, scratching his head. "How did they get up there?"

"Well…umm…they sorta flew up there during all the commotion," Danielle explained.

Turning from the bookshelf, he faced Danielle. "They flew up there?"

"What exactly do you think happened here that's different from what I've told you?" Danielle asked, annoyed with Officer Henderson.

"Someone beat the crap out of Joe and the other guy. When we arrived, they were at opposite sides of the room, with Joe barely conscious."

"So?" Danielle frowned.

"If they had beat the crap out of each other, I wouldn't expect one to be unconscious and the other one barely conscious—and if that was the case—which I'd seriously doubt—I'd expect them to be lying side by side."

"You tell us what really happened," Danielle said.

"I need to slug him again," Walt grumbled.

"It looks to me like someone else was here. Someone else beat up Joe and that other guy."

"Which would mean everything I told you was a lie."

Brian stared at Danielle in stony silence.

Clearing his throat, the chief said, "Brian, I would like you to wait in the hallway while I speak to Ms. Boatman alone. And please close the door on the way out."

Brian flashed the chief a cool look before turning and leaving the room as requested, shutting the door behind him.

"Okay, Danielle. Tell me what really happened. Tell me what you failed to mention to Brian."

Danielle took a deep breath and then exhaled before telling the chief everything that had happened that morning, beginning with losing her cellphone.

"Unfortunately your attacker was wearing gloves, so when we get those guns off the bookshelf, Joe's won't have his fingerprints on it."

"Or my cellphone either. Unless he touched it before putting on the gloves."

"Do you have any idea how he got ahold of your cellphone?" the chief asked.

"I'm almost positive I put it on the charger in the kitchen. When I couldn't find it, I thought maybe I'd taken it off the charger and got distracted when straightening the kitchen, and put it in a box I took to the attic. But that man had it."

119

"You think the last time you saw it was this morning in the kitchen?" the chief asked.

"I'm pretty sure."

"Who was in the house this morning?"

"Well, there was me, Lily, Ian, Lily's nurse—Samantha something—and our guest, Mr. Wayne."

"What about Joanne?" he asked.

"She didn't come in today."

"Where are Lily and Ian now?" he asked.

"Ian took Lily to lunch in Astoria. It's her first real outing since getting out of the hospital."

"What do you know about your guest, Mr. Wayne?"

"Billy Bob Wayne? Oh, I seriously doubt he's involved in this. He's from Phoenix, here on vacation. Used to live in Frederickport years ago. Recently retired. But I know who he is. He's pretty well known in the Phoenix area."

"Well known how?"

"He's a car salesman." Danielle laughed after she said it. "I guess that sounds funny. He used to own a very well-known car dealership in Phoenix. He did a lot of advertising on TV as Billy Bob Wayne, sort of a corny hokey cowboy angle. He was something of a celebrity. I recognized him immediately when he showed up on our doorstep. I used to see his commercials when I visited my friend in Phoenix."

"He would have had access to your cellphone?"

"Yeah, but they all would have. I think everyone was in the kitchen this morning. Of course, I already know it wasn't Lily or Ian."

"So you think it was the nurse?" he asked.

"The nurse?" Danielle considered the suggestion. "I really don't know much about her. She administers Lily's afternoon and evening IVs. Although, now that I think about it, there is one thing that is a little odd…" Danielle frowned.

"What?"

"Today, after administering Lily's afternoon IV, she and Mr. Wayne went on sorta a date thing."

"Date?"

"She took him sightseeing. But she's probably in her twenties, and he's old enough to be my father and he dresses—well, like a cowboy. Not like a Kevin Costner type of cowboy, more along the lines of Roy Rogers."

"Hmmm…you think maybe she took your cellphone and then made sure your guest was out of the way for the rest of the afternoon?"

"I suppose it's possible."

"Did she know Lily and Ian would be in Astoria?"

"Yes. It's all Lily could talk about. She was so excited."

"You need to get me the name of this nurse. But for now, don't say anything to anyone—even Lily—that we suspect she might be involved in this."

"I can't very well do that. How can I have her coming back into my home—twice a day—and take care of Lily? If she's part of this, I don't want her anywhere near us!"

"You have a point. But you have to remember, you can't be a hundred percent certain your guest isn't in some way involved. You did say he used to live here. Perhaps he has some connection to Stoddard."

"But maybe it wasn't any of those people," Danielle suggested.

"You mean someone else took your cellphone?"

"It was in the kitchen on the counter. I don't always lock the kitchen door during the day. It's entirely possible someone slipped in from the side yard and took the phone off the counter sometime this morning."

"I would have seen someone break in," Walt interjected.

"Are you so sure about that?" Danielle asked. "You didn't know Joe and I were being held downstairs at gunpoint."

"You aren't talking to me right now, are you?" the chief asked.

"No. I'm talking to Walt."

OVER AN HOUR LATER, Danielle sat alone in the hospital waiting room. Glancing at the nearby wall clock, she wondered what was going on. Restless, she stood up, preparing to look for a vending machine, when the chief walked into the room.

"How is he?" Danielle asked.

"His tests look good. But they want to hold him overnight for observation."

"Does he remember what happened? He was pretty loopy when he came to."

"Come on, I'll take you to him and you can see for yourself."

"Is he still in the ER?" Danielle asked.

"No, they put him in a room." The chief motioned toward the elevator.

"Do you know anything about the other guy yet?" Danielle asked as she stepped into the elevator with the chief.

"He's in the ICU. Your Walt did a number on him."

"He isn't my Walt, exactly. Any idea who he is?"

"We got an ID back from his fingerprints. He has quite an impressive rap sheet. Including one for a contract hit, which didn't stick."

"When you say it didn't stick, do you mean he didn't kill the person?" Danielle asked.

"No. Someone was killed. This was in Vancouver. The authorities there were certain they had their man, but the case fell apart."

"What's his name?" Danielle asked.

"John Smith."

"Seriously? His name is *John Smith*?"

The chief nodded. "Seriously."

"Do you think someone hired John Smith to kill us, or was he involved with Stoddard's murder?"

"You told me he said he didn't know who killed Stoddard and that you believed him," he reminded her. "What do you think?"

The elevator door opened.

"Sounds like a contract hit," Danielle said dully.

"Does to me too," the chief agreed, ushering Danielle off the elevator.

"You said he's in the ICU. How serious is it exactly?"

"He's still unconscious. They're running tests. I put a guard on his door."

Danielle paused a moment and looked at the chief. "Guard?"

"I don't think whoever hired him will be thrilled to know he botched the job—and his only chance now is to tell us what he knows and hope for a lighter sentence."

"Maybe they'll wait to see how serious he is."

"Perhaps. But if you wanted to keep someone from talking, wouldn't it be best to get rid of them before they had a chance to say anything?"

"I suppose. Do you think Joe and I are still in danger?"

"I suspect John Smith has more to be worried about from whoever hired him than either you or Joe do. If they wanted you both dead to discredit the alibi so we wouldn't keep looking for Stoddard's killer, that's now a moot point, especially after today. Killing you both now won't make us stop looking for Stoddard's killer."

"I hope you're right."

TWENTY-ONE

D anielle peeked inside the hospital room. Joe sat in the bed wearing a hospital gown, with the sheets pulled up to his waist. Brian sat in a chair next to him. The two men quietly discussed something—what exactly—Danielle couldn't hear. She stood with the chief in the open doorway, hesitating a moment before entering. MacDonald cleared his throat. Joe looked in their direction and grinned.

"You don't know how relieved I am to see you standing there, unharmed." Joe greeted her with a warm smile when Danielle and MacDonald walked into the room.

"You are relieved? You scared the crap out of me!" Danielle walked to Joe's side and reached out, giving one of his hands a brief squeeze.

Silently Brian stood up and offered Danielle the chair. She politely declined the offer and remained standing by the bedside. Brian sat back down. The chief's cellphone began to ring. He excused himself and stepped back out into the hallway, leaving Danielle alone in the room with Brian and Joe.

"He tells me it was just the three of you at Marlow House." Brian didn't sound as if he believed it.

"You remember what happened?" Danielle asked Joe. "When you came to, you were really confused, had me worried."

"I don't remember everything. But I remember most of it."

"He doesn't remember how the guns got on the bookshelf," Brian said. "Or throwing Smith against the wall."

Danielle looked at Brian. "It all happened rather fast. And does it really matter? I think the important thing is finding out who hired Smith to kill us."

"I do remember something about the guns. But it really doesn't make sense, so I'm thinking it was just my mind playing tricks on me because of the way I hit my head."

"What do you remember?" Brian asked before Danielle could respond.

"I remember sitting on the floor, thinking Danielle and I were going to die. I was angry at myself for not trying to disarm him before he made me tie Danielle up."

"He would have shot you," Danielle reminded him.

"He was going to do that anyway. I just wanted to distract him, give you a chance to get out of there. But I waited too long."

"Apparently you—or someone—did something. When we got there, Smith was the one tied up, not Danielle," Brian reminded them. "And someone threw those guns on the bookshelf."

"That's when everything gets mixed up for me. I remember my mind was racing. I was desperately trying to think of something to say—anything—to stall him. I figured if I could just get to my feet, it would be easier to lunge at him, possibly take him down. He pointed my gun at me—I figured that was it—and then the gun just seemed to fly out of his hand. A second later, the gun in his belt flew across the room too. I know it couldn't have happened like that, but that's what I keep seeing. I remember jumping up, tackling him and then hitting my head. When I came to, Danielle was there, talking to me, and he was tied up in the corner. I know it couldn't have happened like that. My mind is obviously playing tricks on me."

Brian looked at Danielle. "What do you remember?"

She took a deep breath and glanced from Brian to Joe. "Joe was a hero. When Smith pointed that gun at him, he just leapt from the floor, as if he had a burst of energy. He surprised Smith. Joe ripped the gun out of Smith's hand and flung it across the room. And then he did the same with the other gun. The two men ended up on the floor, rolling around. They both got their heads whacked on the wood floor, pretty hard. It knocked Smith out, and Joe was dazed. He stumbled across the room toward me and then just passed out."

Joe shook his head wearily. "So strange. I don't remember any of that—about the guns or Smith passing out."

"I have one question," Brian asked, looking at Danielle.

"Yes?" Danielle smiled.

"How did you get untied? Joe said when he came to you had his head in your lap and Smith was tied up."

Danielle wanted to kick herself. It was too late to add Joe had untied her before passing out. "I managed to wiggle out of the ropes. Joe didn't tie them all that tight. By the time Smith was down, I was out of the ties and then used the rope to tie him up before he came to."

Brian silently considered Danielle's version of the day's events. Finally, he said, "I guess Joe really is a hero."

"Yes, he is." Danielle grinned.

"I just wish they weren't keeping me overnight. I'd like to get out of here and figure out who's behind this."

"You just take care of yourself, Joe," Brian said. "We'll figure this out. I'm just hoping Smith wakes up, and he can tell us who hired him."

"Are you saying he might die?" Joe asked.

"Apparently his head was hit hard. They're running some tests. But he's still out."

"Damn," Joe muttered, falling back on the pillows. Closing his eyes, he rubbed his temples.

"Joe, what is it?" Danielle asked.

"I've never killed anyone before. I know it comes with the territory, but...damn."

"He isn't dead!" Danielle silently cursed Walt for not intervening sooner—and with less violence.

"Joe, don't beat yourself up over this. If he does die, so? The guy was there to kill you. That's what he does for a living," Brian reminded him.

"You ready, Henderson?" the chief asked from the doorway. "We need to get going."

"Sure, Chief." Brian stood up.

"I wish I could go too," Joe grumbled.

"Just take care of yourself," Brian told him. "And don't worry about Smith."

A few minutes later, Danielle sat in the chair previously occupied by Brian. She and Joe were alone in the hospital room.

"I need to get going in a few minutes," Danielle said. "The chief confiscated my cellphone as evidence, so Lily won't be able to get ahold of me. She and Ian should be getting home about now."

"I've been thinking about that phone call," Joe said.

"You mean the one from me that wasn't from me?"

"Yeah. It really did sound like you. At the time, I didn't doubt for a moment I was talking to you."

"There wasn't anything different about the voice? Is it possible they used some recording thing? Simulating my voice?"

"No. There was a person on the other end of the line. But she was whispering. So I suppose the voice was slightly different, but close enough that I just attributed any difference to the fact that you —I mean, she—was whispering."

"Someone is definitely going to a lot of work to make people think I killed Stoddard. They get a woman who looks like me to drive around Stoddard's neighborhood in a car like mine. They plant the murder weapon in my car. And if you hadn't seen me and come forward—well, I might still be sitting in jail right now. I owe you an apology."

Joe studied Danielle. "For what?"

"I never thanked you for coming forward and telling the chief what you'd seen. And as I recall, I was really pretty snarky about the whole thing when you came over to tell me the charges had been dropped."

Joe shook his head. "You don't owe me an apology or a thank you. I would hope anyone would do the same thing."

"Yes, but if you hadn't gotten involved, then someone wouldn't have tried to kill you."

"Which brings me to a question I need to ask you."

"Okay, ask away." Danielle shifted in the chair, trying to get comfortable.

"Is it possible none of this is about Stoddard, but about you?"

"What do you mean?" Danielle frowned.

"Do you have an enemy? Someone who might go to elaborate lengths to frame you for a murder just to see you locked up?"

"Are you suggesting Stoddard was simply collateral damage to hurt me?"

"You did say someone went to a lot of trouble to frame you. Do you have any enemies? Maybe someone who was upset over either of your inheritances?"

"Well, the only one who ever tried to kill me was Renton, and he's locked up."

"Maybe Renton wants to see you locked up too?" Joe suggested.

Danielle considered the possibility for a moment and then shook her head. "If Renton—or someone else—paid someone to hurt me, why not just kill me instead of Stoddard? Less trouble."

"True, but maybe he wanted to see you in jail, like him, and not dead."

"Then why try to kill me today?"

"Maybe he figured he missed his chance to see you go to jail, so he'd have you killed instead."

"Then why kill you too? According to Smith, he was going to toss me down the stairs to break my neck. He didn't need you to do that. It would have been much easier if he had come to the house when I was alone today, without you there. No, that doesn't make any sense."

Joe let out a sigh and leaned back in the bed. "I suppose you're right."

"Your brain is just working overtime since you're stuck here and can't go back to work with Brian and MacDonald."

"I suppose." Joe lifted his head and studied Danielle. "Then can I ask you one more question?"

"What?"

"How did you really get your hands untied? Smith checked them. I know they were tight."

"I guess not tight enough." Danielle shrugged. "I also know how to get out of duct tape. I'll show you that trick sometime."

"Yeah, I think I've seen that YouTube video," Joe said with a chuckle.

"I really need to go." Danielle stood up, reached to Joe, and took one of his hands in hers. She gave it a little squeeze. When she started to let go, he grabbed it with his other hand and held it for a moment.

Joe looked up into Danielle's eyes. "At least one good thing came out of this."

"What's that?" Danielle asked nervously. He continued to hold her hand.

"This feels like it used to be—after we first met."

Danielle patted Joe's hand and gently pulled away. "Yeah, I suppose it does, in a way. I like you, Joe. I hope we can be friends."

"I was sort of hoping——"

"We've talked about this before, Joe," Danielle interrupted. "I'm not mad anymore, honest. I'm over it. I understand why you had to do certain things—and how some things must have looked to you. And while I'm no longer angry, we really can't go back. But I would like to go forward, as friends."

"Are you seeing someone?"

"Seeing someone?" *Not unless you consider midnight dances with a charming spirit seeing someone.* "No. And frankly, I'm not really looking for a relationship. I just want to get on with my new life here, and hopefully things will finally settle down for me, and I'll be able to do that."

"I wondered if maybe...well...you and Adam..." Joe shrugged.

"Adam Nichols?" Danielle practically choked.

"I heard he took you to Stoddard's funeral. And he did pick you up at the police station after you were released for breaking into Stoddard's house."

"I wouldn't really call attending the funeral of a man I disliked a date." Danielle cringed. "But no. I'm good friends with Marie. And I suppose Adam...well...I guess we have become friends. But no, not that kind of friend."

TWENTY-TWO

It was almost dinnertime when Danielle returned to Marlow House on Monday. She pulled into the drive alongside the house and found Will Wayne sitting on the bench under the shade trees, sipping a glass of wine. Unseen to Will was Stoddard's ghost, who seemed more agitated than normal. Yet this time, he directed his anger at Will and not at Danielle.

After parking her car and turning off the ignition, Danielle sat in the vehicle a few moments, watching Will and Stoddard. Will looked in her direction and raised his glass in greeting before taking another sip. He was oblivious to the ghost, who repeatedly shook a fist in his direction and paced back and forth not three feet from the bench.

"What is this all about?" Danielle muttered to herself before getting out of the car. Reluctantly, she walked to Will and Stoddard.

"Beautiful day, wasn't it?" Will greeted her. "I forgot how lovely the weather is here. So different from Phoenix."

"What is he doing here?" Stoddard demanded. "Is this the real reason you killed me? It wasn't about Lily after all, was it?"

"Did you have a nice afternoon?" she asked with forced cheerfulness. *What is Stoddard talking about? And how much do I tell Will about what happened today at Marlow House? There's sure to be something about it on the radio tomorrow, if not tonight.*

"Yes, it was a most pleasant afternoon. The area has really

changed since I was last here." Will lifted his glass to Danielle. "Would you like some wine? I've more in the kitchen."

"He's just here for my money!" Stoddard shouted.

"Oh, no, thanks." Danielle forced a smile. *Will wants Stoddard's money?*

"He shouldn't be here!" Stoddard shouted before abruptly disappearing.

Danielle glanced around the side yard, looking for some sign of Stoddard. She wondered where he had gone.

"Do you know if Lily's back?" Danielle asked.

"Yes. She and Ian were here when I returned. They were in the library. I didn't see Ian leave, so I assume he's still here. Did she ever get ahold of you?"

"What do you mean?"

"When I got back, she said she's been trying to call you all afternoon, but you weren't answering your cellphone."

Instead of responding to Will's question, Danielle stared at him for a moment. *Did Will take my cellphone? Was he the one and not Samantha?*

"When did Samantha leave?" she asked abruptly.

"Samantha? Oh, she dropped me off about an hour before Lily and Ian returned. Why, did you need her for something?"

"Umm…yes, there was something she was supposed to pick up," Danielle lied. "Did she come in the house when she dropped you off?"

"No." Will shook his head. "I just had her drop me off out front. She was in a hurry anyway, had a patient to see this afternoon."

Confused and troubled over Stoddard's reaction to Will, Danielle excused herself and headed to the house to find Ian and Lily.

SADIE GREETED Danielle in the kitchen. Wagging her tail, the golden retriever ran circles around Danielle, playfully nudging her legs.

"Don't you look pretty," Danielle told Sadie, giving her a pat. "You smell good too. Are Ian and Lily still in the library?" As if she understood the question, Sadie turned quickly and raced from the room, heading to the library.

"Why haven't you been answering your cellphone?" Lily asked the moment Danielle walked into the library a few moments later. Lily sat on the couch with Ian, her feet up on his lap as she leaned against one pillowed arm of the sofa. Ian smiled over at Danielle as he gave Lily a foot rub.

"If Ian hadn't been here, I would have figured out some way to let Lily know what was going on. Write a letter perhaps," Walt said when he appeared in the room a moment later.

Danielle flashed Walt a smile and shut the door behind her. "You guys aren't going to believe the day I've had." She walked to the window and looked outside. Will was still sitting on the bench. If he was involved with the plot to kill her and Joe, he didn't seem upset that she was still alive.

"Well, we had a wonderful day!" Lily boasted. "We went to this restaurant that—"

"Someone tried to murder Joe and me today," Danielle blurted out.

The foot rub abruptly ended. "What?" Ian and Lily chimed in unison.

Danielle sat on a chair across from the sofa and told them about her day, beginning with the missing cellphone. She left out the role Walt played in the drama, yet assumed Lily was able to fill in the blanks. The version she told Ian was not much different from what she'd told Brian. Later she would tell Lily the complete story.

"So you think Samantha was in some way involved?" Lily asked.

"The chief wants to question her." Danielle glanced at the window leading to the side yard. Will was still outside.

"But I...well, I sort of wonder about Will," Danielle muttered.

"Will?" Ian frowned. "Billy Bob Wayne?" Ian was familiar with Will's celebrity status and had seen a number of his commercials when staying in the Phoenix area while working on a story.

"Maybe I'm just being paranoid." Danielle shrugged. "But he did once live in Frederickport. I'd like to find out if he has any connection to Stoddard."

"There is something you aren't saying, isn't there?" Walt asked.

"I definitely don't want Nurse Ratched touching Lily again!" Ian said.

Lily patted Ian's arm. "We don't know if it was her. Samantha seemed nice, but you have a point...I'm not thrilled with the idea of her continuing as my nurse if she was in some way involved. Maybe we could—" Lily stopped talking when her cellphone began to ring. It was sitting on the end table next to the sofa. She picked it up and looked to see who was calling.

"Speak of the devil," Lily said as she answered the phone. "Samantha...hello..."

Ian, Danielle, and Walt silently listened to Lily's side of the conversation. When she finally finished the call, she said, "Well, that was interesting. Sorta takes care of our immediate problem."

"What did she say?" Danielle asked.

"Apparently, the police brought her in this afternoon to interview her. She knows all about the attempt on your life. Of course, she claims she knows because of the police interview. She insisted she had nothing to do with taking your phone. Said she would never be involved with something like that. But she felt under the circumstances she could no longer come here and be my nurse. I guess the morning nurse is filling in tonight until the hospital sends someone else over."

"Do you believe she's telling the truth?" Ian asked.

Lily shrugged and tossed her phone back on the table. "She sounded sincere. But who knows? At least it solves that problem."

"The chief doesn't believe either Joe or I are in danger now, because he thinks the whole point of killing us was to discredit my alibi. But their murder attempt actually had the opposite effect. If someone was trying to stop the local cops from looking elsewhere for Stoddard's killer, they blew it."

"I think all of us would feel a hundred percent better if the police had Stoddard's killer—or killers—behind bars," Ian said.

"It might also solve the local Stoddard problem," Walt told Danielle as he glanced to the window, assuming the angry ghost was nearby the house.

"You think it's more than one person?" Lily asked.

"It has to be," Danielle said. "We know there were at least two people involved—John Smith and the woman who impersonated me."

"Or one person is behind it and they hired the others, like they hired Smith," Ian said.

"And Samantha, if she was the one who took your cellphone," Lily suggested.

"I think what we need to do is follow the money," Ian said.

"If you mean who profits from Stoddard's death, the most obvious person is Darlene," Lily said.

"I know MacDonald doesn't see her as the killer. I guess she was pretty broken up over Stoddard's death," Danielle said.

"Seriously?" Ian scoffed. "Spouses are always prime suspects. I can't believe a few tears would get to MacDonald."

"I'm not saying he's dismissed the possibility, exactly. But if the motive is money, she's just acting a little odd when it comes to the estate."

"How so?" Ian asked. Danielle started to explain about Earthbound Spirits' claim to Isabella's estate and how Darlene made no attempt to contest the will, but he already knew. Lily had told him.

"Maybe she knew she didn't have a valid claim. Earthbound Spirits have a decent legal team. Perhaps she figured she would just cut her losses and take Stoddard's share; it's still a lot of money."

"The thing is…" Danielle wished she could tell Ian everything, but that wasn't feasible. "It's hard to explain, but I have this gut feeling the will Stoddard found was valid."

"We know it was valid," Walt said.

"Gut feeling?" Ian asked.

"It's more a collection of things I've overheard…pieces of the puzzle I've put together."

"Maybe what we need to do is have a closer look at Stoddard's will, Isabella's will, the estate, and Earthbound Spirits," Ian suggested.

"I know Clarence Renton was the one who wrote Isabella's will. I bet he would know which one is the most current," Danielle said.

"If Darlene was walking away from all that money when she was legally entitled to it, that would definitely put a different spin on this," Ian said.

"What would it mean?" Lily asked.

Ian looked at Lily. "Blackmail perhaps?"

"If whoever killed Stoddard wasn't hiring hit men to come into my home to murder me, I suppose I wouldn't have a problem sitting back and letting the Frederickport Police Department sort this out. After all, I wasn't particularly fond of Stoddard in the first place." Danielle glanced to the window and wondered where the angry ghost was now.

"I'll see what I can do about getting a copy of the wills—Stoddard's and Isabella's. It's a start, anyway," Ian said.

"I suppose I could call up that private detective I worked with when Lily was missing, and see what he can find out about Stoddard's company and do a little digging on Darlene," Danielle suggested.

The discussion stopped when Will came into the house. He poked his head into the library to say hello to everyone and then went up to his room. Ian and Sadie went home about thirty minutes later and Danielle, Lily, and Walt retreated to Lily's room.

"Is Walt here?" Lily asked when they were in her bedroom on the first floor.

"Yes." Danielle glanced over to Walt, who leaned against a wall, fidgeting with an unlit cigar.

"I assume there was more to that story you told me and Ian. And one thing I keep wondering, where was Walt when that guy first showed up?"

Lily scooted up on the bed and leaned against the pillows piled against the headboard. Danielle took a seat in the nearby chair. She told Lily, while Walt silently listened, the unabridged version of the day's events, ending with Stoddard's reaction to Will.

"Are you saying nice Will Wayne is in some way involved in all this?" Lily asked.

"I have no idea. But Stoddard was definitely upset. Of course I couldn't ask him any questions with Will there."

"I know what I need to do," Walt announced.

"What?" Danielle asked.

"I'm going to keep a closer eye on your guest." Walt disappeared.

TWENTY-THREE

L ate Monday evening Danielle went outside to find Stoddard. She wanted to know why Will's presence angered him. Unfortunately, the bitter ghost refused to discuss Will Wayne aside from accusing Danielle of plotting with Wayne to destroy his family.

On Tuesday morning, she tried again before Will came down from his room for breakfast. Stoddard remained uncooperative. Danielle wondered if there might be someone else in Frederickport familiar with Stoddard's family history, who might know of Wayne's connection to Stoddard.

Danielle arrived unannounced at Marie Nichols's house shortly before nine, Tuesday morning. She dressed casually for the visit, wearing cuffed faded denims and a white lace blouse, with her hair pulled back into a tidy fishtail braid. Marie cheerfully welcomed Danielle and invited her into her sitting room for a cup of coffee.

"You must have been terrified," Marie said as she poured the coffee. Danielle had just filled her in on yesterday's drama.

"I'm surprised it hasn't been on the radio yet." What Danielle really meant was she was surprised Marie hadn't already heard about the attempt on her and Joe's life. Marie seemed to know what was happening in town before the local newspaper or radio.

"There might have been something in the morning paper, but I'm afraid the sprinkler got to it first." Marie sat down on a chair across from Danielle.

"I didn't look at the paper this morning either." *I was too busy trying to reason with a stubborn ghost.*

"And Joe is going to be alright?" Marie asked.

"Yes. They just wanted to keep him over for observation. I called over there this morning and talked to him. Looks like they're releasing him today."

Marie shook her head. "Quite shocking. Two murders in our little town—and now this attempt on you and Joe. This used to be such a safe place!"

Danielle didn't remind Marie of Walt's murder or the fact Marie's own father had found the body. In fairness, that had happened almost a century before.

"Are they certain you're out of danger?" Marie asked.

"We don't believe it was ever about killing Joe or me, but about deflecting attention off Stoddard's real killers."

"I hope they catch them quick. We don't need those kinds of people in our town," Marie said.

"I did have a question for you," Danielle asked.

"Something to do with the murder?" Marie sipped her coffee.

"No, not really," Danielle lied. She would rather Marie assume her interest in Will was more casual.

"I'll let you ask me anyway," Marie said with a chuckle as she set her coffee cup on its saucer.

"We have a guest staying at Marlow House."

"I thought you weren't going to take anyone until Lily was finished with her treatments."

"I guess we sort of changed our minds." Danielle picked up her purse and pulled out a piece of paper. It was a picture of Will, which she had printed off from the Internet. While Billy Bob Wayne had a web presence—with photographs—it listed no information on his personal or family life. She handed the picture to Marie.

"What is this?" Marie looked down at the picture in her hand.

"He's the one staying at Marlow House this week. His name is Will Wayne. He used to live in Frederickport. I was wondering if you knew him."

Marie shook her head. "Will Wayne?"

"He owned a large car dealership in Phoenix. Actually, he was something of a local celebrity there. Went by the name Billy Bob Wayne and was featured in lots of corny commercials. Always dressed like a cowboy. Still does, in fact. He sold his dealership

137

recently and retired. But he used to live here. He's a widower. Both his wife and daughter are buried in the Frederickport cemetery. I was hoping maybe you knew him when he used to live here."

Marie handed the picture back to Danielle. "Sorry, dear, I don't recognize him."

"From what I understand, he lived here years ago. He probably looked a lot different back then."

"The name's not familiar, either," Marie said.

Danielle stared at the picture a moment and sighed. She slipped it back in her purse. "Oh well, it was worth a shot." *I guess there's always my private detective.*

"You said his wife and daughter are buried here. Do you know when they died?"

"No. But I got the impression it was back when he lived here— and from what I found online, I know he's been in the Phoenix area for over twenty years. I believe he started his car dealership in the nineties."

"And you don't know how they died?" Marie asked.

"No. I never asked."

"Hmmm..." Marie thought a moment. "I remember a horrible car crash—but this was about thirty years ago—where a mother and her daughter were killed. So tragic. The family had just moved to Frederickport, hadn't lived here six months when it happened. But I don't remember their name. The husband, he only stayed a few months after the accident, then moved. I heard he couldn't bear driving on the same highway where his wife and baby were killed."

"Thirty years ago? That might be the right time frame."

"I do recall it was the same week that time-travel movie was released. Hmm...now what was the name of that movie?" Marie frowned, trying to recall.

"Time travel?"

"Yes, with that nice young actor...what was his name? The one who has Parkinson's."

"Do you mean *Back to the Future*?" Danielle asked.

"Yes! That's the movie." Marie smiled.

According to Danielle's memory, *Back to the Future* was released in the mid-1980s.

"Do you remember if the family was connected in any way to the Gusarov family?"

"Stoddard's family?" Marie frowned.

"I was just wondering if they knew each other."

"It was a small town back then. Everyone seemed to know each other. Although, I don't remember that family's name. They weren't here that long. I only remember them because of the tragic circumstances."

"Do you know what caused the accident?"

"It was a drunk driver. The driver wasn't a local."

"What happened to the driver?" Danielle asked.

"He went to jail. I assume he's out by now. But I really don't know. So do you think your guest is the same man whose wife and daughter were killed back then?"

Danielle shrugged. "I don't know. I just assumed they both died around the same time since they're buried here together, and it's been years since he lived here."

"Why did you ask if he knew Stoddard?"

"Well...I figure the subject of Stoddard is bound to come up with everything that's happening and with Lily staying with me. I'd just like to be careful what I say in front of him if he and Stoddard used to be buds," Danielle lied.

"I doubt they ran in the same circles."

The two women chatted for another thirty minutes before Danielle told Marie she needed to be on her way. She had a number of errands to run, which included buying a new iPhone and stopping at the police station to get an update on Joe and John Smith.

By the time Danielle finished most of her errands, it was past noon. She still wanted to stop at the police station, but she was hungry, so she decided to stop by Pier Café and grab something to eat. When she walked into the restaurant, she found Adam Nichols sitting at the lunch counter, eating a burger.

"It's the never-a-dull-moment Danielle Boatman," Adam greeted her when he saw Danielle.

She walked to the lunch counter and looked at the empty seat next to Adam. "Do you mind if I sit here?"

Adam glanced at the empty seat then back at Danielle and grinned. "Is it safe? I heard hanging out with you can get a person killed."

"Ha-ha." Danielle rolled her eyes and sat down. "So you've heard?" She turned the coffee cup sitting on the counter in front of her over to be filled.

"The entire town's heard."

"Are you okay?" Carla, the waitress, asked when she walked up behind the counter and filled Danielle's cup."

Adam nodded toward Carla. "See."

"Yes, Carla, I'm fine." Danielle smiled. "I'd like to order a roast beef sandwich, fruit instead of fries."

"Got it. What would you like to drink?"

"Just coffee is fine. Maybe some water." Danielle took a sip of the coffee.

"You must have been terrified! I heard all about it—" Carla paused mid-sentence when the cook rang the bell. She flashed Danielle a smile and then went to pick up the order in the pass-through window to deliver to a table on the other side of the café.

"So are you really? Fine, I mean?" Adam asked in a more serious tone.

"I'm alive, aren't I?" Danielle took another sip of coffee. "I'm going to regret this."

"Regret what? Being alive?"

"No," Danielle said with a chuckle. "The coffee. I already had a couple cups at your grandmother's and some this morning at home. I don't normally do coffee this late in the day. I'm going to be buzzing tonight."

"I knew you were at Grandma's. She called me, told me about your visit. But I'd already heard about what'd happened yesterday. Scary stuff."

"Yes, it was." Danielle turned her head and studied Adam. "You dated Isabella for a while; you must have spent some time around Stoddard."

"They weren't that close. It's not like we ever had Sunday dinners with them. But I've known Stoddard for years, before I ever started dating Isabella. Knew all Stoddard's wives."

"Do you have any theories about who killed him?"

"Not really." Adam took a bite of his burger.

"What do you know about Darlene?" Danielle asked.

Adam set the burger on his plate and considered the question for a moment. "Not much, really. I know Isabella didn't care for her. But Isabella wasn't thrilled with any of Stoddard's wives. She felt each one got younger—and dumber."

"Do you think Darlene might have killed Stoddard?"

"Hard for me to picture Darlene as the black widow."

"Why? Was she madly in love with her husband?"

THE GHOST WHO WANTED REVENGE

"Not sure I would call it love exactly. She was pretty needy. It wasn't just Stoddard's money she wanted—and I don't doubt that's the main reason she married him—but she relied on him for everything. I simply don't see her going to all that trouble and risk to kill him off, and for what? To get total control of his money? Nahh... she wanted him to take care of her in more ways than just financially."

"Why do you say it wasn't love exactly?"

"Her affair, for one thing." Adam shrugged and finished his burger.

"Her affair?" Danielle practically choked on her coffee. "Darlene has a boyfriend?"

"Had. Yet I wouldn't call him a boyfriend exactly. I just know she had a little fling back when Isabella and I were still together. But she ended it."

"Did Stoddard know?"

"I have no idea." Adam took a sip of his soda and pushed his plate to the far edge of the counter.

"How did you know about it?"

"Isabella saw her go into a hotel with some guy over in Astoria. Would never tell me who it was. She thought it was pretty hilarious at the time, said it served Stoddard right, considering how he kept marrying younger."

"Did Darlene know Isabella saw her?"

"No. I think Isabella found it amusing to keep the secret. Stoddard always acted all high and mighty, tried to push Isabella around, wanted to tell her how to run her life. She took pleasure in knowing he was a clueless cuckold husband. But apparently the affair was brief."

"How do you know that?"

"Isabella told me. I don't really know how she knew. But she was pretty convinced Darlene was faithful after that one time. She joked once that Darlene got boring, throwing herself into the role of the faithful wife. But all that was back when Isabella and I were still dating."

"I'd love to believe Darlene killed Stoddard so she could be with her lover. A nice simple motive. Well, it would be, if the affair hadn't ended so long ago."

TWENTY-FOUR

D anielle was surprised to find Joe at the police station when she
stopped by after lunch later that afternoon.

"I knew they were letting you out of the hospital, but I'm
surprised to see you here," Danielle said from the doorway leading
to Joe's office.

He looked up and smiled. "Where else would I be?"

Danielle stepped into the room. "How are you feeling?"

"A little achy today. I guess I'm not as young as I thought."

"You were slammed against my floor pretty hard."

"I feel it today."

"Has Smith regained consciousness?"

"He's in a coma," Joe said solemnly.

"Too bad. I'd love to know what he has to say."

"If he would say anything."

"True," Danielle agreed. "Is the chief here?"

"Yeah, he was in his office earlier. I think he's still there."

"Thanks. I need to talk to him." Danielle turned to the door
then paused, briefly looking back at Joe. "Don't overdo it today,
okay? You should probably go home and rest."

"Yes, Mom." Joe grinned.

Danielle rolled her eyes and then went to find MacDonald.

The door to MacDonald's office was ajar. Danielle knocked on
it and peeked inside. The police chief was alone, sitting at his

desk, sorting through papers. He looked up and waved Danielle in, motioning for her to shut the door all the way after she entered.

"Any news today?" Danielle asked as she took a seat across from his desk.

"Joe's out of the hospital." MacDonald set his pen down and leaned back in his chair, looking across the desk at Danielle.

"Yeah, I saw him already. I told him he should go home."

"I told him the same thing."

"He said Smith was in a coma. Do they think he's going to come out of it?"

"It looks serious. The way his head hit the wall did some real damage."

"I could kill Walt," Danielle grumbled.

"Wouldn't that be rather redundant?"

"Yeah…" Danielle smiled. "I suppose it would."

"You think he could have disarmed Smith without hurting him?"

"I don't know." Danielle shrugged. "I just wish he would have done something sooner, before Joe got hurt."

"I'm just glad he did something eventually. I'd hate to lose one of my best men."

"And what about me?" Danielle teased.

"You? Well, you're just kind of a pain in the butt so…" MacDonald grinned.

"Gee, thanks."

"On a serious note, I think your nurse Samantha may have been involved."

"Why, what did you find out?"

"We interviewed her yesterday," the chief explained.

"I know. She called Lily and said under the circumstances she couldn't be her nurse."

"The lab found a partial fingerprint on your cellphone. It belonged to Samantha. It's possible she touched the phone at Marlow House before someone else took it."

"What does she say about it?" Danielle asked.

"That's the thing. She's gone."

"What do you mean gone?" Danielle frowned.

"This morning I sent someone over there to see what she had to say about the print, and her apartment was cleaned out. I called the company she works for, and they said she didn't show up for one of her patients this morning."

"Do you have any idea where she went?"

"Not yet. But she seems like the most likely candidate for whoever took your phone. I figured it was either her or your guest."

"Oh…about my guest…" Danielle glanced at the door. "What about him?"

"Something strange happened yesterday when I got home. Stoddard saw him and really freaked out."

"Stoddard?" MacDonald leaned forward, resting his elbows on the desk. "Not sure I can ever get used to the idea his spirit is hanging around Marlow House."

"Well, he is, and it's getting pretty annoying! I'd love to be able to convince him I didn't kill him so he'd just move on."

"What did you mean he freaked out?"

"He must know Will from somewhere. Stoddard was angry Will was at the house, kept asking me why he was there and said Will just wanted to destroy his family."

"Did you…umm…well, ask Stoddard what the problem was?"

"I tried. But he just kept accusing me of being in league with Will, like he thought I was asking something I already knew."

"What did Will say when you told him about what happened yesterday? You did tell him, right?"

"I told him this morning at breakfast. He acted shocked. And afterwards, got really quiet."

"I could see some people checking out after hearing something like that. I don't see how that kind of publicity would be good for business."

"Last night, after Stoddard freaked, I wondered if Will was in some way involved with the killer. And if that were the case, he would naturally expect to return to Marlow House and find the police there and the place taped off. Lily got home before he did, and she and Ian would have found our bodies. But according to Lily, when Will came back to the house, he acted perfectly normal. And when I saw him later, when I got back from the hospital, he was rather mellow, just chilling in the backyard, drinking a glass of wine."

"Isn't it possible Stoddard thought Will was someone else? Are spirits always rational?"

"You have a point." Danielle silently considered the possibility for a moment. "After all, he did think I killed him."

"I don't want you to worry, Danielle. I can't tell you everything I know right now—we're still following up on some leads. But I don't believe you're in any danger, and whoever tried to frame you really has no reason to hurt you anymore. So go home, and try to get some rest."

Danielle stood up. "But there is still Stoddard."

"Sorry. But I can't help you there."

"Maybe I should stop by the Catholic church, and see if they can help me." Danielle walked to the door.

"Catholic church?" MacDonald frowned.

"Sure, for an exorcism."

WHEN DANIELLE ARRIVED home from the police station, there was a black Mercedes parked in front of Marlow House. Will's car was gone and so was Ian's. Lily was home alone—except for Walt and perhaps whoever was driving the Mercedes.

Instead of pulling down the driveway, she parked behind the Mercedes and got out of the car. *I really should get me one of these,* Danielle thought as she walked by the expensive vehicle and admired its shiny and clean exterior. As she made her way up the front walk, she looked around for Stoddard, expecting him to jump out at any minute. When she reached the front door, he still hadn't made an appearance. The front door was unlocked, which didn't please her, considering the previous day's events. Entering the house, she heard voices coming from the parlor.

Walt appeared in the entry. "You're finally home."

"Who's here?" Danielle whispered, pointing to the parlor.

"They're talking to Lily. The men from...let me see...what do they call themselves? Ahh yes...Earthbound Spirits. A ridiculous name."

"Earthbound Spirits? What are they doing here?"

"They said they wanted to discuss the lawsuit. At first, I thought she was going to turn them away, but you know Lily. I think her curiosity got the best of her, and she wanted to hear what they had to say."

Danielle frowned and walked to the parlor. She found Lily

sitting on the sofa, talking to two men who sat in chairs facing her. The moment they saw Danielle enter the room, they stood and greeted her.

"Danielle, this is Peter Morris," Lily introduced, pointing first to the taller of the two men, "and Cleve Monchique from Earthbound Spirits. Gentleman, this is Danielle Boatman, the owner of Marlow House."

They definitely didn't get those off the rack, Danielle thought to herself as she noted the men's tailored silk business suits.

"A couple of dandies," Walt quipped as he leaned against the parlor desk.

"Very nice to meet you, Ms. Boatman," Peter Morris said as he took her hand and gave it a brief shake.

"Ms. Boatman," Cleve greeted her, shaking her hand after Peter.

"We heard what happened to you yesterday," Peter said. "We're so relieved to hear you survived the ordeal unscathed. If there is anything we can do to help, we want you to know we're here for you."

"Thank you, but why exactly are you here today?" Danielle asked with hesitation.

"We wanted to introduce ourselves to Ms. Miller," Cleve Monchique explained. "You probably haven't heard, but Isabella Strickland left her estate to Earthbound Spirits, which of course includes a fifty percent share of Dignity Care and Life."

"We're aware of the pending lawsuit against DCL by Ms. Miller," Peter Morris continued.

"Yes," Danielle interrupted. "There is a lawsuit. I'm not sure this is such a good idea, you speaking with Lily without her attorney present." Danielle looked at Lily. "Lily?"

"I thought I could at least listen to what they had to say," Lily said with a shrug.

"Oh, please understand," Peter Morris explained. "We are in no means attempting to circumvent Ms. Miller's legal counsel. But technically speaking, we haven't assumed ownership of DCL yet; therefore we're not yet part of any lawsuit."

"And I'm sure Lily's attorney would not want her to discuss the case with anyone at this point," Danielle said politely.

"We just wanted to make Ms. Miller aware of all the worthwhile projects Earthbound Spirits funds," Cleve explained. "We understand and sympathize with her plight and certainly support her lawsuit against the personal estate of Stoddard Gusarov for the pain and suffering she has endured. But dear Isabella was in no way part of that injustice; therefore we hope Ms. Miller would at least consider dropping her claim against DCL, which will only hurt innocent people who had nothing to do with Stoddard Gusarov's actions and could financially cripple the company, thereby hindering funding for numerous worthy projects."

"I'd like to know what worthwhile projects these palookas fund," Walt snorted.

"Would you mind if I ask a question?" Danielle asked politely.

"Of course we wouldn't," Peter said with a smile.

"What exactly is Earthbound Spirits? I understand you are some sort of a—religious order—but your organization has a very...well, interesting name."

"It's a stupid name," Walt said.

"And you are curious as to what it means?" Peter smiled.

"I suppose I am."

"Why don't you sit down, Ms. Boatman, and I will be happy to explain it." Peter motioned to the empty spot on the sofa next to Lily.

How charming, he is inviting me to sit down in my own house. "No, that's okay. I've been sitting all morning. Please go on. I am curious."

An expression akin to annoyance flashed briefly over Peter's face, yet was quickly replaced with a smile—one that seemed oddly fake to Danielle. He glanced over to Cleve and then back to Danielle. Both men remained standing.

"It's very simple, really," Peter began. "You see, we are all earthbound spirits, on earth for a very short time. While here, we are preparing for our next—the ultimate journey for our souls. If we spend our time selfishly, waste the opportunities given to us by indulging in personal petty pleasures, we return to earth in our next life to learn lessons—often painful lessons—instead of moving on. We will continue to return, destined to repeat the painful cycle."

"You mean reincarnation?" Danielle asked.

"Something like that," Peter said. "This is my last life on earth. When I die, I'll finally be able to move on, to truly embrace the wonders waiting for me."

"Umm...how do you know that?" Danielle asked.

Lily remained quiet, sitting back in the sofa, curious to see how

Danielle would react to what Peter had to say. She had already heard it all before Danielle arrived home.

"I had a vision. Saw my past lives—and I finally understood. My mission in this life is to show others how they can move on to their ultimate destination. By dedicating my life to the Earthbound Spirits' calling, I am not only helping myself, but also others. I want to help you, Danielle Boatman, like I helped Isabella. And I want to help Ms. Miller."

"You mean you want Lily to drop the suit against DCL, which will inadvertently be a suit against Earthbound Spirits' assets?"

"Yes, but not for just Earthbound Spirits—for her own spiritual health."

"Oh bushwa!" Walt spat. "Tell it to Sweeney!"

TWENTY-FIVE

Darlene sat alone on the boardwalk park bench overlooking the ocean. Glancing down at her watch, she wondered what was taking Brian so long. He had promised to meet her at 4 p.m. sharp, and it was already five minutes after the hour.

"You're late," Darlene said when Brian showed up five minutes later.

"I had things to do." He took a seat next to her.

"I heard what happened at Marlow House yesterday." Darlene stared out at the ocean, not looking at Brian.

"Oh yeah. What do you know about it?"

Darlene briefly glanced at Brian. "What is that supposed to mean?"

"Just that. 'What do you know about it?' Fairly straightforward question."

Darlene gazed out at the ocean. "Just what I heard on the news. Do they know who hired that man?"

"Why do you think someone hired him?" Brian asked. "Maybe he just wanted to kill Boatman and Joe."

"Because according to the news, he's a hit man."

"Then, that must be what happened." Brian sat back on the bench. "Why did you want to see me?"

"What are you doing about Danielle Boatman? You promised you'd help me."

149

"Do about her? That was when you were convinced she killed Stoddard."

"When? I still think she killed my husband. I heard him," she said stubbornly.

"I don't know why Stoddard said what he did, Darlene. But it's fairly obvious to everyone Danielle Boatman didn't kill your husband."

"Just because of what happened yesterday?"

"Darlene, someone hired that man to kill Joe—to make it look like Danielle did it because he was retracting his alibi."

"So she says," Darlene snapped.

"So Joe says."

"Then they're in this together!"

"Are you listening to yourself? What do you think happened; Danielle hired the hit man?"

"It's possible."

"Oh yeah, that makes a lot of sense," Brian scoffed. "Right, the hit man was in on it too? Agreed to be part of a bungled contract hit?"

"Obviously, he didn't plan that part. They tricked him. That way it looks like poor Danielle Boatman is being framed."

"Darlene, I've known Joe for a long time. He's one of the most honest men I know. If he thought Danielle was guilty, he wouldn't hesitate arresting her." *He had done it before.*

"I just know what I heard."

They sat in silence for a few moments. Finally Brian asked, "Darlene, do you know anyone who would have wanted Stoddard dead?"

"You mean aside from Danielle Boatman?"

"Obviously."

"No one. Everyone loved my husband."

"Stop it, Darlene. It's me you're talking to. And I knew Stoddard. You do know you're now on the top of the suspect list."

"I didn't kill my husband."

"I never said you did." Brian studied Darlene's profile. Tears filled her eyes as she continued to stare out to sea.

"I didn't know all my husband's acquaintances. As far as I know, he had no enemies."

"I heard Earthbound Spirits is inheriting Isabella's estate."

Darlene glanced briefly at Brian. "Yes."

"So the will Stoddard claimed to have found was fake?"

"Todd wasn't a perfect man."

"Maybe someone from Earthbound Spirits killed Stoddard."

Darlene frowned at Brian. "They didn't have a motive."

"Didn't they? After all, Stoddard tried to circumvent their inheritance with a fake will."

"They had nothing to do with Stoddard's death! It's not fair to start pointing the finger at them when Stoddard was the one who did something wrong by putting that fake will in probate. But all that has been straightened out. You're not helping if you start accusing innocent people."

"I didn't know you had a relationship with the people at Earthbound Spirits."

"I don't," Darlene snapped. "I've never even met any of those people over there."

"You never met any of them when Isabella was involved with the group?"

"No. Stoddard wanted nothing to do with Earthbound Spirits."

"And you still say they didn't have a motive to kill him?"

Darlene turned abruptly to face Brian. "Why are you doing this, Brian? I just want to see the person responsible for killing my husband behind bars. I don't want to chase after innocent people just because Todd disliked them."

"Someone killed Stoddard, and it wasn't Danielle Boatman. You need to come to terms with that."

Darlene took a deep breath and looked down the beach. "Does MacDonald think I killed Stoddard?"

"I imagine he's going to be looking at everyone who was close to Stoddard."

IAN AND SADIE arrived at Marlow House just as the men from Earthbound Spirits drove off in the Mercedes. Desperate for a little fresh air to clear her mind, Danielle offered to take Sadie for a walk along the beach while Lily filled Ian in on the visit from Earthbound Spirits.

Leaving by the front door, Danielle glanced around for Stoddard. She hadn't seen him for a while and wondered if he had finally moved on. Not wanting him to follow her to the beach, should he suddenly appear, Danielle jogged with Sadie by her side across the street and down to the portion of the beach that allowed dogs.

Wagging her tail, Sadie walked with Danielle along the boardwalk.

"If the cops show up," Danielle said as she showed Sadie the leash she carried, "I'll have to put this on you. I really don't want to get arrested again." Danielle laughed when Sadie responded with a bark. She had no idea if the dog understood what she was saying, but she found it hilarious that Sadie often responded as if she did.

They had walked for about five minutes when Danielle spotted a woman sitting alone on a park bench—it was Darlene Gusarov. Danielle was about to turn around and go in the opposite direction, to avoid running into Stoddard's widow, when Sadie took off, chasing a pigeon.

"Sadie! Come back here!" Danielle called out. When the dog didn't listen, Danielle took off in a sprint, catching Sadie just a few feet from the bench where Darlene sat.

Darlene looked over to Danielle and Sadie. "Dogs are supposed to be on a leash."

"Yes, I know," Danielle said, trying to catch her breath. Leaning down, she snapped the leash on Sadie's collar.

Darlene continued to stare at Danielle. Finally, she said, "I guess you didn't kill my husband."

"You believe it now?" Danielle stood a few feet from Darlene, the golden retriever sitting by her side.

"I suppose I have to." Darlene sighed. "I heard some man tried to kill you and Joe Morelli. Do you know who hired him?"

"Not yet. But I imagine the police will figure it out." Danielle was tempted to ask did you hire him? But then she took a second look at Darlene and noticed the tears in the widow's eyes. Darlene had lost her husband and, according to Stoddard, was pregnant. Danielle felt a surge of sympathy for the widow.

"I'm sorry about your husband. I had my issues with him, but never wanted to see him dead," Danielle said seriously.

Darlene, her expression devoid of emotion, studied Danielle for a moment. Finally, she said, "Thank you for that."

"How are you feeling?" Danielle asked.

"I suppose as well as can be expected. I'm taking one day at a time. It's all so overwhelming."

"I imagine it's been very stressful. But it's important to take care of yourself—for the baby and all."

"Baby?" Darlene scowled.

"I heard about the baby—you being pregnant."

"I'm not pregnant," Darlene snapped. She glanced down at her cotton blouse and sat up straighter. "Are you saying I look fat?" She ran her palm over her belly.

"Fat?" Danielle frowned in confusion. "No. But I heard you were pregnant."

"Who told you that?"

"I…someone mentioned it…I can't remember who," Danielle lied.

"They were wrong. Stupid rumors."

"So you've never been pregnant?" The question just popped out of Danielle's mouth. She instantly regretted it.

"No, I haven't. Although, I really don't see how that's any of your business." Darlene sat rigidly on the bench, her hands folded primly on her lap.

"You're right. It isn't any of my business." Danielle gave the leash a little tug. "Come on, Sadie, let's go." As she walked away, she told Darlene, "Have a nice day."

Danielle could feel Darlene's stare at her back as she walked back down the boardwalk toward Marlow House. She paused a moment and glanced back. Darlene continued to look in her direction.

Turning her back to Darlene again, Danielle suddenly recalled something Stoddard had reportedly said with his last breath. She didn't doubt Stoddard had said it, since he told her the same thing. According to Stoddard, his killer had threatened to kill Darlene after she finished with him. However, from what she could tell, Darlene never seemed particularly fearful of the threat—or had she been? *What would I do if I thought someone was going to kill me?*

Danielle pulled her cellphone out of her back pocket and dialed Chief MacDonald. She continued to walk down the boardwalk, holding the phone by her ear.

"Hi, Chief, I have a quick question for you," Danielle said after he answered the call.

"I'll see if I have a quick answer."

"When I was released on bail, did Darlene ever ask for protection?"

"Not really. I did tell her you were wearing an ankle monitor."

"But afterwards, when Joe came forward and she still thought I killed her husband, did she demand any protection?"

"No, why?"

"Do you know if she hired any security guards?"

"You mean someone to protect her from you?"

"Yes. According to Stoddard, I was coming after her next. Brian and Darlene heard him say it before he died. And I don't doubt it, because Stoddard said the same thing to me."

"I don't think she hired anyone. Why?"

"Don't you think it's odd? If I felt someone I knew planned to kill me and the police didn't believe it, I would hire someone to protect me. After all, I can afford it. And so can Darlene. If she didn't hire someone to keep me from killing her, why didn't she?"

"You think Darlene killed her husband?"

"Someone killed Stoddard, and the only thing I do know, it wasn't me. There's something else odd about Darlene."

"What's that?"

"According to Stoddard, Darlene was pregnant."

"Darlene's pregnant?"

"According to her, she isn't."

"You talked to her?"

"I'm down at the beach right now, taking Sadie for a walk. I ran into Darlene, and I stopped to talk to her. She told me she no longer believes I killed Stoddard."

"That's a good thing, isn't it?"

"Well, if she killed him, then she knew all along."

"But what about this supposed baby?"

"I sorta mentioned something about her being pregnant. Kinda pissed her off. She made it clear I was misinformed."

"Maybe she lost the baby."

"No. According to her, she was never pregnant. Which I can believe, since Adam mentioned he saw Darlene at a bar not long ago, doing some serious drinking. Not really something I'd expect a pregnant woman to do. But why would she let Stoddard think she was pregnant?"

"Did Stoddard say how far along he thought she was?"

"No. But I assume he thought she was in the early stages, considering she wasn't showing."

"Hmmm...I can think of one reason."

"What's that?"

"He insisted on seeing me days before his death. Wanted to make a sworn statement."

"Sworn statement?"

"He was emphatic Darlene was not involved with Lily's abduction. Gave a sworn affidavit that his wife was completely innocent, insisted Darlene believed Lily was Isabella."

"You think he did it because he thought she was pregnant?"

"He might have done it anyway. But considering how adamant he was at the time, wanting to put it on record, insisting he did not want her subjected to any questioning—"

"Because of the baby."

"Exactly."

TWENTY-SIX

"W here's Will?" Ian asked Danielle and Lily when he arrived at Marlow House on Wednesday morning. He and Sadie had come through the side gate and entered the house through the kitchen door. He found Danielle and Lily sitting at the kitchen table, drinking coffee. Sadie raced through the kitchen, into the hallway, and up the stairs to find Walt.

"He told us he was driving into Portland for the afternoon and would be back later this evening," Lily told Ian as he kissed her cheek on his way over to the counter to pour himself a cup of coffee.

"I saw your nurse leaving. Figured it was safe to come over with this." Ian waved a large envelope in the air.

Danielle hadn't noticed he was carrying anything when he first walked into the house. "What is it?"

"Copies of Isabella's two wills. Very interesting." Ian tossed the envelope on the table and sat down.

Danielle picked up the envelope. "Where did you get them?"

"The magic of the Internet." Ian sipped his coffee. "So why did Will go to Portland?"

"He didn't say, and we didn't ask," Lily said.

"He seems like a nice guy, even though I'm not big on cowboy hats." Ian grinned.

"That's only because they don't make Cubs cowboy hats," Lily teased.

"They don't?" Grabbing the bill of his Cubs baseball cap, Ian removed it from his head and tossed it on the empty chair next to him.

Danielle sat quietly thinking of Will. Hiring someone to look for a connection between Will and Stoddard no longer seemed critical. She was fairly certain Samantha was the one who had taken her cellphone. Will was a respected businessman who hadn't been to Frederickport in years. She suspected MacDonald was correct; Stoddard was confused about Will. It was entirely possible; after all, Stoddard had been confused about her.

She had planned to hire the investigator she had used to look for Lily, yet changed her mind when she realized he was probably not the ideal choice for digging into Stoddard and Darlene's past, considering his locale and expertise. She wondered if Ian might have a recommendation.

"What did you find that was interesting?" Danielle asked as she removed the documents from the envelope.

"By just looking at them, one would assume they are both Isabella's wills—with the Earthbound Spirits' will being an older version and Stoddard's the newer, revised one. By appearances, they were both prepared by Renton."

Danielle shuffled through the pages. "You have three wills here."

"Yes. I ran off a copy of Isabella's two wills and Stoddard's will, the one Darlene filed."

"I assume Darlene gets everything," Lily said.

"That one had an interesting provision," Ian said as he took Stoddard's will from the pile of papers in Danielle's hands.

"How so?" Lily asked.

"Stoddard has a provision in his will that if Darlene ever cheated on him during their marriage, she is disinherited."

Danielle looked up from the papers. "You're kidding me?"

"Nope." Ian found the section in the will with the infidelity clause and showed it to Danielle.

"That's interesting, because Darlene cheated on Stoddard during their marriage," Danielle said.

"How do you know?" Ian asked.

"Adam told me. I guess Isabella caught Darlene meeting some guy on the sly in Astoria. But she never told Stoddard or let Darlene know she knew."

"Did you tell MacDonald this?" Ian asked.

"No. It happened over a year ago."

"It gives Darlene a motive to kill her husband," Lily suggested.

"Why, because she once had a lover? Like I said, it was over a year ago, and according to Adam, Isabella told him Darlene ended the affair and seemed even more committed to the relationship afterwards," Danielle argued.

"Maybe it's a flimsy motive for murder after all this time, but even if she ended the affair, she would lose her inheritance if it was proven to the courts she'd been unfaithful to Stoddard during their marriage," Ian said.

"I doubt that will happen after all this time." Danielle said.

"If she is disinherited, where would the money go?" Lily asked. "I understood Isabella was his only family, and with her gone, who'd inherit after Darlene?"

"Another thing I learned, Darlene isn't Stoddard's sole beneficiary. He leaves a portion of his estate to something called KS Trust. But if Darlene is disinherited due to infidelity, then his entire estate goes to KS Trust," Ian told them.

"What is that?" Danielle asked.

"I don't know. I need to do more digging," Ian said.

"Any more surprises with Stoddard's will?" Lily asked.

"Not really. Basically he leaves everything to Darlene and the trust, with the lion's share going to Darlene."

"I imagine whoever is behind KS Trust would be interested in learning about Darlene's indiscretion," Lily said. "And considering what she tried to do to me, I'd be happy to tell them."

"Telling them about the affair wouldn't get her disinherited," Ian said. "You'd have to have some sort of proof." He looked at Danielle. "Do you know who she had an affair with?"

"No. Adam didn't know either. Isabella never told him."

"So what about Isabella's wills? Learn anything interesting there?" Lily asked.

"In the will where she leaves everything to her uncle, she named a second beneficiary should Stoddard predecease her."

"Who did she name?" Lily asked.

"Her father."

"Her father? Didn't you once tell me he skipped out on her mother before she was ever born?" Danielle asked.

"Yes. I always assumed he was dead, since he never came

forward after Isabella's mother died. Figured he might try to get his hands on some of the Gusarov money, through Isabella. It's interesting; it doesn't actually give his name. In the will it simply refers to the alternate beneficiary as Isabella's biological father."

"Isn't that a little odd to state it that way?" Lily asked.

"What I find odd, if that will is forged, as Darlene claims, why would Stoddard stick something in the will like that? Obviously there was no love between Isabella's father and the Gusarov family, so what was the point of putting that in the will?"

"I told you I don't believe the will is fake," Danielle said.

"Maybe Isabella's father is the one who killed Stoddard," Lily suggested.

"And the motive?" Ian asked.

"Let's assume the will isn't a fake. If he knew Isabella named him as a beneficiary in the will after Stoddard, maybe he bumped off Stoddard so he could inherit Isabella's estate," Lily suggested.

"It doesn't work that way," Danielle said.

"What do you mean?" Lily frowned.

"Danielle's right. Assuming the will Stoddard filed isn't fake, then the only way Isabella's father would have inherited her estate would be if Stoddard died before Isabella—not after."

"Ahh…that's right," Lily said with a sigh. "Because it hadn't gone through probate yet, my brain was looking at it as if Stoddard died before Isabella. That was stupid of me."

"Maybe it doesn't give us an extra suspect, but it does give me more reason to question Darlene's story that the will was fake," Ian said.

"I imagine the only one who can straighten this out would be Clarence Renton. But I sure don't want to talk to him, considering the man killed my cousin and tried to kill me." Danielle downed the rest of her coffee.

"I'll talk to him. They sent him to Oregon State Penitentiary, didn't they?" Ian asked.

"If that's the one in Salem, yes," Danielle said.

"That's about two hours from here. I could drive down there and talk to him. See what he has to say," Ian said.

Lily picked up her iPhone and began surfing the web.

"What are you looking for?" Ian asked.

"Visiting hours." Lily glanced up at Ian, and then looked back at her phone. "According to this site you can visit inmates daily from

7:15 a.m. to 10:15 a.m. and then again from 12:30 p.m. to 3:45 p.m."

"If I left now, I could get there in time to make the afternoon visiting hours. I'd have to leave Sadie here."

"You should probably call first, just to make sure. Who knows, maybe Clarence got into some mischief, and they threw him into the hole," Danielle suggested.

"Do they still do that?" Lily asked.

"In his case, I hope so," Danielle grumbled.

"I wish I could go with you," Lily said.

"Sorry, babe. By the time I get in to see Renton you'll probably be hooked up to the IV again."

"I lead an exciting life." Lily sighed.

"I hope you understand why I don't want to go," Danielle asked.

"Absolutely. I wouldn't even suggest it."

"Do you think Renton will even talk to you?" Lily asked.

"All I can do is try."

***

IAN ARRIVED in Salem a few minutes past two in the afternoon. By the time he was brought to the waiting area, it was almost three.

It had been almost two months since he had seen Danielle's ex-attorney, Clarence Renton—the man who had embezzled from Brianna Boatman's estate, murdered Danielle's cousin Cheryl, and tried to murder Danielle. When they brought Renton into the visiting area, Ian's first thought was that the man had lost weight, something he could afford to do.

Danielle had once described Renton as a clean-shaven Santa Claus. Later, she retracted her description, insisting that comparing a man of Clarence Renton's caliber to Saint Nick was blasphemy. Ian thought he looked like a short, stout, defeated man.

"When they said you were here to see me, I was surprised. What would the famous Jon Altar want with me? To write a story on me perhaps?"

"I just want to ask you a few questions. About one of your clients."

"You know I can't talk to you about my clients. Client confidentiality and all." Clarence smiled.

"It's Isabella Strickland. She's dead, so I don't think it will be an issue."

"Ahh…Isabella. I heard about her death." Clarence leaned back in the chair. "All that money, and she never appreciated what she had."

"I wanted to ask you about her will. I know you prepared it for her."

"I prepared several wills for Isabella. She kept changing her mind." Clarence laughed. Ian wondered what Clarence thought was so funny.

"I need to know, which is her most current will?"

"The wills are dated. The one with the most current date, of course."

"That's not what I mean. Stoddard put a will into probate and so did Earthbound Spirits. I wanted to know if you prepared the will Stoddard put into probate."

"I prepared hundreds of wills for various clients. You can't expect me to remember them all."

Ian removed a document from an envelope and handed it to Clarence. "This is the will Stoddard put into probate."

Clarence took the document and flipped through its pages. "Looks like one of mine." He handed it back to Ian.

"Stoddard's widow is saying her husband forged the will. That it's fake. I need you to verify it isn't forged. That you wrote it for Isabella."

"Well, if she says Stoddard forged the will, he must have. I can't really remember every will I prepared. And this is only a photocopy."

"Please try to remember. In one will, Isabella left her estate to Earthbound Spirits. But about six months ago, she went to you and had you prepare a new will leaving everything to her uncle."

Clarence smiled. "Earthbound Spirits gives me a lot of comfort."

"Excuse me?" Ian frowned.

"They've showed me I'm on this earth to learn, improve my soul. I've made mistakes, but I no longer have to return and continue making the same ones."

"What are you talking about?"

Clarence stood up. "I'm glad Isabella left her estate to Earthbound Spirits."

TWENTY-SEVEN

"So what does this mean? Is Renton lying for Earthbound Spirits?" Lily asked when Ian returned to Marlow House that evening. He shared a pizza with Danielle and Lily while Walt sat with them at the kitchen table, and Sadie napped nearby.

"If you're positive the will Stoddard put into probate wasn't a fake, then, yeah, it appears that way." Ian took a swig of his beer.

"I really don't care who gets Isabella's money," Danielle said as she picked up a slice of pizza. "All the possible beneficiaries are sleazy in my book—Darlene and Earthbound Spirits. I'd just like to know if any of this has something to do with Stoddard's murder. It must mean something, but what?"

"You think Renton is a true follower of Earthbound Spirits?" Lily asked.

"More than likely he's getting some sort of payoff," Ian suggested. "We already know he's not exactly ethical."

"That's a major understatement," Danielle scoffed.

"That pizza looks good," Walt said as he watched them eat. Danielle glanced briefly in his direction.

"I'm sorry you had to go to Salem for nothing," Lily said.

"It was interesting," Ian told her.

"When was the last time I ate something? What has it been, almost ninety years? I remember hearing about pizza when I was alive. A friend of mine from New York told me about it. I always meant to try some. Apparently he was right, it must be good, considering the commercials I've seen on television promoting it and the amount of times you seem to eat it."

"It's just an easy meal," Danielle said.

Ian looked over at her. "What?"

Suspecting Danielle's comment was directed to Walt, Lily began to giggle.

"What's so funny?" Ian asked, looking from Lily to Danielle.

"Don't mind Danielle," Lily said. "Sometimes she thinks aloud."

"Yes, I was just thinking about how pizza is an easy meal," Danielle lied.

"You mean it doesn't taste that good?" Walt asked.

"Sure it tastes good," Danielle replied.

"I see what you mean." Ian chuckled. "I confess there have been a few times I thought Danielle was talking to herself. Not sure if I should be concerned or relieved to know Lily considers it's the norm."

"There is nothing normal around here," Lily said.

Danielle's startled gasp was not in response to Lily's comment about there being nothing normal around Marlow House—yet it was fitting. Stoddard had taken that moment to show himself, appearing outside the kitchen window, pressing his face against the glass pane while howling silent screams.

"He's back," Walt said dryly.

Ian looked toward the window where Danielle stared. He saw nothing out of the ordinary.

"You okay?" Ian asked.

"I'm fine. Just thought I saw something. My imagination," she lied.

A few minutes later, Danielle had a fairly good idea why Stoddard was back and making himself known. Will had returned from Portland. He walked into the kitchen with a cheerful hello, oblivious to the fact an angry spirit hovered just a few feet away, cursing his presence.

"How was your afternoon?" Lily asked.

Will walked to the table. "It was nice."

"Want some pizza, a beer?" Ian offered.

"I already ate, thanks. But I will take a beer."

"In the fridge, help yourself," Danielle said.

Will grabbed a beer and started to sit down in the chair occupied by Walt.

"Damn, I hate when that happens!" Walt cursed, jumping up from the chair. Annoyed, he walked toward the window. Danielle and Lily exchange glances, both aware the spirit of Marlow House had just lost his seat at the table.

"What are you looking at?" Walt asked of Stoddard. They stood just a foot from each other—the glass window separating them.

Stoddard pointed to Will. Walt glanced to Will and then back to Stoddard.

"So what's the deal? You don't like cowboys?" Walt asked. Stoddard responded by shaking a fist at Walt.

"Idiot," Walt muttered and then closed the blinds.

Ian jerked his head up and looked to the window. "That blind just closed."

"It does that sometimes," Lily said, taking a bite of her pizza, trying to suppress her giggles.

Ian stood up from the table and walked to the window.

"I guess I shouldn't have done that," Walt said with a sigh. He watched as Ian toyed with the window blind. Ian reopened the blinds and then fidgeted with the pull to see if the blind would fall down again.

Sadie woke up and lifted her head. She spied Stoddard standing outside the window, looking in the house, making contorted facial expressions while pounding on the glass. She jumped up and raced to the window, barking.

"Sadie!" Ian shouted. She continued to bark.

"Sadie, enough," Walt snapped. The dog stopped barking and sat down, still looking out the window. She began to growl.

"Maybe you did see something out there." Ian scratched his head.

"Why don't you shut the blind," Lily suggested. "Something outside is bothering Sadie."

"Maybe I should go out there and see what it is," Ian said. "Considering what happened the other day."

"I'll go with you." Will stood up.

"Guys, sit down," Danielle said. "It's nothing."

"I'm going to check," Ian said stubbornly. He and Will went out to the side yard, taking Sadie with them.

THE SUN WAS JUST STARTING to set. Will and Ian stood in the side yard of Marlow House, with Sadie. They glanced around the yard, trying to determine what had upset the dog, yet Sadie no longer seemed agitated and sat quietly by their side.

"Go back to where you came from, Bobby!" Stoddard shouted at Will. Instead of barking or growling, Sadie stood up and walked to Stoddard, giving him a little sniff. Neither Will nor Ian paid attention to what Sadie was doing.

"Get away from me, you stupid dog," Stoddard ordered. Sadie walked to where he stood. Stoddard looked down. The golden retriever appeared to be standing in his legs. "Get out of there!" Instead of abiding by Stoddard's command, Sadie squatted and started to pee.

DANIELLE STOOD at the window and started to laugh.

"What is it?" Lily asked.

"Sadie just peed on Stoddard. Well, not on him exactly, but as close as possible considering he no longer has a body."

Walt took a drag off his cigar and then exhaled. "Smart dog."

Danielle continued to look outside. "Until Sadie peed on him, looked like Stoddard was still railing against Will."

"Do you still think Stoddard is confusing Will with someone else?" Lily asked.

"Stoddard thinks I'm the one who shot him, so he's not exactly a reliable witness."

Walt stood by Danielle and looked out the window. "He definitely thinks Will is someone he knows," Walt said.

"But who?" Danielle asked.

"But who what?" Lily asked with a frown.

"We were wondering who Stoddard thinks Will is. It's obviously not some old friend."

"Looks like they're coming in," Walt said.

Danielle returned to the table with Lily and sat down. Will, Ian, and Sadie walked back into the kitchen. Before Ian shut the door, Danielle could hear Stoddard shouting at Will, telling him to leave Frederickport.

"I guess she just needed to go out," Ian said when he sat back down. If Stoddard were looking in the window again, Sadie wouldn't be able to see him, since Danielle had shut the blinds.

"So you guys didn't find anything out there?" Lily asked, glancing over at Danielle with a grin.

"No. But I have to admit, something about your backyard is... well...makes me feel uneasy," Will confessed.

"It's probably just because of what happened in here the other day," Ian suggested.

"Maybe." Will glanced over at Danielle. "Has that man come out of his coma yet?"

"No. And he may not." Danielle looked at Walt.

"What?" Walt asked, slightly offended at the scowl Danielle flashed his way. "The man was going to kill you. A thank you would be nice."

"I can't believe Samantha was involved in all that." Will had been interviewed by the police earlier, since he was one of the last people to see Samantha before she disappeared. "She seemed like such a nice woman, offering to show me the sights."

"It was her idea?" Lily asked, trying to sound casual.

"More or less." Will shrugged.

"So when you lived here, you didn't know Stoddard Gusarov, the man who was murdered?" Danielle said.

"I knew who he was." Will sipped his beer. "His family was well known back then."

"Did you know Stoddard's niece, Isabella, or Stoddard's sister?" Lily asked.

Will set his beer can on the table and looked over at Lily. "I knew his sister. But I never met his niece."

"Did you ever meet Isabella's father? His last name was Strickland," Lily asked.

Will shook his head. "I never met a Strickland. So why all this interest in what appears to be ancient history?"

"Someone killed Stoddard and tried to frame Danielle. And then tried to kill Danielle and Joe," Ian said. "We're just trying to figure out who in Stoddard's life would want him dead."

"I imagine anyone who ever met him," Will said.

"Why do you say that?" Danielle asked.

Will shrugged. "I just remember from when I lived here. I didn't know him well, but when I talked to people who did, they all seemed to agree on one thing. He was a jerk."

"Someone thought he was enough of a jerk that they wanted him dead," Danielle said.

"Who runs the company now?" Will asked.

"Stoddard's right-hand man. Chuck Christiansen."

"Christiansen is still with the company?" Will laughed.

"What's so funny?" Lily asked.

"Christiansen was such a little weasel back then."

"So you knew Christiansen?" Danielle asked.

"Sure. Not well, but enough to know he was always looking out for himself. He's actually running the company now?"

"From what I understand," Danielle said, "he has been for a long time."

"While I really didn't know Stoddard, I knew his parents. They started the company. Even back then, Christiansen was trying to worm his way into management. I guess he got everything he always wanted." Will downed the last of his beer.

"Do you think Christiansen would have a motive to kill Stoddard?" Danielle asked. "If he's as conniving as you say."

Will set his beer can on the table and looked at Danielle. "Did he stand to inherit anything if Stoddard is out of the picture?"

"No," Ian said. "We've looked at the wills, and Stoddard left his estate to his wife and a trust, with his wife getting the lion's share."

"Then no. I can't see why he'd kill him if he weren't in line to inherit anything. I'd assume he'd want to maintain his status quo," Will said. "But then, I've been away for years. My money would be on the wife."

"You mean for the killer?" Lily asked.

"Yes. If she's the one who inherits Stoddard's estate, sounds like she's the one with the best motive."

"I agree. Unfortunately, Darlene seems genuinely devastated over losing her husband."

"Over losing Stoddard?" Will shook his head in disbelief. "This Darlene is either a very stupid woman or a very good actress."

TWENTY-EIGHT

"Look who just walked in," Cleve Monchique told Peter Morris. The two men sat in a back booth of the Pearl Cove Restaurant.

Sipping his merlot, Peter glanced in the direction of Cleve's gaze. It was Darlene Gusarov. She was alone. "Do you think we should go over and introduce ourselves?"

Cleve laughed at the suggestion. "That would be interesting."

DARLENE ADMIRED HER RECENT MANICURE. *Black nail polish has a certain dramatic flair—especially for a widow.* Smiling, she sipped the apple martini and glanced at her watch. Chuck would probably be angry that she had already started drinking, especially if he found out this was her second cocktail.

When he had called her an hour earlier, asking her to meet at the restaurant so they could discuss business, he sounded serious. While he would want her sober for such a discussion, she preferred conversing with Chuck while slightly buzzed.

"Drinking alone?" a male voice asked. Darlene looked up to find Brian Henderson standing over her. Instead of his uniform, he wore dark slacks and a dark gray shirt. She wondered if he was at the restaurant with a date.

"No, I'm waiting for someone." Darlene ran a finger over the rim of her martini glass.

Brian looked down at her black nail polish. "I never figured you'd go for the Goth look."

"It's not Goth. I'm in mourning." Darlene picked up her drink and took a sip.

"I can see that," he said dryly. Without asking, Brian sat down at Darlene's booth.

"What are you doing?" Darlene glanced around.

"I'm sitting down, talking to an old friend. After all, you're the one who started this."

"I didn't start anything. But you have to leave. Chuck Christiansen is meeting me here."

"Christiansen?" Brian raised a brow.

"It isn't like that. Get your mind out of the gutter. He does run my business. We have important things to discuss. You have to leave. Now."

"I never pictured you as a corporate head. More like someone who needed a man to take care of her. Or is that it? Is Christiansen taking Stoddard's place?"

"Don't be crude. Chuck is my employee. Nothing more. He works for me. I call the shots."

"Is that why you're so anxious for me to leave? Why do you keep looking around as if Christiansen might appear at any moment? So afraid to have your employee see you with me?"

Darlene leaned toward Brian and hissed under her breath, "That isn't it and you know it! People can't see us together!"

"Why not? What does it matter now?"

"It's complicated, Brian."

"It may be complicated, but it was just the other day you begged for my help."

"I didn't beg." Darlene glared at Brian.

"What would you call it? You even tried resurrecting those old feelings."

"I was distraught, vulnerable. I thought that woman had murdered my husband, but I guess I was wrong."

"And you needed me to make sure she was punished for the crime?"

"You are a police officer. It's your job."

169

"I should have known that's all it really was. Hell, I did know." Brian sat there a moment, staring at Darlene.

"Why are you looking at me like that?" Darlene shifted nervously in the booth's seat.

"I'm just always amazed how a woman can be one thing one moment and then transform into something entirely different the next. I suppose it's just in a woman's DNA to be manipulative."

"I don't know what you're talking about, but I need you to leave." Darlene gulped the rest of her martini.

Brian leaned across the table and snatched Darlene's right hand, holding it tightly. He glared at her.

"You're hurting me!" Darlene hissed under her breath. She looked around to see if anyone was watching.

"Did you kill Stoddard?" Brian refused to release her hand.

"Of course not!" With a quick jerk, she pulled her hand from his grip. Pouting, she began to rub her free hand. Darlene glared at Brian.

"I've done a lot of thinking these last few days. I didn't want to believe you could do something like that. That I could be such a damn fool...again." Brian leaned back in the booth and studied Darlene.

"You know me, Brian. You know me better than anyone. You can't believe I'd do something like that."

"Do I know you? Did I ever? Why did you really want me to make sure Boatman got what was coming to her? So you could get away with murder?"

"How can you even think I would do something like that?"

"For one thing, you basically kidnapped Lily Miller."

"It wasn't me! It was Stoddard! I had no idea it was Lily Miller and not Isabella. You know I was never close to Todd's niece. I didn't see her at the hospital, and when they brought her to the estate, she was partially bandaged. She was in a coma, and Stoddard hired round-the-clock nurses to care for her. I had no reason to visit her."

Brian shook his head. "I find that hard to believe."

"How can you say that? Even Joe Morelli thought Lily was Isabella. Why would you expect me to tell the difference if he couldn't?"

"You were living in the same house with her. I find it hard to believe Stoddard didn't confide in you."

"Todd kept his own secrets. He was trying to protect me. There was no reason for me to know what he was up to. He didn't want me to worry. Before he died, Todd made a sworn statement declaring I had no prior knowledge of the crime."

"Yes, I know. I was there when he came in to make the statement. I agree; he was trying to protect you. I'm just not certain he was telling the truth."

"And if he wasn't telling the truth, what would any of that have to do with my innocence or guilt regarding Todd's murder?"

"It just makes me wonder what you're willing to do to get what you want. And it isn't just about Stoddard; did you hire Smith to kill Joe and Boatman? Joe's one of my best friends."

"How would I even know how to find a hit man?"

"You've always been a resourceful woman."

"Why would I kill Todd after all this time? Why? I chose him over you. Is that why you're so angry now, why you're making these ugly accusations, because I chose to stay with my husband?"

"The other day you insisted I was the one you really wanted. Of course, at the time you wanted something from me. Yet now, well, now you don't even want to be seen with me."

"It isn't that, Brian. Can't you see? I could lose everything."

"Yes, I suppose you would lose everything if you went to prison for Stoddard's murder."

"That's not what I mean!"

"What did you mean?"

Darlene glanced around nervously. "Us. People can't know about us," Darlene whispered.

"There is no us, Darlene."

"There used to be. I don't want people to start asking questions about us."

"What do you care? It's not like Stoddard will divorce you. You've got everything you ever wanted."

"I just don't want anyone to ever know I was unfaithful to Todd."

"I never thought you murdered your husband for me. You worried others will think that?"

"Brian, have you told anyone about us?"

"Like I said, there is no us."

"You know what I mean. When we were together, did you ever tell anyone about us? Joe perhaps?"

"I don't tell people my personal business, not even my partner."

"So you never told anyone, not even afterwards?"

"No, never. But why does it matter now? Hell, now we can shout it to the world if we want." Brian started to stand, pretending he was going to shout to the world of their affair. Darlene let out a horrified gasp.

CARLA STOOD at the hostess station, trying to memorize the menu. She had taken a night job as hostess, hoping it would turn into a waitress position. Servers at the seaside dinner house had to be bringing in bigger tips than she was earning at Pier Café.

So far, she hadn't memorized any of the menu items. Since coming on shift, she had been distracted, watching the interaction between Darlene Gusarov and Officer Henderson. Carla knew Brian; he was a regular at the café. She had waited on Darlene a number of times, but the woman wasn't particularly friendly.

Carla remembered Brian was the officer who had been with Darlene when she found her husband shot and dying. Brian had been the one to hear Stoddard accuse Danielle Boatman of his murder. However, if the last newspaper article she read was correct, Danielle was innocent.

Two men walked into the restaurant, interrupting Carla's train of thought. She recognized one of the men; he occasionally came into Pier Café. She had never seen the second man. From their manner of dress, she assumed they were at the restaurant for a business dinner. While Pearl Cove was upscale compared to Pier Café, the male clientele rarely wore suits.

"Good evening," Carla greeted them, picking up two menus. "Do you have a reservation?"

"We're meeting someone. She might already be here, Darlene Gusarov," the man she recognized said.

"Oh yes, she and Brian Henderson are already here."

"Brian Henderson?" The man frowned. "Officer Henderson?"

"I thought we were meeting Mrs. Gusarov alone?" the second man said, looking at his companion.

Carla dropped her voice to a whisper. "Brian was at the bar when Mrs. Gusarov came in. When he went over there, I just assumed that's who she was waiting for, because he sat right down."

"We're running a little late. I suppose we should be grateful she had someone to keep her company," the man she recognized said.

"Well, frankly, I think she'll probably be relieved when you get to the table so she'll have an excuse to get rid of him."

"Really? Why do you say that?" the second man asked, glancing over at the man Carla recognized.

"They seem to be having some sort of argument. She didn't look happy, and he seemed angry. He even grabbed her."

"Grabbed her?" the men said in unison.

"Well, just her wrist, but it did seem to upset her. Of course, he let it go. Brian is a police officer. Maybe it had something to do with her husband's murder investigation." Carla's mind spun. She could imagine a dozen titillating scenarios for the display at Darlene's table.

"How so?" one of the men asked.

"Considering how Officer Henderson was the one to find her husband after the man had been shot, and how Mr. Gusarov practically died in their arms. I know there's that ongoing investigation, what with Danielle Boatman being arrested for Mr. Gusarov's murder and then released. And then that man getting arrested for trying to kill Danielle Boatman and Joe Morelli, and someone trying to frame Danielle for the murder." Carla stopped talking and tried to catch her breath. Her heart pounded. "Maybe they are discussing the murder!"

"PLEASE, BRIAN, LEAVE. CHUCK IS HERE," Darlene pleaded.

Brian glanced up to the front of the restaurant. "Who's that with him?"

"Just someone else who works for DCL. Please, Brian."

Without saying another word, Brian stood up and walked from the table.

TWENTY-NINE

"What's wrong with Carla?" Bill Jones asked Adam as they sat at the Pier Café lunch counter, eating breakfast.

Adam glanced over to Carla, who stood at the waitress station, her palms resting on the counter and her head bent down. If Adam didn't know better, he'd swear she was sleeping standing up.

"I heard she took a night job at Pearl Cove. By the looks of it, I'd say she worked last night." Adam took a sip of coffee and resumed eating his breakfast.

"So what's going on with the Boatman woman? She's been in the paper all week. First she gets arrested, then they drop the charges, and now I hear someone tried to kill her," Bill asked.

"Yeah, her and Morelli."

"I heard that. So what's the deal?"

"Looks like someone's trying to frame her for Stoddard's murder."

"She does know how to get herself in trouble." Bill chuckled.

"You should have seen Darlene tear into her at Stoddard's funeral."

"I'm surprised you went," Bill said. "Gusarov was a jerk."

"Grandma wanted to go. Danielle went with us."

"You two getting kind of chummy?" Bill snickered.

"She's alright." Adam shrugged.

"Yeah, alright to look at, if you can get past the ditzy."

"Whatever." Adam took a bite of toast.

"When you say someone's trying to frame her, what do you mean?" Bill asked.

"The murder weapon was planted in her car. And around the time Stoddard was killed, the trash truck was on the street, and the guys on the truck claim they saw a car like hers in the neighborhood and a woman matching Danielle's description leaving Stoddard's house. But Morelli claims it couldn't have been her. He saw her over on Sea Cliff Drive at the time of the murder."

"So they think they were lying?"

"Nah. The cops think whoever killed Stoddard had someone dress up to look like Danielle and then drive through the neighborhood around the time of the murder."

"Doesn't she drive something like a Focus? I know at least half a dozen people in town with the same car and color."

"No. She recently got a new car. A red Flex."

"Hmmm…can't recall seeing any of those in town. Of course, when I leave here, I'll probably see a dozen today," Bill said.

"Yeah, that's usually how it works." Adam downed the rest of his coffee. "According to the article in the paper, there's only one red Ford Flex registered to an owner in Frederickport: Danielle Boatman." Adam popped his last bite of food in his mouth and then pushed his now empty plate to the other side of the counter.

"I'm trying to remember what a Flex looks like."

"I don't know—a short Suburban maybe? Although, Danielle's sort of reminds me of a Woody with its grooved side panels and the white top."

"Thought you said her car was red."

"It is, with a white top."

Bill looked up at Joe. "I've seen a car like that in town. But I can't remember where."

"It was probably Danielle's."

"No." Bill shook his head. "It wasn't. So I take it they haven't figured out who was in that car, if it wasn't Boatman."

"As far as I know. No."

"This is really going to bug me." Bill tossed his napkin on his plate.

"Why?"

"Trying to remember where I saw that car. It was just the other day. Damn…"

"They say the memory is one of the first things to go." Adam snickered.

"Oh, shut up." Bill stood up to get his wallet.

"I'll get it."

"You sure?" Bill asked.

"Yeah, anyway I can write it off on my taxes."

Bill was gone when Carla returned to the counter to pick up the empty plates and drop off the ticket.

"You paying for Bill's?" Carla asked between yawns.

"Nah, he said since you took so long to get back here, you could pick up his tab."

"What?" Panicked, Carla looked to the door. For a moment, Adam thought she was going to run after the handyman.

Adam started to laugh. "I'm just kidding. Simmer down. What's with you today?"

Carla let out a sigh and leaned against the counter. "I'm just tired. I got home so late last night and had to be up before five this morning. These hours are going to kill me."

"Is the other job worth it?" Adam asked.

"Hard to tell. They just have me hostessing right now." Carla then grinned and said, "But I must say, my first night was very interesting."

"How so?" Adam asked.

"Darlene Gusarov came in for dinner last night," Carla explained.

"Darlene is a regular merry widow," Adam mumbled.

"Why do you say that?"

"I saw her the other night at The Gray Whale, throwing back one too many and having a pretty good time."

Carla shook her head. "Well, this wasn't like that."

"What do you mean?"

"She was alone at the table, waiting for the rest of her party, when Brian Henderson joined her. They got into a fight. It got nasty. At one point, he even grabbed her. I thought they were going to start throwing punches."

"Brian Henderson? As in Brian Henderson the cop?"

"None other."

"What were they arguing about?"

"I don't know, but it seemed pretty intense—and personal."

"Hmmm…"

"I heard Darlene tore into Danielle at her husband's funeral. Really made a scene. But I don't know if it's true," Carla whispered.

"It is. I was there. Danielle went to the funeral with Grandma and me. Darlene lit into her." Adam paused for a moment, as if remembering something.

"What?"

Adam shrugged. "When Darlene was pitching her fit, Brian Henderson intervened. Took her off somewhere to calm down."

"Did he have to force her?"

"Force her?" Adam wasn't sure what Carla meant.

"To go with him—when she was yelling at Danielle."

"No. In fact, she seemed pretty comfortable with him."

"Well, they weren't comfortable with each other last night."

"So what happened?" Adam asked.

"Brian was still with her when the rest of her party arrived. They were just walking to her table when he took off. Didn't say anything to them or me, just stormed out of the restaurant."

"Stormed out?"

"Like he was pissed."

"Was he in uniform?" Adam asked.

"No. Before she came in, he was sitting at the bar, having something to drink."

"Alone?"

"Yeah, I guess." Carla shrugged.

"So you don't have any idea what they were arguing about?"

"No. But like I said, it looked intense and personal. I tell you what, I certainly wouldn't want to get Brian Henderson pissed off. He gets a little scary."

BILL JONES SAT in his truck, smoking a cigarette while flipping through the work orders on his clipboard. Adam kept him busy maintaining the rental houses for Frederickport Vacation Properties, yet that didn't stop Bill from taking on side jobs. Sorting through the work orders, he removed the ones that had been completed and tossed them on the passenger seat.

He added one of the completed work orders to the pile when a memory sparked. Frowning, he picked it back up, studying the paper a moment. It was for a vacation rental house on the south side of town.

The job was a simple one: replace a fluorescent lighting tube in the garage. But he was running late that day, and he didn't have time to stop at the hardware store, located on the north side of town, to purchase one. He decided to borrow one from a rental house a few blocks away on Sea Cliff Drive. The second property was empty, and he had a key. He knew there were a couple spare fluorescent lighting tubes in the garage—he had put them there. He could borrow one; they were the same size, and then later, when he was at the hardware store, he could purchase a replacement. He didn't call the owner of the Sea Cliff Drive property to ask permission; he didn't see the point. After all, no one would miss the lighting tube.

Tossing the work order and the clipboard on the passenger seat, Bill threw his cigarette out the window and started up his truck. Curiosity sent him back to the vacant rental property.

A few minutes later Bill turned down Sea Cliff Drive. There weren't any vehicles on the street and no sign of life. Most of the houses in this neighborhood were rentals and typically vacant this time of year, save for an occasional weekend visitor and the cat lady who lived on the corner.

He pulled in front of the house where he had borrowed the fluorescent lighting tube. Parking the truck, he looked around and turned off the engine. Technically speaking, he wasn't supposed to go into any of the houses he occasionally worked on without a work order. Some of the property owners, like this one, had given him a house key, making it more convenient to go in when needed.

Rummaging through his glove compartment, he looked for the right key. Once he found it, he got out of the truck and sprinted up to the house. Standing at the front door, he glanced around, looking for any nosey neighbors. It took him just a moment to get into the house and make his way to the door leading to the garage. Once in the garage, he turned on the light. There it was: a red Ford Flex.

"Damn," Bill said aloud, walking toward the vehicle. When he had been here the other day, he was in and out and paid little attention to the red car. Yet he had seen it. The owner of the house had half a dozen vehicles, if not more. It wasn't uncommon for one of them to be parked in the garage during the off-season when the house wasn't being rented.

Bill remembered what Adam had told him—no one in Frederickport, other than Danielle Boatman, owned a red Ford Flex. But the owner of this house lived in Frederickport. So who was the car's registered owner? Was this the car the trash men had claimed to see on the day Stoddard was murdered?

Curious to check out the vehicle's registration, Bill walked around to the passenger side and opened the door. Leaning into the car, preparing to open the glove compartment, he froze. There on the passenger seat was what looked like a long brown braid. He almost picked it up, yet thought better of it. There was something on the seat next to it—a red purse, a knit cap and gloves. Looking closer, yet not touching, he could see there was also something sitting on the middle console. A ski mask?

Backing away from the car, he closed the passenger door.

"Crap," he muttered, heading to the door leading to the house. As he exited the garage, he turned off the light and hastily made his way to the front door. With his heart pumping, he locked up the house and returned to his vehicle.

Once in the truck, he grabbed his cellphone off the dashboard. He was already driving down the street when he reached the person he was calling.

"It's Bill Jones. I think I found something you might be interested in."

THIRTY

U sing the remote control, he opened the gate leading to the
Gusarov Estate's private drive. After entering, he closed the
gate behind him and parked the car at the side of the house, where
it wasn't visible from the street.

Darlene had let the household staff go the day before. He
wondered if it had been a shock to them. They had worked for
Stoddard since before Darlene arrived. Yet unlike Stoddard,
Darlene could not speak Russian. It was never an issue when Stoddard was alive, and Darlene was more than content letting Stoddard
direct the domestic help. As long as things were clean, laundry done,
and food on the table, life was good. Unfortunately, being unable to
communicate with the household staff proved frustrating. The new
help would not be starting until next week, but by then, Darlene
wouldn't need them.

Using the key given to him, he let himself into the house. Killing
Darlene was never the plan—yet they had known it might be necessary should things start falling apart. Things were falling apart.

DARLENE DIDN'T KNOW why he couldn't just explain on the
phone, but he insisted he needed to show her. It had something to
do with Isabella's estate. She drove Stoddard's little T-Bird. He had

rarely let her drive it when he was alive, yet since his death it was the only vehicle she drove. Of course, they—now she—owned a half dozen other cars. But the T-Bird was fun to drive, especially on windy roads like this one.

Just as she was about to keep driving, she saw him. She almost passed him by. Darlene didn't recognize the vehicle. He must have gotten a new car. Pulling off the road, she looked in the rearview mirror, backed up and parked. Grabbing her purse, she got out of the car.

It was sunny and in the high seventies. She wondered why he was wearing gloves and a bulky jacket on such a lovely day.

"Thanks for coming," he greeted her, giving her a friendly wave when she walked toward him.

"I really don't see why we couldn't have done this on the phone," she said, making no attempt to conceal her annoyance.

"You'll understand when I show you." He pointed to the view point along the nearby bluff.

With a sigh, Darlene walked alongside him toward the view point. Glancing over to him, she asked, "Are you cold?"

"No. But sometimes it's a little cool up here. I suppose I overdressed." He laughed.

When they reached the edge of the bluff, she looked at him again, waiting for his explanation.

"Be careful," he warned. "It's a little precarious up here. But I need to show you the land Isabella purchased and explain why it might be a concern."

"Here? What did she think she was going to do with this? No way to build anything, it's so steep."

"Maybe you'll understand when you see what someone built along the shore."

"I don't see anything." Darlene squinted as she peered over the cliff.

"Watch where you're stepping. Some of the rocks might be loose."

Darlene glanced down to her feet. Something sparkling caught her eye. There wedged between some rocks was what appeared to be a diamond ring.

"Look at this!" Darlene said excitedly as she kneeled and reached for the ring.

SOMETIMES DARLENE COULD BE SO predictable. He watched as she eagerly knelt down, oblivious to any possible danger. From his coat pocket, he removed a heavy paperweight he had hidden there. With steady hands, he brought the paperweight down on her skull, crushing it. She crumpled to the ground without a whimper.

Glancing around, he hastily pulled a knit cap from his pocket and slipped it on while kneeling beside Darlene. While this stretch of roadway was normally quiet, there was always a possibility another car could come by at any minute.

Feeling for a pulse, he was surprised to find there was none. He expected a second blow would be needed to finish the job. Picking up the diamond ring next to her body, he slipped it in his pocket. It wasn't actually a real diamond, but a high quality cubic zirconia with plenty of sparkle. Enough sparkle to attract Darlene's attention.

He shoved her body over the bluff's edge and watched it roll down the hill. It was about two hundred feet from where they stood to the desolate stretch of beach below. Before standing, he picked up her purse and opened it up.

"Wasn't sure if you'd leave your purse in the car, but this saves time," he said aloud. Pulling her cellphone from the purse, he used it to send a text message. Waiting a few seconds for a reply, he glanced around nervously. A reply came, to which he responded. A brief text exchange ensued. When he was finished, he slipped the cellphone back into the purse. Setting the handbag on the ground, he picked up the paperweight. There was blood on one side. He set it atop the leather handbag, blood side down.

Standing up, he jogged toward the car he had borrowed. Borrowed was putting it nicely. He had procured the vehicle from one of his employees. He needed to return the car before anyone knew it was missing and before someone drove down the road and noticed the T-Bird. His manner of dress might make it difficult for someone to identify him, yet he couldn't take any chances. He had already taken enough chances these last few weeks to last a lifetime.

BRIAN HENDERSON STARED at his cellphone. He had just had the oddest text exchange from Darlene. During their affair, she had never sent him text messages, fearful Stoddard would see them on her phone. With Stoddard gone, Brian figured she no longer had that worry. Of course, she still didn't want to be seen with him, considering her behavior the previous night. Perhaps that was why she wanted him to meet her at such an isolated location. Silently, he reread the exchange.

Her: *Meet me at Pilgrim's Point as soon as you can. Come alone. Urgent.*
Him: *Why?*
Her: *You were so angry last night. We need to work this out.*
Him: *There is nothing to work out.*
Her: *You hurt my arm last night. I thought you were going to break it.*
Him: *It wasn't that bad.*
Her: *You scare me when you get violent. I hate when you are mad at me.*
Him: *I'm not mad.*
Her: *I still love you. Please forgive me for what I did. Please meet me.*
Him: *When?*
Her: *Now.*
Him: *Okay.*

BRIAN DROVE along the desolate stretch of highway leading to Pilgrim's Point. According to local folklore, Frederick Marlow had named the landmark. Why the town's founder chose that name, Brian had no idea.

He spied the T-Bird up ahead, parked along the side of the road. He didn't see Darlene. Pulling behind the T-Bird, he put his car in park and turned off the ignition. Getting out of his car, he looked around. It didn't feel right. Walking to Darlene's car, he peeked inside. He didn't see keys in the ignition or a purse on the seat. She must have taken them with her. But where did she go?

Surveying the desolate area overlooking the ocean, he noticed what appeared to be a woman's handbag abandoned on the ground near the edge of a cliff. His heart lurched. "Darlene!" he shouted. With a sprint, he rushed to the cliff's edge. A paperweight sat atop the leather handbag. It was always breezy at Pilgrim's Point. The heavy paperweight helped prevent the handbag from blowing off the side of the cliff. Picking the paperweight up, he tossed it aside and opened the purse, looking for identification. The purse belonged to Darlene.

Once again, he shouted her name. Clutching the handbag in one hand, he stood up and looked over the edge of the cliff. A lifeless body lay on the beach below. Frantic, he looked for some way to climb down to Darlene, praying she was still alive. Unfortunately, the only way to get to her now would be to drive down the highway a half mile, take the dirt path leading down the hill, and walk back up the beach. Racing to his car, he pulled out his cellphone and called for help.

REMOVING his baseball cap briefly and repositioning it on his head, Chief MacDonald let out a weary sigh. Silently, he watched the coroner examine Darlene's body. It had been one hell of a day, and for once Danielle Boatman wasn't in the center of the drama.

"What was she doing up there, so close to the edge?" MacDonald asked as he looked up the sheer cliff to the roadway. The T-Bird remained parked along the side of the road. He couldn't see it from his position on the beach, but he knew it was still there.

Brian stood with Joe next to MacDonald. The three looked up to where the fatal fall had probably taken place. Trying to wrap his head around the tragic event, Brian remained silent after MacDonald asked the question.

"She didn't just fall," the coroner said as he stood up and turned to face the three officers.

"What do you mean?" MacDonald asked.

"By her injuries, I'd say someone hit her over the head first. With something hard. And then just pushed her over the cliff. She rolled down that hill. Judging by her injuries, I'd say the hit to the head is what killed her. But I'll know more when I give her a thorough exam." The coroner turned his back to the police officers and instructed his men to move the body.

MacDonald got on his radio and relayed the coroner's information to the officers up on the road by the T-Bird.

"I wonder if this has something to do with what Bill Jones found in her rental," MacDonald murmured.

"What are you talking about?" Brian asked.

"When you were out of the office this morning, we got a call from Bill Jones. He found a Ford Flex, one that looks just like

Danielle's, parked in the garage of a rental house owned by Darlene."

"What was Bill Jones doing in the garage?" Brian asked.

"He does repair work for the rental," Joe explained.

"Are you saying Darlene was the one framing Boatman?" Brian asked.

"It sure looks that way," Joe said. "After Bill called, we got a warrant, and I went to check out the house. The car's there. Looks just like Danielle's."

"I don't understand; when we checked registrations for Ford Flexes similar to Boatman's, no one in town owned one that color aside from Boatman. Who does the car belong to?" Brian asked.

"It's registered to some guy who lives in Washington," MacDonald said. "According to him, a woman approached him at the supermarket parking lot in Vancouver and offered to pay cash for his car. She was offering about five thousand more than what the car was worth, so I guess he didn't question it. By the description he gave of the woman, it might be Darlene if she was wearing a red wig."

"I also found a hairpiece—a braided ponytail—in the car," Joe said. "Along with a hat, gloves, red purse, and ski mask. Plus, the Washington license plate had been covered with paper, making it look like a temporary dealer plate like the one on Danielle's car. Even the numbers matched Danielle's."

"I think we found something, Chief," a voice called over the radio.

"What is it?" MacDonald asked. Both Joe and Brian could hear the conversation.

"Maybe the murder weapon. It looks like blood. We may have a fingerprint," the voice over the radio told him.

THIRTY-ONE

D anielle sat with Marie in a booth at Lucy's Diner. They had just ordered lunch.

"This is nice. It was sweet of you to invite me," Marie said as she unfolded her napkin, placing it on her lap. "How is Lily doing?"

"Much better, although she's going stir-crazy. She's counting the days, can't wait to be done with the IV treatments. It really is confining."

"She has been able to get out a little, hasn't she?" Marie asked.

"Just once. Remember, she was out with Ian the day the hit man tried to kill Joe and me."

"Shocking." Marie shook her head. "I understand he's still in a coma."

Before Danielle could respond, the waitress arrived with their beverages. They resumed their conversation when they were alone again.

"I wanted to ask you something," Danielle said. "Ian got copies of Stoddard's and Isabella's wills. We figure whoever killed Stoddard might have done it for the inheritance."

"I would assume Stoddard left his estate to Darlene, since he doesn't really have any other family."

"He did leave most of it to Darlene. But he also left a portion to something called KS Trust. Do you have any idea what that might be?"

"KS Trust?" Marie frowned. "No, sorry, I've never heard of it before."

"I've tried to play detective online, but from what I've learned, trust information is private. I doubt Stoddard's attorney would share that information with me."

"Do you know who Stoddard's attorney is?" Marie asked.

"Some guy in Portland. Never heard of him before. But his name was on the will Darlene filed with probate."

"Perhaps it's some charity," Marie suggested. "Although I never knew Stoddard to be very charitable."

"I figure KS is an acronym or someone's initials."

"Initials? Those were his sister's initials."

"Isabella's mother?" Danielle asked.

"Yes, Karen Strickland."

"Her married name," Danielle murmured.

"Yes and no." Marie chuckled.

"What do you mean?"

"Strickland wasn't Bobby's last name. And it obviously wasn't her maiden name."

"Who's Bobby?" Danielle asked.

"Isabella's father. Karen's husband."

"Who was Strickland?"

"Some name they grabbed out of a hat, I suppose." Marie sipped her iced tea.

"I don't understand?"

"After they ran Bobby off and then found out Karen was pregnant, they really didn't want her going by her maiden name. How would that look? But Stoddard's father was not about to have his daughter use Bobby's name."

"Now I'm really confused. What do you mean—they ran him off? According to Ian, Isabella's father only married her mother for the Gusarov money, and when they disinherited her and she got pregnant, he abandoned her."

"I imagine that's the story Ian dug up when he did his research. Some folks believe if you repeat a falsehood often enough, others will start accepting it as fact."

"Are you saying that story wasn't true?"

"It's the version Karen's father wanted the world to believe. The only problem, that's not what happened," Marie said. "I was there when Karen and Bobby eloped. I remember how furious Karen's father was. Considering poor Karen's mental state, it didn't take much to break them up."

"Mental state?"

"Karen was always fragile and a bit of a scatterbrain, like her mother. Needy might be one way to describe her. She seemed to adore Bobby, and he her, but she also adored her father, and his fury over the elopement was too much for her. Once they ran Bobby off, Old Man Gusarov couldn't wait to erase all memory of him from their lives. Unfortunately, Karen was with child by that time, so having Karen take a new surname was how he was able to erase Bobby without making his daughter look like an unmarried mother."

"Is that why Isabella didn't mention her father by name?" Danielle murmured. "Didn't she know it?"

"What do you mean?"

"I told you Ian got copies of the wills. Isabella's will, the one Stoddard put into probate, left everything to her father should Stoddard predecease her. Yet she doesn't mention him by name, just refers to him as her biological father."

"Interesting." Marie sipped her tea. "That would mean she found out Strickland wasn't the name of her father."

"I think it's bizarre Karen would take some random name. You'd think she'd want her child to carry the name of the man she loved."

"Poor Karen never had much of a backbone. And frankly, I don't think she was all there."

"All there?" Danielle frowned.

Marie tapped a finger against her temple. "Her screws were a bit loose. I suspect a few were missing. After Isabella was born, she seemed to unravel completely. According to rumors around town, she was addicted to pain medication. She was in and out of rehab. I remember the last time she was in rehab, she ran away. It was quite a scandal at the time. But then they found her, and not long after that she died."

"So do you think this KS Trust is some sort of charity, perhaps in the memory of Karen?"

"It's possible." Marie shrugged.

"So what do you remember about Isabella's father?"

"I met him a few times. I found him rather charming. Unfortunately, he was as poor as a church mouse. From what I recall, his parents died when he was quite young, and he was raised by some distant relative who promptly showed him to the door when he turned eighteen."

"Were Bobby and Karen teenagers when they started dating?"

"He moved to town not long after he turned eighteen. He and Karen met right after that. They secretly dated for a few months. I suppose Karen always knew her father wouldn't approve."

"I wonder why he moved to Frederickport."

"There used to be a little used-car lot on the south side of town. The man who owned it was a friend of mine. He passed away about fifteen years ago. He's the one who told me about Bobby's family situation. Apparently, he'd met Bobby through some mutual friends, heard his story, felt sorry for him, and offered him a job washing cars. Within six months, Bobby was a car salesman. He was quite industrious, as I recall."

"But not quite good enough for Karen?"

"Her parents didn't think so." Marie looked up as the server brought their food to the table. She moved her glass of ice tea to one side to make room for her plate of food.

"I'm curious," Danielle said after the server left their table. "When Adam was dating Isabella, did she ever discuss her father with you? You said something a moment ago—that Isabella thought her father's name was Strickland."

"No, I never discussed her parents' situation with her. But I always assumed she thought her father's surname was Strickland. I'm sure there are others in town—those who were around back then—who are aware of what really happened. But no one would ever say anything, at least not openly. Some found the Gusarov family quite intimidating, and they didn't want to cross them, so they remained quiet. Of course, the family never intimidated me. I just felt, what was the point after all this time? Perhaps if Isabella had shown some interest in finding her father, I would have said something."

"It's interesting she mentioned him in her will."

"If it is her will, since the people at Earthbound Spirits now claim to be the true beneficiaries."

"It's complicated." Danielle took a bite of her burger.

"I will tell you a little secret," Marie whispered, glancing around to make sure no one could hear. "I was secretly relieved when Adam broke up with Isabella."

Danielle arched her brows. "Really?"

"Isabella was a sweet girl. I liked her, in spite of that horrid tattoo. What are young women thinking these days?" Marie shook her head. "But I was worried about the great-grandchildren." Marie tapped a finger against her temple again. "Bad genes."

"Oh, you mean because of Karen's mental issues?"

"Yes. I had a cousin who married the loveliest girl. Her mother was nuttier than a fruitcake. When they had children, goofiest bunch you ever saw. All in the genes."

"What do you think happened to Isabella's father?"

"I know there was some sort of row. What happened exactly, I don't know. It was all very hush-hush. But one minute Karen and Bobby are newlyweds, the next her father is busting a gasket and then Bobby just vanishes. Moves out of town. Never to be heard of again."

Danielle's eyes widened. "You don't think…they killed him?"

Marie laughed. "No. Although that thought did cross my mind when I heard he just upped and disappeared. But my friend, the one who gave the boy a job, later told me in confidence that he got a call from Bobby several months later, apologizing for leaving so abruptly. He didn't explain what had happened, but he wanted to know how Karen was. From what I understand, he'd call my friend every month. Continued to call after Karen died. But then he was asking about Isabella."

"How long did that last?"

"You mean the calls?" Marie asked.

"Yes."

"I assume until my friend died, about fifteen years ago."

"And you never mentioned any of that to Isabella?"

"The opportunity never came up." Marie sighed. "But now that I think about it, I probably should have said something to her."

"Do you remember Bobby's last name?"

"So this is why you aren't answering your phone." A male voice interrupted their conversation. The two women looked up. It was Marie's grandson, Adam.

"Adam, dear, what a nice surprise."

Adam leaned down and kissed his grandmother's cheek. She scooted over, making room for him to sit down.

"Hi, Adam," Danielle greeted him.

"I noticed your car out front," he told Danielle as he sat down.

"Wondered if you heard the news. I've been trying to call Grandma to tell her."

"News? What news?" Marie asked.

"Nothing official, just what we heard over the police scanner in the office."

"You have a police scanner in your office?" Danielle asked.

"Yep. Brand new. I was just trying it out."

"Is that legal? Should you be eavesdropping on the police?" Marie scolded.

Adam laughed. "It's okay, Grandma. You want to know what I heard or not?"

"Is it about Stoddard's murder?" Danielle asked.

"Did that horrid hit man finally wake up?" Marie asked.

"Darlene Gusarov is dead. Looks like murder," Adam announced.

"Are you serious? What happened?" Danielle remembered the killer had told Stoddard Darlene was next. Had the killer made good on his promise?

"Looks like someone pushed her off Pilgrim's Point after bashing her head in."

"Another murder? What is happening to our town?" Marie shook her head.

"Dang, I wish I was still wearing that stupid ankle monitor," Danielle muttered.

"Why do you say that?" Adam asked.

"Before Stoddard died, he not only claimed I was the shooter, he told Brian Henderson I was planning to kill Darlene next."

"Brian Henderson?" Adam laughed.

"A poor woman has been killed, Adam!" Marie chided. "Not a laughing matter."

"Sorry, Grandma. It's just that according to what I heard on the scanner, Brian is the one who found her. And according to Carla, Brian and Darlene got into quite an argument last night. She claimed Brian even got physical."

"Carla from Pier Café?" Marie asked.

"Yeah," Adam said with a nod.

"Carla's a little gossip," Marie grumbled. "I'd take anything she says with a healthy dose of salt."

Adam shrugged. "Just telling you what I heard."

"I wonder what they were arguing about," Danielle said.

"I don't know, but for now it takes the heat off you." Adam grinned.

"I was going back and forth about Darlene. But now this," Danielle muttered.

"What do you mean?" Adam asked.

"One minute I'm convinced Darlene is behind Stoddard's murder—and the next I think it has to be someone else. I wonder who inherits the estate now?"

"That would be Darlene's heirs, whoever they may be," Marie said.

"Knowing Stoddard," Adam said, "I'm sure his attorney prepared Darlene's will, leaving everything to him. I know he purchased some real estate with Darlene, a couple rental houses here and some along the coast. Isabella told me. No way would he let her bequest those to her family. Now it's probably going to his other heirs."

"Unless she prepared a new will," Danielle suggested.

"You mean since Stoddard's murder?" Adam asked.

Danielle responded with a nod.

"I doubt she had time." Adam then added with a shrug, "I suppose it is possible."

"If her estate now goes to Stoddard's other heirs, it is not a person, per se—it's KS Trust," Danielle said.

"What's that?" Adam asked.

"We have no idea," Marie said.

"Now with Darlene gone, I wish there was some way to learn more about Isabella's will, the one Stoddard put into probate. I still don't believe it's fake. For some reason Darlene lied."

"Renton was Isabella's attorney," Adam said.

"Ian already talked to him. All he found out was that Renton seems to be a fan of Earthbound Spirits."

"He saw him at the prison?" Marie asked.

"Yep." Danielle nodded. "But he didn't say much one way or another about the validity of the will, just that he was glad it was going to Earthbound Spirits."

"There's always Gloria; she'd know," Adam suggested.

"Gloria Comings, Renton's assistant? From what I understand, she left town, and no one knows where she went," Danielle said.

"I went to school with Gloria. She was one of those girls who always had to follow the rules. Took her job seriously. Renton's arrest came as quite a blow to her. She couldn't get out of town fast enough," Adam explained.

"Well, if she didn't know what he'd done, she wasn't to blame," Danielle said.

"True, but that's not how she sees it. Gloria would know if that will was Isabella's or not. She'd tell you the truth," Adam said.

"Adam, you know how to contact Gloria, don't you?" Marie asked.

"Sure I do." Adam grinned.

"You know where she is?" Danielle asked.

"Yeah. Like I said, Gloria and I go way back. I'll call her for you. See what she says."

"Thanks, Adam. I'd appreciate that. If the will is legit, you think she'd be willing to give MacDonald a statement?"

"I'm sure she would. Like I said, Gloria is a straight arrow."

"Another thing," Danielle said. She looked at Marie. "Before Adam showed up, I was asking you if you remembered Bobby's surname."

"Who's Bobby?" Adam asked.

"That was Isabella's father," Marie explained.

"Then wouldn't it be Strickland?" Adam asked.

"No, dear." Marie patted Adam's knee and then looked at Danielle. "I remember it was the same last name as one of my favorite actors. I once asked him if they were related. Of course, I knew they weren't."

"What was the name?" Danielle asked.

"John Wayne. I loved his movies. Don't you just love John Wayne?" Marie asked.

THIRTY-TWO

Danielle tossed her keys and purse on the kitchen counter at Marlow House. After parking her car in the driveway a few minutes earlier, she had dodged Stoddard's ghost, who hurled curses at her the moment she stepped out of her car.

A sound from the kitchen window caught her attention. Looking toward the sound, she saw Walt, who had just closed the blinds.

"Thanks," Danielle greeted him. "I was going to do that."

"The police need to solve his murder so we can get rid of him. I prefer the windows open so I can smell the sea air." Walt waved his hand, summoning a lit cigar.

"So we get to smell cigar instead?"

Walt shrugged and took a puff.

"Is Lily sleeping?" Danielle asked.

"No, she went out with Ian. They took Sadie to the beach for a walk."

Danielle glanced to the corner of the kitchen, where Lily had parked her walker. "She didn't take it?"

"I don't imagine it would work very well on the beach. Plus she seems to be doing much better today."

"I'm glad she's getting out more. I saw Will's car out front. Where is he?" Danielle glanced to the doorway leading to the hall.

"Up in his room. He just took a shower. I think he's getting ready to go out. I heard him tell Lily that he's leaving in the morning." Walt leaned against the counter and watched Danielle. "Is there something wrong?"

"Wrong?"

"You seem…edgy. Nervous."

"Where do I begin?" Danielle sat at the kitchen table. "But if Will comes in here, you stick around. Don't leave me alone with him."

"What's wrong?" Walt took a seat at the table.

"I think Will might be Isabella's father."

"Her father?"

"At lunch Marie told me Isabella's father was named Bobby Wayne. Strickland was just a name her mother took after the two separated."

"I thought you showed Marie Will's photograph, told her his name, and she didn't recognize him."

"She knew Isabella's father as Bobby Wayne, not Will Wayne or Billy Bob Wayne. She didn't recognize the name. It's been years since she's seen him. He was just a teenager back then, so the picture didn't trigger anything. Not to mention the fact that Marie is ninety."

"So it's Isabella's and her mother's graves he came to visit," Walt murmured. "Interesting, considering he abandoned Isabella's mother before Isabella was born."

"That may not be the true story."

"He didn't abandon them?"

"Not exactly. According to Marie, Isabella's grandparents broke up the marriage and drove their son-in-law from Frederickport. I guess they really were in love, and Marie doesn't believe he married her for the Gusarov money. I'm not sure how or why he left, but he kept in contact with one of Marie's friends up until the friend died, checking on Isabella and her mother."

"I thought you said Will had a lot of money."

"I'm sure he does. His car dealership was very successful. I have no idea why he stayed away."

"I could see how an inexperienced young man might be intimidated by the Gusarov family. From how it sounds, they were once influential in the same way my family was. Yet once he got older and financially successful, I would expect him to return if he were truly interested in his daughter and wife's welfare."

"Ex-wife. From what I understand, they were divorced."

"But still, Isabella was his daughter. I know if I ever had a daughter, I would never abandon her."

"That's not all the news. Darlene is dead."

"Darlene? You mean…" Walt nodded to the kitchen window, its blind closed. "His wife?"

"Yes." Danielle stared at the closed window.

"What happened?"

"I don't know all the details, but apparently she fell from Pilgrim's Point."

"That's quite a fall. What was she doing up there?"

Danielle shrugged. "Like I said, I don't know all the details. Adam stopped in the restaurant when I was having lunch with his grandmother. He'd heard it on the police scanner."

"Police scanner?" Walt frowned.

"It's a device that picks up the radio frequency used by the police. So you can listen in to what they're saying."

"Hmmm…interesting…I think I saw something like that on a television show."

"Adam says it sounded like someone hit her over the head and then shoved her off the cliff."

"I imagine the fall alone would kill her."

"All I know for sure is that she's dead."

"Are you worried?" Walt asked.

"Worried? How?"

"Stoddard did tell Brian Henderson you planned to kill her next."

"The police understand Stoddard didn't know what he was talking about."

"I hope you're right." Walt nodded toward the closed window. "Does he know yet?"

"Stoddard? No. But that doesn't surprise me. After all, for decades you never knew your wife had died."

"Yes, but Stoddard's experience seems to be quite different from mine. Even different from Cheryl's," Walt said.

"How so?"

"Neither Cheryl nor I realized we were dead. At least, not right away. I lived here for close to a century, not realizing the truth. And if you hadn't told Cheryl, she might still be stumbling around in a haze."

"You have a point. Stoddard knows he's dead. Knows he was

murdered. Unfortunately, he gets confused on the who murdered him part."

"I thought someone was in here with you," Will said from the doorway.

Danielle stood up and turned to Will, blushing. "Hi. I guess I was thinking out loud."

"I do that sometimes too." Will laughed and walked into the kitchen.

"What have you been up to today?" Danielle went to the sink, getting herself a glass of water.

"I took a drive this morning," Will said as he walked to the table and sat down. "I'll be leaving in the morning, and I wanted to tell you how much I appreciate you letting me stay here."

"We had our share of excitement—glad you didn't walk into it and get caught in the crossfire."

"Glad you're okay." Will smiled.

Danielle walked back to the table and sat down. "You said you took a drive this morning? Where did you go?"

"You don't think he had something to do with Darlene's death, do you?" Walt asked. Silently, Danielle glanced at Walt.

"Just drove up the coast a ways."

"You didn't happen to go by Pilgrim's Point, did you?"

Will stood up abruptly and walked to the sink. "You don't mind if I help myself to a glass of water, do you?"

"No, help yourself." Danielle watched Will as he silently got himself a glass of water without answering her question.

"So did you drive by Pilgrim's Point?" she asked again.

"Pilgrim's Point?" Will turned to face Danielle and took a sip of his water. "I'm afraid I don't know where that's at."

"Really? It's a well-known landmark around here."

Will shrugged. "Doesn't sound familiar." He finished his water and set the glass in the sink. "Why do you ask?"

Danielle shifted uncomfortably in her seat. Will remained standing by the sink, staring at her, waiting for an answer.

"I heard there was an accident up there today. Just wondered if you saw any of the commotion. Lots of police cars, ambulances, that sort of thing."

"Accident? What kind of accident?"

"A woman fell. She was killed."

"How sad," Will said. "Was it someone you knew?"

"It was Darlene Gusarov." Danielle watched for his reaction.

"Isn't her husband the one who was murdered?"

"Yes. The one they arrested me for."

"Do they know what happened?" he asked.

"I don't know. I just heard about the fall. I don't know any of the details." She failed to mention Darlene's fatal head injury.

"Too bad." Will stood up.

"What are you doing this afternoon?" Danielle asked.

"I'm going to visit my girls one last time. Then grab something to eat and get to bed early. I have a long drive ahead of me."

"Do you still think he's Isabella's father?" Walt asked when Will left the room.

"I don't know. But there is one way to find out."

"What's that?"

"I could go down to the cemetery and see whose grave he visits."

"You would do that? You hate cemeteries!"

"Considering how it's been in my own backyard since Stoddard died, I think I can handle a cemetery."

"Does it really matter if Will is Isabella's father?" Walt asked.

"I don't know, maybe. What if he's in some way involved with Stoddard's murder? And Darlene's?"

"What's his motive?" Walt asked.

"I don't know. Revenge maybe."

"Why take his revenge out on Stoddard? Sounds like his parents were the ones who interfered with the marriage. As for Darlene, she wasn't even around back then. Why kill her?"

"I don't know." Danielle stood up and started pacing the room. She paused a moment and looked at Walt. "Don't you think it's a strange coincidence he showed up now? Right after the murder?"

Walt shrugged. "And maybe he's not Isabella's father."

"Why are you finding excuses for Will? Not long ago you seemed to be suspicious of him. You said you were going to keep an eye on him."

"I did. But from what I've seen, he just seems like a nice guy. I simply like him. I thought you did too."

Danielle sighed. "I did...I do." She sat back down. "But still, if he is Isabella's father, it seems odd he showed up now...and wanted to stay here. You have to admit, wouldn't most people check out after a murder attempt on the premises?"

"Then follow him to the cemetery. See what graves he visits. If you're worried he's in some way involved in the murders, don't let him see you. You can always question him later when he returns to Marlow House."

"So you can protect me? Like you did with Smith?"

"Are you ever going to let me live that down?"

"Live that down? Not the best idiom, considering your state," Danielle smirked.

"I promise I won't put the guy in a coma if he gets out of hand. And I promise to intervene before things get too out of hand."

Danielle grinned, but didn't say anything as the kitchen door opened and Sadie rushed in, followed by Ian and Lily. Lily leaned on Ian, who helped her into the room.

Danielle stood up and faced the open door. Behind Lily and Ian was Stoddard, who jumped up and down, flailing his arms. She tried to ignore him, focusing her attention on Lily. "Will told me you took a walk. How did it go?"

"I think I wore her out." Ian chuckled, leading Lily to a chair.

"It was nice getting out, but I am such a wimp," Lily grumbled.

Danielle slammed the door shut on Stoddard and turned to the table, where Ian and Lily now sat with Walt. Sadie curled up under the table on Walt's feet.

"I don't imagine you two have heard yet," Danielle said as she sat down.

"What?" Lily asked.

"Darlene Gusarov is dead."

"Seriously?" Ian asked.

"If Adam Nichols is to be believed. I was having lunch at the diner with Marie when he stopped by. He heard it on his scanner. She fell at Pilgrim's Point."

"What happened?" Ian asked.

"I don't know the details. But from what Adam could pick up, sounded like someone hit her over the head then shoved her off the cliff. I haven't turned the radio on yet, so I don't know if the news has picked it up."

"Wow...dead...Darlene..." Lily glanced to the kitchen window. She knew why the blinds were closed.

"And there's something else too." Danielle stood up and shut the door leading to the hallway. When she returned to the table, she told them what Marie had said about Bobby Wayne.

"I'm a little curious too," Ian said. "Are you serious about following him when he goes down to the cemetery?"

"Yeah. Considering everything that's happened, I'd like to know if he's in some way connected with the family."

"I'll go with you," Ian said. "I don't think it's a good idea for you to go alone."

"You think Will is dangerous?" Danielle asked, glancing from Ian to Walt.

"He's been staying here almost a week," Lily said. "I really like him."

"I do too," Ian said. "But it wouldn't hurt us to proceed with caution."

"I'm not planning on letting him see me, and if we both go, it'll be more difficult to stay out of sight. I'll be okay." What Danielle didn't want was Ian by her side should spirits from the cemetery start vying for her attention.

THIRTY-THREE

"I can explain, Chief." Brian sat at the table in the interrogation room. He had never been on this side of the interview before.

"Your fingerprints were on the murder weapon," the chief said as he sat down at the table.

"You think I would just leave it there if I'd used it to kill Darlene? I told you it was sitting on her purse. I thought Darlene had put it there to weigh it down so it wouldn't blow away."

"You're telling me you thought she just set her purse on the side of the road and left it, with a paperweight to keep it safe?"

"No." Brian combed his fingers through his hair. "That's not what I meant. Everything happened so fast. When I saw her car, the purse, and she wasn't there—I got worried. I checked to make sure it was her purse. I didn't even notice the blood. The killer must have left it."

"Explain again why you were there?"

"Darlene asked me to meet her."

"You said she called you. What did she say exactly? Why did she want you to meet her there?"

"I don't know." Brian shook his head.

"You said you talked to her on the phone. She must have said something."

Brian looked up into the chief's eyes. "It wasn't exactly a phone call."

"What was it, a carrier pigeon?"

"It was a text message."

MacDonald extended his hand, waiting for Brian to hand him his phone. With a reluctant sigh, Brian handed over the phone. Quietly MacDonald read the text messages. When he finished, he looked up and stared at Brian as if seeing a stranger.

"I can explain, Chief. It isn't as bad as it seems."

"Go ahead." MacDonald set the cellphone on the table.

"Darlene and I had an affair. It was brief. Ended over a year ago."

"She said you almost broke her arm?"

"She was exaggerating. I grabbed her wrist. It was at Pearl Cove. I was there having a drink; she came in to have dinner. I went over to her table, and we got into an argument. I swear I never got violent with Darlene."

"What were you arguing about?"

"She wanted me to make sure Boatman went to jail for killing Stoddard. But after Smith attacked Joe and Boatman, I knew Danielle hadn't killed him. And I started wondering…if maybe it was Darlene all along. I wanted to know if she'd sent a hit man after one of my best friends. And by what Joe found in Darlene's rental, it looks like I was right."

"Are you still in love with her?"

"No." Brian shifted nervously in his seat.

"Are you sure?"

"Okay, I have some unresolved feelings for her. But we aren't seeing each other, and I didn't kill her. I just wanted to know what she had to say."

"Why did she accuse you of getting violent?"

"I don't know. But ask Carla; she saw the entire thing. She'll tell you it was no big deal."

"Carla?"

"Carla, the waitress from Pier Café. She's working part time at Pearl Cove as a hostess. She was there last night. I noticed she kept looking over at us."

"Did you see anyone else there?"

"I wasn't really looking. I was pretty focused on Darlene—wondering if she was behind Smith."

"Why didn't you say anything to me?"

"I was going to. Honest. But first, I wanted to be sure. You have to understand, I really didn't want to go public about my affair with Darlene. But I would have. She kept begging me not to say anything to anyone about it."

"I'm not surprised."

"Why do you say that?"

"I've read Stoddard's will. Darlene could have lost everything if you came forward about the affair. Stoddard had a provision in the will stipulating she'd be disinherited if she was ever unfaithful during their marriage. Had you made the affair public knowledge, it would have complicated things for her, since the will just went into probate."

"She never told me."

"I'm going to put you on paid leave."

"Why?" Brian sat up straighter in the chair.

"This is an ongoing investigation, and right now you are the lead suspect."

"I didn't kill her," Brian said dully.

CARLA SAT across the table from Chief MacDonald in the interrogation room.

"I can't believe she's dead; I saw her just last night," she said.

"How well did you know Darlene Gusarov?" the chief asked.

"I really didn't know her. Oh, I knew who she was. She came into the café sometimes."

"Tell me about last night. How did Mrs. Gusarov seem?"

"She seemed fine when she came in. She was meeting Mr. Christiansen and some other man for dinner. I took her to her table. I remember she ordered a couple martinis before Mr. Christiansen arrived."

"So nothing unusual happened?"

"Unusual? Well…" Carla lowered her voice and glanced over at the two-way mirror. "Officer Henderson was there."

"That's okay, you don't have to whisper. Officer Henderson isn't here; he's gone home."

"Well," Carla said in a clearer voice, "he was in the bar, having a drink when she came in. He went over to her table, I assumed to say hello. But then they got in this argument."

"Argument? Do you know what about?"

"No. I couldn't hear what they were saying, but I could tell Mrs. Gusarov was embarrassed. She wanted him to leave."

"How could you tell that?"

"By the way she kept looking around. Like she was worried people were staring."

"Were people staring?"

"Well...no...there really weren't many people in the restaurant yet."

"What happened?"

"At one point he grabbed her. That's when it really got heated."

"Did you ever consider going to her table?"

"Go to her table, why would I do that?" Carla frowned.

"Well, if one of your customers is being bothered by another customer, don't you think it's your job to do something?"

"But he's a police officer! I figured it wasn't any of my business."

"Okay, after he grabbed her, then what?"

"She pulled away from him, rubbing her wrist like it really hurt. Gave him a dirty look. A few minutes later Mr. Christiansen and the other man arrived, and by the time they got to the table, Officer Henderson had left."

"You said it wasn't very busy last night. Do you remember who was there during Darlene and Officer Henderson's argument?"

"No...not really..." Carla considered the question a moment. "But everyone paid by credit card. Does that help?"

"Are you sure?"

"Yes. About an hour after Mrs. Gusarov's party left, I remember ringing up a customer's ticket and thinking it was the first cash sale of the evening."

"I'd like to get a list of the customers who were there last night during the time Mrs. Gusarov was at the restaurant."

"THANK YOU FOR COMING IN," MacDonald greeted Chuck Christiansen, shaking his hand.

"I can't believe she's gone. I just had dinner with her last night." Chuck sighed wearily. He followed MacDonald down the hall to the interrogation room.

"I hope you don't mind if we talk in here," MacDonald said, opening the door for Chuck. "It's more private."

"This is fine," Chuck said, walking into the room. He took a seat at the table. MacDonald sat across from him, a notepad in hand.

"You mentioned you had dinner with her last night?" MacDonald asked.

"Yes. Bart Haston and I."

"Bart Haston?"

"He manages the Western Division," Chuck explained.

"So was this a business dinner?"

"Yes. We've been trying to get Darlene up to speed on what's going on with the company. She was never involved when Stoddard was alive." Chuck took a deep breath and rubbed his temples. "I can't believe she's gone. What happened exactly? They told me she fell from Pilgrim's Point. How did that even happen?"

"We're not sure. The coroner hasn't finished his report yet, and we're still processing the crime scene."

"Crime scene? I thought it was an accident?"

"It's an open investigation. We'll be able to tell you more later. But for now, could you please tell me how Mrs. Gusarov was last night. Did she seem concerned about anything?"

"She was rather upset about her run-in with Brian Henderson."

"Run-in? What do you mean?"

"Before we arrived at the restaurant, Henderson approached her table. According to Darlene, he'd had too much to drink and got a little forward."

"Forward?"

"Apparently, he felt Darlene was ready to start dating. And he wanted to be her first date."

"Are you suggesting he made a pass at Mrs. Gusarov?"

"I'm not suggesting anything. I'm just telling you what Darlene told us when we arrived at the table. She was upset, claimed Henderson got forward with her—even grabbed her. I offered to come down here and talk to you about it. After all, he is one of your officers."

"What did she say?"

"She didn't want to get Henderson in trouble. Insisted he simply had too much to drink. But she seemed genuinely afraid of him."

"What was her and Stoddard's relationship like?" the chief asked.

"Stoddard? I'm not sure what that has to do with what happened last night."

"It doesn't."

"Well." Chuck shifted in his seat. "They're both dead now. I feel strange talking about them."

"Yes, they are both dead. Under more than questionable circumstances."

"They had their problems. All married people do."

"Do you think Darlene was happy in her marriage?"

"I don't know…" Chuck stammered.

"You suggesting they weren't happy?"

"I know Darlene was furious over the Lily Miller situation. She blamed Stoddard for the legal problems, insisted she didn't know it wasn't Isabella. But honestly, I can't believe she didn't know. Stoddard confided in Darlene."

"Do you think she was angry enough to kill him?"

"I hate to say this, especially with Darlene dead now, but when I heard he'd been murdered, my first thought was that Darlene had done it. Then I heard Stoddard supposedly told Henderson it was Danielle Boatman…but now…" Chuck shook his head.

"Now what?"

"Now I have to wonder. Were Henderson and Darlene in this together? I read about Sergeant Morelli seeing Danielle Boatman at the time of the murder. She couldn't have killed Stoddard. Henderson must have lied about what Stoddard said. Which means they had to be in this together; after all, Darlene was there too when he supposedly accused Boatman."

"You're saying Officer Henderson and Darlene conspired to kill Stoddard?"

"How can I not wonder that? Maybe she planned to pay him off. Maybe it was something more personal between them. All I know is they had a fight last night, and today Darlene is dead."

THIRTY-FOUR

Ian didn't insist on accompanying Danielle to the cemetery, providing she agree to send him regular text messages to let him know everything was okay. When Danielle arrived at the cemetery, she parked by the chapel. There were more cars in that area and she felt Will would be less likely to notice the red Ford Flex there, as he had parked around the corner.

After locking her car, she stood in the parking lot a moment, mustering her courage. It wasn't Will who made her apprehensive, but the spirits lingering nearby.

Before leaving home, Danielle had changed into denims, a gray T-shirt, and a dark gray hoodie. The late afternoon sea breeze cooled the air. Standing by her car, she pulled the hood of her jacket up over the back of her head, covering her braid. She had left her purse under the driver's seat and tucked her car keys and cellphone into the hoodie's pocket along with her hands.

Making her way to the walkway leading to Karen's and Isabella's gravesites, Danielle watched for Will. If necessary, she would duck behind a tree; there were plenty in this section of the cemetery.

Passing a number of grave markers, Danielle rounded a corner and almost stumbled over an elderly woman who knelt by a grave. Coming to an abrupt stop, Danielle looked down.

The woman turned her head and smiled up at Danielle. "You

again. I was hoping you'd stop by." It was Chief MacDonald's grandmother. The woman had died a year earlier.

"Hello, Kathy," Danielle greeted her. "By any chance, did a man wearing a cowboy hat pass by this way?"

"Why yes. He was carrying some lovely flowers. Roses. Red roses. I love when they bring flowers." Kathy stood up and pointed in the direction of the Strickland graves. "He took them down there. When he came back, he didn't have the flowers anymore."

"So he's already been there," Danielle said under her breath. "Where did he go when he came back?"

"Down there." Kathy pointed in the direction of the walkway leading to the side street where Will had parked his car.

"That was quick. He didn't stay long," Danielle said more to herself than Kathy.

"I see you didn't bring flowers." Kathy sounded disappointed.

"No, but I will next time, I promise."

"How is my grandson?"

"He's doing well. I understand he's seeing a lovely woman who his boys like."

"I was rather hoping he was seeing you."

"Me?"

Kathy shrugged and knelt back down by the grave and began brushing imaginary leaves from the marker. "Perhaps later when the other one doesn't work out." Kathy disappeared.

Danielle smiled and shook her head before hurrying down the walkway toward the Strickland graves. At least now, she didn't have to worry about running into Will, since he had already made his visit. If she found flowers on Isabella's and Karen's graves, she would have her answer.

Danielle stopped a moment and pulled her cellphone from her pocket to send a quick text message to Ian: *No worries. Will has already left.*

Slipping her cellphone back in her hoodie pocket, she headed down the path leading toward Isabella's and Karen's gravesites. Off in the distance she spied a couple going in the opposite direction. Aside from the two people, the cemetery seemed deserted. She wondered who belonged to all the cars parked by the chapel. Perhaps they were attending a funeral, yet she thought it seemed rather late in the day for a service.

She came to Stoddard's grave first. His marker hadn't yet been set. Next to his site was an empty plot, which she assumed was intended for Darlene someday. Who would have thought that day would be so soon?

Danielle wasn't surprised that Stoddard or Darlene weren't lurking around. She knew Stoddard was busy haunting the grounds of Marlow House, while Darlene probably wouldn't show up at the cemetery until her funeral—or maybe not at all. As far as Danielle knew, Stoddard's murdered wife might have already moved on.

Walking past Stoddard's grave and then his parents', Danielle came to the gravesites of Isabella and Karen.

"Oh my," Danielle gasped when she spied the red roses on Isabella's grave. For some reason she expected to be wrong—expected to learn that Will Wayne was not Bobby Wayne. But he was. Kneeling down to Isabella's grave, her fingertips brushed gently over the red buds. She noticed Isabella's marker had been set. It wasn't here the last time she had been at the cemetery.

Glancing at Karen's grave, she noticed there were no flowers. Frowning, Danielle wondered why Will hadn't divided the roses between the two graves. There were no wilted and dying blossoms scattered about, which either meant this was the first time Will brought flowers, or someone from the cemetery's landscape crew had already removed them.

She couldn't feel Isabella's presence and had never felt Karen's. Both women had probably moved on to their next destination, wherever that might be. She thought briefly of Kathy MacDonald and wondered why she remained at the cemetery. Perhaps Kathy was waiting until her grandson remarried.

"I didn't expect to find you here," a male voice broke the silence.

Startled, Danielle turned and looked up into the face of Will Wayne, who stood over her, cowboy hat in hand.

"Will," Danielle greeted him nervously, stumbling to her feet.

With his cowboy hat, he motioned to Isabella's grave. "A friend of yours?"

"I…I suppose I feel like she's a friend, even though we never met." *Well, not until after she died.* "I was admiring the roses someone left."

Will cocked his brows. "Were you?"

"I was just heading back to Marlow House." She glanced to the walkway leading back to the chapel.

"Through the cemetery? I could swear you were just at Marlow

House thirty minutes ago."

"I come down here sometimes and walk. It's peaceful," she lied.

"How long have you known?" Will asked.

"Excuse me?"

"Don't play dumb, Danielle. It doesn't suit you."

Danielle let out a sigh. "I had no idea. Not until I had lunch with Marie Nichols today."

"I remember Marie." Will tapped the brim of the hat against his thigh. He stepped closer to Danielle and looked down at the grave. "Why didn't you just tell us? Why all the secrecy?"

"I really didn't expect to arrive in the midst of my brother-in-law's murder investigation."

"So it's just a coincidence you came now?" Danielle asked without thinking.

He looked in Danielle's eyes. "You think I was involved in Stoddard's murder?"

"Of course not," Danielle said too quickly. "I just meant..." *What did I mean?*

"I'm a private person, Danielle. Maybe you don't believe that, considering all the Billy Bob Wayne crap. But he wasn't me, just a persona to help me sell cars. But you should know about that. I understand you were something of a marketing guru."

Danielle didn't comment. She watched Will, who stared off into the distance.

"I never met her, you know." Will looked down at the grave.

"Isabella, your daughter?"

Will nodded.

"Why not?" Danielle continued to study Will.

"I shouldn't have left in the first place. I was young and dumb. Karen was fragile. I had no idea how fragile. Or how easy it was for the old man to manipulate her."

"Old man? Her father?"

"Yes."

"The story Ian heard was that you left Karen after she was disinherited and you found out she was pregnant."

"I didn't leave Karen. Her father convinced her to annul the marriage. I was so devastated at the time, felt such betrayal, I went along with it. I thought she didn't love me anymore, but I was wrong."

"Why didn't you come back when you found out she was pregnant?" Danielle asked.

"I did. Her parents insisted the baby wasn't mine—that she had briefly married someone name Strickland. They tried to keep me from her."

"Did they?"

"No. I managed to see her. She was about eight months pregnant at the time. She told me she still loved me, that she had never wanted to annul our marriage, that her parents had forced her. Karen was always terrified of her parents."

"Why didn't she just leave with you?"

"At the time she believed there was something wrong with the baby. I realize now it was all a lie her parents told her. They convinced her if she left with me, the baby would die. They said they would only pay the medical bills if she remained with them."

"They actually told her they would let their grandchild die if she went with you?"

"They weren't candidates for grandparents of the year."

"What about after the baby was born?"

"I had already moved to Phoenix when I found out about the baby. I decided to stay in Phoenix, work my butt off and make something of myself. And then after the baby was born, I'd come back to Frederickport and collect my wife and child."

"But you never did."

"No. Time has a way of moving along quickly. I kept track of them through my old employer. When I found out Karen's mental state had deteriorated, I began questioning how equipped I was to take care of a child, much less a mentally ill woman who was no longer my wife."

"So you forgot about them?"

Shifting his gaze to Danielle, Will narrowed his eyes. "I never forgot them. I knew Isabella was thriving. She didn't seem to have her mother's mental problems."

"I'm surprised you didn't return after Karen's parents were both gone."

"Why, and have everyone think I only returned to cash in on my daughter's inheritance? I wanted to return at a time when Isabella wouldn't question my motives. When I had my own fortune behind me that she would one day inherit. I had no idea she wouldn't be here when that time came."

"You were planning to come after you sold your dealership,

before she died?"

"Yes. Obviously, I was too late." Holding his hat by its crown, he fitted it on his head.

"Can I ask you a question?" Danielle said after a moment of silence.

"Not sure I'll answer, but go ahead."

"What about when Isabella was supposedly in a coma? Why didn't you come back then?"

"I didn't know about the accident. It wasn't in the Phoenix news."

Danielle remembered Marie telling her about Will's former employer, the one who Will had used to keep tabs on Isabella and Karen. According to Marie, the man had died over a decade earlier. She wondered if Will had ever bothered to check on Isabella during all that time.

"Are you going to tell Chief MacDonald?" Will asked.

"Tell him what?" Danielle shifted nervously.

"Who I really am."

"You're still Will Wayne, aren't you?"

"You know what I mean."

"I don't know." Danielle shrugged. "I suppose it doesn't matter. I can't see where you'd have a motive anyway. Not sure what you'd have to gain by seeing your ex-brother-in-law dead."

"Stoddard was a jerk. He was the one who told his parents about our elopement. If it wasn't for him, we would have been able to get out of Frederickport without his father manipulating Karen into going for an annulment."

"Gee, Will, are you trying to get hauled in for questioning?"

"Why would they haul me in for questioning if they don't know I was Stoddard's brother-in-law?"

"What time are you leaving tomorrow?"

"Changing the subject?" Will laughed.

"No...I was just wondering." Danielle glanced at Karen's grave. "I thought you were bringing them both flowers."

"I did."

Danielle glanced from the roses on Isabella's grave to Will. "You left them all on Isabella's grave."

"No. I took Karen her flowers."

Danielle looked back to Karen's grave, void of flowers.

"Karen's not buried there, Danielle. She's not dead."

THIRTY-FIVE

D anielle sat in her car at the cemetery parking lot, the engine running. She replayed Will's parting comment back in her mind. She had stood there like an idiot, saying nothing.

"Why didn't I ask him what he meant?" she said aloud. Annoyed with herself for not asking him to explain, she put her car in reverse and backed out of the parking space. When she got home, she would have some questions for Will Wayne.

Turning down her street a few minutes later, she didn't see Will's car. He hadn't returned to Marlow House. Earlier he had mentioned going out to dinner. This was probably better, she told herself. It would give her time to discuss the situation with Ian and Lily before talking to Will again.

The gate was closed, so she decided to park in front of the house. Just as she turned off the ignition, a police car pulled in behind her. Looking up into the rearview mirror, she saw it was Chief MacDonald. Snatching her purse off the passenger seat, Danielle got out of her vehicle and walked to the patrol car.

"Hey, Chief. Just saw your grandma," Danielle greeted him.

"I take it you were at the cemetery." MacDonald remained in the driver's seat, the window down, engine running.

"Yeah. She's still holding onto hope that you and I will get together," she teased.

"Who has time for romance?" MacDonald grumbled. "I need your help, Danielle."

"What's wrong?" She stood by his open window.

He nodded toward the passenger side. "Get in."

"Are you arresting me?"

"Not today."

Danielle walked to the passenger side of the car and opened the door.

Peeking inside, she asked, "Are you sure you aren't arresting me?"

Not turning to look at Danielle, MacDonald stared down the road, his hands gripping the steering wheel. "Get in."

With a sigh, Danielle climbed into the car, closing the door behind her. "What do you need?"

"I was hoping you could talk to Darlene."

"Excuse me?"

MacDonald turned to look at Danielle. "As we speak, Brian is being arrested for Darlene's murder."

"Brian?" Danielle almost laughed, but she caught herself in time and stifled the urge. After all the times Brian had delighted in her unfortunate situations, she couldn't help but think it was karma. However, she genuinely liked Chief MacDonald—he had always been fair with her. Arresting one of his officers, someone he considered a friend, was obviously painful for the police chief.

"This is between you and me. Agreed?" he asked.

"Certainly, Chief. What's going on?"

"Remember when I told you about that woman Brian dated after his divorce?"

"The one that left him a little bitter?"

"It was Darlene."

"Darlene? Stoddard's Darlene?" Danielle choked out.

"The very one." MacDonald glanced over to Danielle.

"I did not see that coming."

"Brian insists they ended it long ago. But after Stoddard was killed, Darlene wanted his help making sure you were arrested."

"Now that, I could see coming."

"Brian and Darlene ran into each other at Pearl Cove last night. After Smith's attempt on your life, Brian started wondering if Darlene was involved in the murder. They argued. It was heated. There were witnesses."

"So? Brian gets in heated arguments with me all the time, and he hasn't killed me yet. Of course, he wouldn't be opposed to letting the state do the job for him."

"Chuck Christiansen, CEO of DCL, believes Brian and Darlene conspired to kill Stoddard. They both claimed to hear Stoddard name you as his killer, when in fact you have an ironclad alibi. He believes their deadly alliance to kill Stoddard and frame you went off the rails and Brian ended up killing his co-conspirator."

"But we know Stoddard did tell Brian I was the shooter."

"I know. But Brian found Darlene's body, and his fingerprints were all over the murder weapon."

"What murder weapon?"

"Someone crushed her skull with a paperweight before pushing her over the cliff."

Danielle winced. "Ouch."

"Brian claims he arrived on the scene, her car was there and her purse was sitting on the side of the road, with a paperweight sitting on it."

"Don't tell me; he picked it up without knowing what it was."

"Yes. He didn't see the blood on the paperweight, just tossed it aside. Later, when we were processing the crime scene, they found it with Brian's fingerprints."

"But that should be easy enough to explain."

"The thing is..." MacDonald removed his cap and wiped his brow with his wrist. He tossed the cap on the dashboard. "It looks like Darlene killed Stoddard."

"While that doesn't particularly surprise me, how do you know?"

"We found the other red Flex parked in the garage of a rental house owned by Darlene. A brown braid and ski mask were in the car."

"Stoddard said the shooter was wearing a ski mask."

"There was also a red purse," he said, nodding to Danielle's handbag. "Like yours. Darlene's fingerprints were all over the car, the handbag."

"So why arrest Brian?"

"A few hours ago we got a search warrant for the Gusarov Estate. Joe went over there with several officers. In her desk were some...umm...compromising photographs of Darlene and Brian.

Her computer was turned on and a document open, as if she was in the middle of writing a letter to Brian."

"What kind of letter?"

"Part love letter, part confession. She wrote how they had everyone believing Stoddard named you as the killer, and it would have worked had Joe not interfered."

"But Stoddard did name me."

"That's why I don't believe Darlene wrote that letter. I'm sure she killed Stoddard, and probably had a partner, but I don't think it was Brian."

"So why did you arrest Brian if you don't believe he did it?"

"The same reason I arrested you for murdering Stoddard. I had no choice, considering the evidence."

"What do you need from me?"

"I want to see if you can contact Darlene. See if she'll tell you who helped her kill Stoddard, who killed her."

"It doesn't work that way, I told you before. I don't do séances. And I can't choose who I see and hear."

"But it might be possible. Maybe we'll find her where she was killed or at her house."

Danielle closed her eyes and tossed her head back on the car seat. "Uggg...I don't even like Brian."

"But you can't let an innocent man go to jail for a crime he didn't commit."

"He was prepared to let me go to jail for a crime I didn't commit...multiple times."

"Yeah, but in all fairness to Brian, he actually thought you did those crimes."

Lifting her head and opening her eyes, Danielle glared at MacDonald.

"Ahh, come on, Danielle, please. You don't want the people who tried to frame you—who tried to have you and Joe killed—go free...do you?"

Danielle considered his request for a moment. Finally, she said, "You know what really irritates me?"

"What?"

"If this works and I do help you...help Brian...he won't even know I saved his sorry butt."

"Danielle, you don't seem the type of woman who does things just for a pat on the back. You're better than that."

"Oh pfff…stop trying to flatter me, Chief. I'll try to help you. Because you're right, I do want to see the people who tried to kill me arrested."

"So where should we go, to the beach where we found Darlene's body or her house?"

"I don't see Darlene lingering on the beach. It's possible. But if she didn't realize she was dead, she might have gone home. Of course, she might have already moved on."

"Moved on where?"

"I'm not sure exactly. In Darlene's case, probably somewhere with a warmer climate."

"But she has the choice to stay? Stoddard hasn't moved on."

"It seems some spirits can linger for a while. But I don't think indefinitely." She glanced at Marlow House and thought about Walt. He seemed to be lingering indefinitely, yet from what she understood, once he was weary of his confinement to Marlow House, he would move on.

Danielle pulled out her cellphone.

"Who are you calling?"

"I'm going to let Lily know I'll be gone for a while. I don't want her looking outside and seeing my car and wondering where I went."

MacDonald put the car in gear and pulled out into the street as Danielle called Lily. Driving away from Marlow House, they passed Will Wayne's car going in the opposite direction.

"That was your guest?" MacDonald asked when Danielle got off the phone.

"Yeah." Danielle shoved her phone in her purse and stared out the side window.

"What's wrong?" MacDonald asked after several minutes of silence.

"I discovered something today. I don't think it has anything to do with Stoddard's murder, but it's a strange coincidence."

"There are no coincidences."

Danielle turned to look at MacDonald. "Do you really believe that?"

"Pretty much. So what did you learn? Let me be the judge of whether it has anything to do with the murder."

"If I have to vote who gets nailed for Stoddard's murder, Brian or Will, I vote Brian."

"Will? Your guest? The cowboy car dealer?"

"He used to be known as Bobby Wayne. Moved to Frederickport after he turned eighteen. Married Karen Gusarov."

"Stoddard's sister?"

"Yep. He's Isabella's father."

"I thought Isabella's father's name was Strickland."

"No. Actually, it was Marie that told me about it. I guess the story about Isabella's father taking off after her mother was disinherited was a fiction created by Stoddard's father. After they got Karen to have the marriage annulled and they found out she was pregnant, they had her take another surname."

"Why?"

Danielle shrugged. "Stoddard's dad was a jerk."

"What reason does Wayne give for being in Frederickport?"

"He's retired now. Sold his dealership a few months back. Initially the plan was to finally meet his daughter, and then he found out she had died."

"Why did he wait so long? Even if his in-laws broke up the marriage, they've been dead for years."

"Who knows?" Danielle leaned back in the seat and looked ahead. "He's not the first man who made excuses for abandoning his child."

"You think he abandoned her?"

"I don't think he wanted to at first. But as time went by, I think he made excuses for why he didn't come back to see her."

"Did he say why he came back now? What's the point now that she's dead?"

"To visit her grave." Danielle glanced over to the chief. "You think it's just a coincidence he showed up when Stoddard was murdered?"

"Probably."

"I thought you didn't believe in coincidences."

When MacDonald didn't reply, Danielle asked, "You know what else he said?"

"What?"

"He told me Karen wasn't buried in the grave next to Isabella's."

"Oh really? And where is she buried? Wait…I know, the Marlow Crypt."

Danielle rolled her eyes. "Funny."

"So tell me then, where is she buried?"

Danielle watched MacDonald's expression, waiting for a reaction. "My guess would be nowhere."

"Nowhere?"

"According to Will, Karen isn't dead."

THIRTY-SIX

C hief MacDonald pulled the police car in front of the Gusarov Estate and parked. Turning off the ignition, he faced Danielle.

"What do you mean she isn't dead?"

"That's just what he said." Danielle shrugged.

"Did you ask him to explain what he meant?"

"He sort of caught me by surprise. It was when we were at the cemetery."

"Why were you at the cemetery?"

"I wanted to see whose graves he was putting flowers on."

"And did you?"

"Yeah, Isabella's. But he didn't put any on Karen's, and when I asked him why, he said because she wasn't there, she was still alive."

"And you just walked away after he said that?"

"No. Actually, he walked away. I was kind of speechless. But then I figured I'd quiz him about it when we got back to Marlow House."

"So what happened?"

"You." Danielle smiled.

"Me?"

"Yeah."

"Oh." MacDonald sighed. He opened the door and got out of the car. "When we're done here, I'd like to find out what Wayne meant."

"Fine, but you have to let me talk to him. I don't want you coming into Marlow House and interrogating him." Danielle got out of the car and slammed the door.

"No, Danielle, I'm going to talk to him."

Danielle opened the car door and climbed back in. Sitting on the passenger seat, she slammed the door shut.

"What are you doing?" MacDonald asked.

Stubbornly folding her arms across her chest, she said, "I told you about Will because I thought you should know. But I really don't want him to think I went tattling to you the first chance I got. If you don't let me talk to Will—without you—then you can talk to Darlene without me."

Shaking his head, he walked to her side of the car and opened the door. "Fine, you talk to him. Just let me know what he says. But if I've good reason to believe he's in some way involved in Stoddard or Darlene's murder, deal's off."

"Fair enough." Danielle stepped from the car.

Together they made their way up the walkway to the massive front door. The mansion looked more industrial than residential in design, a sterile blending of metal and glass.

"I wonder what's going to happen to this monstrosity now?" Danielle asked.

"I suppose that's up to Darlene's heirs."

"Which is probably KS Trust, whoever they are," Danielle murmured.

MacDonald stopped walking and looked at Danielle. "What do you know of KS Trust?"

Stopping in her tracks, Danielle looked back at the chief. "Nothing really, just that Stoddard made a stipulation in his will that should Darlene ever be unfaithful during their marriage, his estate would go to KS Trust. And considering what you told me, looks like that's going to happen."

"I know about KS Trust, but how do you?"

"Ian got us copies of the will. So what is KS Trust?"

"We're still looking into that."

They started walking again.

"I asked Marie if she ever heard of it before. She hadn't, but she noted KS are Karen Strickland's initials."

The moment the words left Danielle's mouth, she and MacDonald froze. They faced each other.

"Is it possible? Was Will serious when he said Karen was still alive?" Danielle asked.

"I think we need to see what you can find here and then get back to Marlow House so I can talk to Will Wayne."

"I thought you were going to let me do that," Danielle grumbled.

"Sorry, bet's off."

"Fine," Danielle said with a sigh and started walking toward the front door again.

"You mean you're still going to do this for me?"

"Yeah, why not. But if I help Brian, before you let him go, you have to first let me visit him in lockup so I can laugh at him."

"Sounds fair."

When they reached the front porch, MacDonald paused again and faced Danielle. "Before we go in, there's more you need to know, so if you do see Darlene, you can ask for her side of the story."

"If she'll tell me. But sure, go on."

MacDonald took a few minutes filling Danielle in on the facts of the case. When he was done, he unlocked the front door.

"The alarm wasn't on?" Danielle asked.

"It wasn't on when we came over earlier." MacDonald opened the door.

"You have a key? Did you have to call a locksmith?" Danielle walked through the doorway ahead of MacDonald.

"No. When Chuck Christiansen came into the office, he told me he had a key to the estate and offered to give it to me," MacDonald told her as he shut the door behind them.

It was still daylight outside. With all the high windows and skylights in the mansion, it wasn't necessary to turn on the interior lights. Danielle had been in the mansion before—back when Stoddard had held Lily upstairs, telling the world the comatose girl was his niece, Isabella.

Danielle walked through the entry to the living room. The moment she stepped onto the carpet from the tile floor, she heard it: muffled sobs. Turning toward the sound, she found Darlene curled up on the sofa, her arms wrapped around her legs as she cried.

"Oh crap," Danielle groaned.

"What is it?" MacDonald asked, glancing around the room. He didn't see anything out of the ordinary.

Darlene stopped crying. She looked up from her place on the sofa and sniffled. Instead of standing up or saying anything, she silently watched Danielle and the police chief walk into the room.

"Darlene. She's on the couch," Danielle explained.

Darlene sat up straight and put her feet on the floor. "You can see me?"

"Yes. But the chief can't."

"Why can you see me, and no one else can?" she asked. "Sergeant Morelli was here with some other cops, they just came right in. Didn't even ring the bell. They went through my things. They all ignored me! It was so frustrating!"

"They went through your things because they found your Ford Flex. Looks just like mine, imagine that."

Darlene pulled her feet back on the sofa and scooted back, retreating into the cushions.

"You killed your husband, didn't you?"

"I don't want to talk about it. Please leave my house." Darlene wrapped her arms around her legs again.

"And you tried to frame me." Danielle sat on a chair facing Darlene.

"Don't go into that now," the chief said. "Find out who murdered Darlene."

Darlene's head snapped up. She stared at the chief. "What's he talking about?"

Letting out a weary sigh, Danielle looked over to MacDonald. "Please don't say anything else. Leave us alone. Go." Danielle pointed to the hallway.

"But..."

"I'm serious, Chief, trust me."

"I'll go in the kitchen and wait," he grumbled, leaving the room.

"When you're in the kitchen, pour me a glass of wine!" Darlene called out. "I think a glass of wine will help."

"He can't hear you."

"Why? I don't understand."

"Why do you think?" Danielle asked.

"I didn't write that letter," Darlene said.

"What letter?"

"That disgusting letter Sergeant Morelli was reading on my computer. I don't even know how to type."

"What do you mean you don't type?"

"Just that. If I wanted to write a letter, I'd use a pen and paper. I don't even have a printer hooked up to my computer, so why would I use it to write a letter?"

"Email the letter to Brian?" Danielle suggested.

"Who sends emails? It's faster to call or text."

"Do you have an email account?" Danielle asked.

"Of course. I need one when I shop online. But I don't use it to send people letters."

"Did Brian have anything to do with Stoddard's murder?" Danielle asked.

"Brian? Are you serious?" Darlene laughed. "Hardly."

"But you killed him, didn't you?"

"I told you I don't want to talk about it."

"Darlene, why do you think no one can see you except for me?"

"I don't know." Darlene shifted nervously on the sofa.

"Did you go up to Pilgrim's Point today?"

Darlene looked up. "How did you know?"

"Why did you go up there?"

"Someone asked me to meet him." Darlene looked away from Danielle. She tapped her feet nervously.

"Who?"

"I can't say."

"Could you at least tell me if it was his idea to meet you up there or yours?"

Darlene shrugged. "His. I didn't want to go up there."

"So you didn't send Brian a text message asking him to meet you at Pilgrim's Point?"

Darlene jerked her head around to look at Danielle. "Of course not. I don't do text messages."

"Just a minute ago you said you'd send a text message instead of an email."

"So? Just meant, if I had to do one or the other, I would choose to send a text. It doesn't mean I'm going to start text messaging people."

"So you didn't send Brian a text message asking him to meet you?"

"Didn't I just say that?" Darlene snapped.

"I'm curious about something. I know your husband really told Brian I shot him."

"I was there, remember?"

"What I can't figure out is, how did you pull that one off?"

"I said I don't want to talk about it," Darlene said stubbornly.

"They found the braid and ski mask the shooter wore. I know the shooter wore a ski mask, Stoddard told me."

Darlene narrowed her eyes. "You talked to Todd? How?"

"He was convinced the person in the ski mask, wearing the fake braid, was me. How is that possible? How did you find someone who sounded just like me? It couldn't have been you; your husband would have recognized your voice."

Darlene began to laugh. "Todd always underestimated me! He didn't appreciate my talent!"

"I don't understand. Explain it to me."

"I'm an actress."

"Actress?"

"Well, I could have been. My drama teacher said I was the most talented student he ever had. Impersonating voices always came easy to me. I suppose I could have done something with my talent, but then I married Todd and I thought, why bother? I didn't need to work anymore. No more tedious casting calls. I liked being married to Todd."

"Then why did he have to die?"

"I didn't want to go to jail over Lily. It's not like we were the ones who hurt her. We were paying her medical bills; she should have been grateful."

"I still don't understand why your husband had to die. Just days before the murder he went to the police station and swore out an affidavit that he was solely responsible for kidnapping Lily, that you weren't involved. They weren't going to charge you with anything."

"And what would have happened when Todd realized I wasn't pregnant? He would have been furious! He would have blamed everything on me!"

"So that's why you told him you were pregnant?"

"It's what he wanted to hear. He died happy."

Danielle didn't know how to respond to that, so she changed the subject.

"Those photographs Joe found today, of you and Brian…"

"I knew I should have destroyed those!" Darlene groaned.

"They didn't look like something you took." While Danielle hadn't actually seen the photographs, MacDonald had described them.

"Of course not, do you actually think we'd take pictures like that?"

"Then who took them?"

Darlene stared at Danielle a moment before answering. "I suppose there's no reason to keep it a secret now. After all, Sergeant Morelli already took the pictures with him. Anyway, it would serve them right."

"Serve who right?"

"Earthbound Spirits. They were blackmailing me."

"Earthbound Spirits?" Danielle repeated. Then she remembered. "Isabella's will. You knew it wasn't a fake!"

"Of course I knew. But it was either lie about Isabella's will or risk losing everything. But it looks like everything will now be going to KS Trust anyway. If only Morelli hadn't found those pictures!"

"Darlene, what's KS Trust?"

"I have no idea," Darlene said before disappearing.

THIRTY-SEVEN

Danielle sat with MacDonald in the police car outside of the Gusarov Estate. The sun was starting to set.

"She didn't say who she met at Pilgrim's Point?" the chief asked. He hadn't yet turned on the engine.

"Just that it wasn't Brian, but it was a he, and whoever he was, it was his idea to meet up there, not hers. She confirmed she was the shooter, yet I suspect she didn't do it alone. And I bet whoever pushed her off that cliff was her accomplice."

"That's what I'm thinking." He studied Danielle's profile as she looked out the window. "Why did you make me leave the room?"

"Because Darlene is in that hazy period between life and death. Part of her realizes she's no longer alive, yet she hasn't embraced the fact she's dead. I didn't want to upset her."

"Sounded to me you were already asking questions that could upset her."

"No, it's different. A spirit might be reluctant to admit certain things, yet they seem to innately know confessing to a crime isn't going to get them into deeper trouble. After all, they're already dead. However, this doesn't mean they've actually accepted their death or acknowledged it. I know that sounds a little contradictory, but that's how it is."

"Yes, it is contradictory. If she already knows confession won't

227

get her in deeper trouble because she's dead, how can she not recognize the fact she's dead? It doesn't make sense."

Danielle laughed. "Whoever said death made sense? Once a spirit is forced to face his new state, I never know how he or she is going to respond. Cheryl threw a tantrum and cried for hours when it was her time. Walt, he was pretty mellow about it, yet he'd had almost a century to get used to the idea."

"So all we really know...it wasn't Brian. Did she give you anything that might clear him?"

"A couple things, but I'm not sure how it will help. According to Darlene, she didn't write the letter Joe found on her computer. In fact, she insists she doesn't type. I imagine you might be able to somewhat confirm that by checking out her computer. The same with the text message—she claims she never sends text messages. Oh, and a biggie. She was being blackmailed by Earthbound Spirits."

"What?"

"Yep. Those racy pictures Joe found were blackmail pictures sent to Darlene. It's what got her to lie about Stoddard forging that will. She figured it was better to lose Isabella's portion of the estate than all of it."

"That really doesn't surprise me. I suspected it might be something like that. Let's head back to your place so I can have a little chat with Will Wayne. See what he knows about KS Trust—the one entity who'll definitely benefit from this turn of events. Even if Darlene had her own will drawn up, leaving her estate to someone other than KS Trust, those photographs Joe found today would nullify her beneficiary in favor of the trust."

On the way back to her house, Danielle told MacDonald everything she could recall from her conversation with Darlene's spirit. When they drove up to Marlow House, Danielle noticed Stoddard hovering by the windows on the second story. He hadn't yet noticed she'd pulled up in the police car. She imagined once he did, he'd swoop down and continue with his tedious taunts.

"Do me a favor," Danielle asked before getting from the car.

"What's that?"

"Let's not discuss any of this, especially the fact that Darlene is dead, when we're outside Marlow House. I don't want Stoddard getting more upset than he already is."

"Wouldn't he already know she's dead?"

228

"No. Not unless their spirits bumped into each other. Take Walt, for example, he's been stuck at Marlow House for almost a century while his wife is down at the cemetery. Those two haven't seen each other. Angela seems to have an idea of what is going on with Walt, I suspect that's because she interacts more with other spirits at the cemetery."

"I won't say anything."

The moment they stepped onto the walkway leading to the front door, Stoddard was at their side. He appeared even more agitated than normal, which concerned Danielle, who felt the agitation energized his obsession. It might result in his ability to harness his energy in the same way Walt had. If that was the case, she worried Stoddard would then be bound to the perimeter of Marlow House, making him a permanent and potentially dangerous entity. She had never worried about spirits hurting her before. However, she had never encountered one quite like Stoddard.

Sadie met Danielle and MacDonald in the hallway and followed them to the library, where Lily was alone with Walt. Perhaps Lily and Walt could not hold a conversation during Lily's wakeful hours, that didn't mean they couldn't play chess. Lily sat at a small table facing what appeared to be an empty chair.

"Hi, Lily, we're back," Danielle greeted her when she and the chief walked into the library.

Lily gave an absent wave yet focused her attention on the chessboard sitting on the table in front of her. "Hi. Hold on, let me just make my move."

"Playing chess alone?" MacDonald chuckled.

Lily moved her chess piece. A moment later, an opposing chess piece seemingly moved on its own volition.

"Umm…I guess not." The chief gulped.

"So where have you guys been?" Lily asked, turning from the board.

"I guess we can finish this later," Walt said, standing up and walking to the other side of the room to light up a cigar.

"We went over to the Gusarov Estate. Long story, I'll explain later. I didn't see Will's car out front. Did he say when he'll be back?"

"He's not," Lily said.

"What do you mean he's not?" Danielle frowned.

"Right after you called, Will came in and said he was going to have to leave early, something came up. Told me to tell you thanks for everything. I was wondering if the sudden departure had something to do with you seeing him at the cemetery."

"Did he say anything about it?" the chief asked.

"Nothing. And I only know what Dani told me on the phone when she called to tell me she was going with you. I didn't mention anything to Will about it."

"Where's Ian?" Danielle asked.

"He went to get us something to eat."

Danielle sat down at the table. "Then let me get you up to speed with what's going on, before Ian gets back."

"WHAT ARE you going to do about Will?" Danielle asked as she walked MacDonald to the door, leaving Ian and Lily in the kitchen, eating take-out burgers.

"I still want to talk to him. Don't imagine he'll be too difficult to track down, considering who he is. But right now, I'm going down to the station and check on Brian."

"I was wondering…do you think before you do that, we could go back to the Gusarov Estate?"

"Why?"

"Yes, why?" Walt parroted when he appeared the next moment, standing next to MacDonald.

"I want to give it another try; see if she'll tell me who she met up with at Pilgrim's Point. There's really nothing holding Darlene here. Once she leaves, we may never get our answers."

"And you said you didn't like Brian." The chief smiled.

"This has nothing to do with Brian. It's about him." She pointed to the window next to the front door.

MacDonald glanced in the direction she pointed. "Stoddard is standing outside the window, isn't he?"

"Yes, he is. And it's becoming more difficult each day to put up with him. I need some way to convince him I wasn't involved in his murder."

THE CHIEF WENT into the Gusarov house first, turning on the

lights. He sat alone in the living room as Danielle wandered through the house, searching for Darlene. She found the spirit in the master bedroom, sitting on the edge of the king-size bed.

"You're back?" Darlene didn't bother standing up.

"I was hoping we could talk again."

"You should have at least knocked. Rather presumptuous, just coming and going whenever you feel like it."

"I wasn't sure you'd hear me."

"Well, no one seems to hear me. Except you, of course."

"Do you know why people can't hear you?" Danielle asked gently. She stood at the side of the bed next to Darlene.

"Yes. But I can't figure out why you can hear me."

"Tell me, why can't people hear you?"

"Good grief, must you address me as if I'm an idiot?" Darlene snapped. "I'm dead, not stupid!"

"Okay…just wanted to make sure you understood." Danielle glanced at the chair sitting next to the vanity. "Do you mind if I sit down?"

"Whatever." Darlene shrugged indifferently.

Danielle sat down. "I'm here to help you."

"Help me? How can you help me? You have a magic potion that will bring me back to life?"

"No. But I can see that whoever murdered you is punished."

Darlene turned to look at Danielle. She studied her a moment. "I suppose I'd like that. He was a jerk to kill me."

"Who?"

"Chuck Christiansen."

"Your CEO?"

"Yeah. And I bet that little weasel Bart Haston was in on it too."

"Why would Christiansen want to kill you?"

"Are you saying you don't believe me?" Darlene asked angrily.

"No. But if I'm going to see he gets arrested, I'll need a motive."

"How is murder for a motive?"

"Murder?"

"Sure. Wasn't my idea to kill Stoddard. It was Chuck's."

"Why?"

"Because Christiansen and Haston helped Stoddard cover up Isabella's death. They knew she was in the tomb. They knew it was Lily. We all did. None of us wanted Earthbound Spirits to inherit Isabella's share of the company. And when it all fell apart, they were afraid Stoddard was about to fold and drag them into it to reduce his sentence. They didn't want to go to jail and lose everything; neither did I."

"But you ended up letting Earthbound Spirits have Isabella's share anyway."

"I had no choice. That all came down after we killed Stoddard. They sent me those damning photographs in the mail. Called me up, told me if I didn't lie about the will, they'd turn the photos into probate, and I'd end up losing everything. Chuck was furious."

"He knew about the blackmail?"

"Of course not! He wouldn't have cared if my share went to KS Trust. He would have preferred it."

"Why is that?"

"I don't really know what the trust is. I just remember Stoddard saying Chuck would remain the CEO of the company if the trust ever inherited after Stoddard died."

"What did you tell Christiansen? How did you explain Earthbound Spirit's claim on the estate?"

"I told him the will was forged. He always suspected it anyway. He found it hard to believe Stoddard just happened to find Isabella's new will conveniently shoved in a file drawer at our house."

"What happened the day you were killed?"

"Chuck asked me to meet him at Pilgrim's Point. Said he wanted to show me something, that it had to do with Isabella's estate. The last thing I remember was looking down to pick something up off the ground, when suddenly my head felt as if it was about to explode. Everything went black. He must have hit me over the head."

"Who hired Smith?"

"Chuck and Haston handled that. I'm afraid I don't know any of the details. We needed someone convicted of Stoddard's murder so the police wouldn't start looking at us. After all, we were the closest to him."

"So you chose me?"

"Nothing personal." Darlene shrugged. "But everyone in town knows you've had issues with the local police. You had a motive."

"You took a gamble. Stoddard could have just as easily died before you brought Brian here."

"True. But we also made sure the trash men saw your car—or what looked like your car. And the police found you with the murder weapon. Anyway, it would have worked had Morelli not seen you. That's the one detail we missed. Christiansen was certain the houses on either side of the one we chose to send you to would be vacant."

"Is there any way we can prove Chuck and Haston were in on Stoddard's murder? That Chuck killed you?"

"I doubt they left any kind of paper trail. Knowing Chuck, he's already put any incriminating evidence through the paper shredder. My diary might have helped. But when the cops were going through my things, I didn't see it. I suspect whoever wrote that nasty letter on my computer took my diary."

Danielle mulled over all that Darlene was telling her, and then she remembered Will and Karen.

"Do you know if Stoddard's sister is still alive?" Danielle asked.

"What are you talking about?"

"Isabella's mother, Karen Strickland."

"She died years ago before I ever met Stoddard. Her grave's right next to Isabella's. Why would you ask if she's alive?"

"Just something I heard," Danielle muttered. "Do you know anything about Will Wayne?"

"Who?" Darlene frowned.

"He was Isabella's father. Back then he was known as Bobby Wayne."

"Are you suggesting Todd's sister wasn't married to Isabella's father?"

"No. They were married."

Darlene shook her head. "That wasn't Isabella's father. Todd told me his sister was married to some guy named Strickland and he ditched her after his parents disinherited her. That was Isabella's father."

Danielle didn't bother explaining the truth about the Strickland name to Darlene. What was the point? Plus, Danielle doubted Darlene would care one way or the other. From what Darlene was telling her, Chuck and Haston were her accomplices, and it was beginning to look like Will's trip to Frederickport was nothing more than a coincidence.

"I have an idea," Danielle said. "Tell me something—a secret—something no one but you and Chuck Christiansen know."

THIRTY-EIGHT

Someone needed to loan Brian Henderson a comb. A toothbrush would also be nice. From the condition of his wrinkled shirt and slacks, it was obvious he had slept in his clothes. He stood alone by the watercooler in the back section of the police station, across the hallway from Chief MacDonald's office. He had just been released on bail, yet the chief asked him to wait. They needed to talk.

The door leading from the reception area opened, and in walked Danielle Boatman. By the spring in her step, it was apparent she'd had a good night's sleep—something Brian had missed. She wore a crisply pressed lavender blouse and denim slacks. Danielle was the last person Brian wanted to see.

"Did you have a good night's rest?" Danielle asked with a cheeky grin. Stepping up to Brian, she looked him up and down. "That bed in lockup really sucks, doesn't it?"

"I bet this makes you happy," Brian grumbled.

"Happy? Oh, not happy, exactly. Karma comes to mind."

"I didn't kill Darlene. But I don't expect you to believe that." He glared at Danielle. "I don't care what you believe."

"Really? Sheesh, you're even a jerk when you're on that side of the law."

"What are you doing here? Did you just come to gloat?"

"No. Actually I'm here to get your sorry butt out of this mess."

As if on cue, Chief MacDonald opened the door to his office. "Danielle, good, you're here. Come on in."

"I thought you wanted to talk to me," Brian stammered as he watched Danielle practically skip into the chief's office.

"I do. Stay there. But first I need to talk to Danielle."

"I THINK you're enjoying this too much," the chief said when he closed the office door, leaving Brian alone in the hallway. MacDonald sat at his desk while Danielle took a seat across from him.

"Just a little. Although, he looks so miserable it sort of takes the fun out of it for me."

"This is serious, Danielle. I understand your issues with Brian. But we both know he didn't murder Darlene."

"I know." Danielle leaned toward the desk. "But considering I may have a way to help Brian, don't be too annoyed with me."

"Help him how?"

"When I was talking with Darlene, I had an idea. I didn't want to say anything to you about it last night, until I could work it out in my head. But I think I've come up with a way that will allow you to arrest Chuck and Haston, get the charges against Brian dropped, and convince Stoddard I had nothing to do with his murder."

"What's your idea?"

DANIELLE SAT on the park bench in the side yard of Marlow House, sipping a tall glass of iced tea. Stoddard stood a few feet away, glaring at her in stony silence. Since she had come into the yard, he had hurled repeated threats at her, yet she failed to respond. He was beginning to wonder if she could no longer see him.

When he heard the side gate open, he turned to see who was entering the yard. "What are they doing here?" he asked. It was Chuck Christiansen and Bart Haston.

Lifting her glass while remaining seated, she said, "Thank you for coming, gentlemen."

"You said you wanted to discuss an out-of-court settlement for

Lily Miller. Although I don't know why you insisted Haston be here. Where is she?"

"Oh, Lily? She went to Astoria today with Ian. I'm the only one here." Danielle smiled.

"You're lying to them. Lily is in the house with the cops. I saw them all going in there. What's going on?" Stoddard demanded.

"I don't understand?" Haston frowned. "You don't represent Ms. Miller."

"No. I represent myself." Danielle sipped her tea.

"Yourself?" Chuck asked.

"I know about Stoddard's private art collection. And I want it."

"Who told you?" Stoddard demanded.

"I don't know what you're talking about." Chuck glanced around nervously.

"Oh, don't play dumb. You know what I'm talking about."

"Even if an art collection was part of the Gusarov estate, we aren't at liberty to sell it to you," Chuck said.

"Oh, I don't want to buy it!" Danielle laughed. "I want it in exchange for keeping quiet. And since no one knows about the art collection but the three of us, then there shouldn't be a problem."

"Darlene knows," Stoddard said.

Chuck narrowed his eyes and glared at Danielle. "Are you blackmailing us?"

"Ouch, ugly term. But yeah, pretty much. I know you conspired with Darlene to kill Stoddard because you were afraid he'd let the world know the two of you helped him cover up Isabella's death and Lily's kidnapping."

"Darlene wouldn't kill me. She was carrying my child."

Danielle prayed her next words wouldn't send Stoddard over the edge. "I know Darlene told Stoddard she was pregnant so he'd give the cops that sworn affidavit. Of course, that was only a temporary solution. She knew once he realized she wasn't pregnant, he could throw her under the bus—with the two of you."

"Is this some fantasy you and Morelli cooked up?" Chuck accused.

"Sergeant Morelli? No. Joe has no idea I'm talking to you today. No one does. It will be our little secret."

"I don't understand..." Stoddard looked from Danielle to Chuck.

"You can't prove anything," Chuck said.

"Sure I can. You see, I have a penchant for breaking and entering. You should know that. After all, I was the one who broke into the Gusarov Estate when Lily was held there. Of course, this time it was much easier, as the alarm wasn't on."

Chuck and Haston exchanged glances.

"Sometimes Joe tells me more than he should. He told me about the letter he found at the estate. It was considerate of you to turn off the security alarm before giving the key to Chief MacDonald. You just wanted to help out the cops, so they wouldn't be distracted and could easily find that bogus letter you left on Darlene's computer."

"So what, I gave him the key so he wouldn't have to break down the door. They had a warrant," Chuck said.

"See, the thing is, whoever you sent to the house earlier didn't do a terrific job of getting rid of Darlene's incriminating evidence. I mean, gosh, that house is enormous. Of course, the cops didn't do a terrific job either."

"What are you saying?" Chuck asked.

"Being a woman, I know where women like to hide things. Didn't take me long to find Darlene's diary."

"That's not true. We took—" Chuck smacked Haston's arm before he could finish his sentence.

"So Darlene had a second diary? Lots of women do that. They have one diary for the hubby to find, and another where they write their deepest darkest secrets."

"So what did this diary say?" Chuck asked.

Danielle glanced over to Haston, who looked as if he were about to pee his pants. Chuck, on the other hand, looked chillingly calm.

"That's how I found out about the art collection," Danielle lied. She looked over to Stoddard, who stood mute. "What I found most enlightening was her detailed account involving Stoddard's murder. Every time she spoke on the phone or met with either of you, she made a note, with date and time, on what was said. I learned Bart Haston staked out the Sea Cliff Drive house, where he discovered Joe was my alibi witness, and how after that, Chuck contacted Smith to kill us."

"That's enough." Chuck pulled something from his pocket.

Danielle's eyes widened in surprise when she realized what he held.

"I didn't see that coming," Danielle squeaked. "You keep a gun in your pocket?"

"It comes in handy," Chuck said, glancing around.

"What are you doing with that?" Bart asked nervously.

"What does it look like? We're going to escort Ms. Boatman into her house, and she's going to hand over that diary."

"And then what?" Danielle asked.

"This has to end! We can't just keep killing people!" Bart blurted.

"Shut up, Bart, and get a hold of yourself."

"This is out of control. I knew I should have refused to help Stoddard hide Isabella's body."

"I said shut up!" Chuck said.

"And what if I refuse to give you the diary?" Danielle asked.

Chuck pointed the gun at Danielle's face. "We don't need you to give us the diary. I'll make it look like a suicide. It's a good drive from here to Astoria, plenty of time to find where you hid Darlene's diary. And if Lily happens to show up before we're done, then too bad for Lily."

"You can't do this, Chuck!" Bart gasped.

Danielle wondered if MacDonald and his men were waiting for Chuck to force her into the house before disarming him, or if they planned to storm the side yard. She would prefer to have them wait, knowing she would be safer having Walt take the gun from Chuck. Chuck was starting to make her nervous, the way his hand shook and finger seemed overly anxious to pull the trigger. He and Haston were arguing, and she suspected Chuck might turn the gun on his accomplice. After all, he had already gotten rid of Darlene. At least now, Chuck was no longer aiming the gun at her head.

From the corner of her eye, she noticed someone slinking around the perimeter of the house in her direction. *Damn, they plan to disarm Chuck outside—beyond Walt's reach.* Movement then came from the opposite direction. This time Chuck noticed. He started to raise the gun again in Danielle's direction when Stoddard let out a ghostly scream before lunging at Chuck, snatching the gun from his grasp and hurling it into the sky.

To the amazement of the five police officers now in the side yard, Chuck's gun sailed effortlessly overhead before landing on the porch roof.

DANIELLE STOOD by the gate and watched as they loaded Chuck Christiansen into the back of one patrol car and Bart Haston into another one. She suspected the chief wanted to keep the men separated from each other, giving them less of an opportunity to agree on some alternate story before interrogation. It looked like Bart was prepared to tell them everything they wanted to know.

"It was really Darlene?" Stoddard asked, sounding heartbroken. "There is no baby?"

Danielle reached under her blouse and pulled off the wire. There were some conversations she would prefer the police not record.

"I'm sorry. There never was a child," Danielle said.

Instead of a response, Stoddard vanished.

Danielle glanced around and then muttered, "I think he's really gone." She turned back to the house when she noticed Brian Henderson walking out the kitchen doorway and coming in her direction.

"They got the gun off the roof," he called out.

"Yeah, I noticed," Danielle said, walking to Brian. He followed her back to the house.

"I was surprised the chief let me come today. Although he told me I had to stay put."

Danielle didn't respond.

"How did you know those things?"

"An educated guess," she lied.

They stopped when they reached the door to the kitchen.

Brian turned to her. "Thank you, Danielle. You don't know how much I appreciate your help."

"I'm sorry about Darlene," Danielle said after a moment of reflection. When her comment seemed to confuse him, she continued. "We don't choose who we fall in love with. In spite of the things she did, I imagine losing Darlene is painful for you."

"I would never have helped her frame you. I need you to know that."

"Oh, I do." Danielle smiled. "I know you're a jerk. But not that big of a jerk."

THIRTY-NINE

The ocean breeze made its way through the open bedroom window. Danielle hadn't closed the curtains the night before, and they remained open. She wasn't in a hurry to get out of bed. It was Saturday morning, and there were no guests to feed. Lily was downstairs with her nurse, getting her morning IV medication.

"I see you're enjoying having your windows open again," Walt said when he appeared in the bedroom.

Danielle automatically scooted over on the mattress, making room for Walt. "I think he's really gone."

Walt stretched out next to Danielle, folding his arms across his chest while leaning against the headboard. "Do you think he went back to his estate, or has he moved on?"

"I don't know. I suspect he might have moved on."

"And Darlene?"

"Can't imagine what would keep her here. Although, I'm not sure either will be thrilled with the next leg in their journey."

"You're only guessing, Danielle. You don't really know how this all works."

"Maybe." Danielle shrugged. "But I like to think there is an element of karma in the hereafter."

"Before Stoddard left, it looked like he learned how to harness his energy. He sent that gun flying."

"Yeah. I had been worrying about that. I never really figured he could hurt me, but then when he scratched me at the funeral, I started to wonder. Maybe I've been wrong all these years."

"So what's happening to Christiansen and Haston?"

"Joe called me last night. I guess once Haston started talking, they couldn't get him to shut up. Confessed to everything from being complicit in hiding Isabella's body to hiring Smith, who, by the way, came out of his coma last night. Christiansen lawyered up, but I'm not sure how much that's going to help him considering half of the local police department witnessed him holding me at gunpoint."

The cellphone sitting on the nightstand began to ring. Danielle grabbed it and looked to see who was calling.

"It's MacDonald."

"You two are getting awful chummy."

"Oh, hush," she said with a grin before answering the phone. When the call ended a few minutes later, Danielle jumped out of bed.

Walt watched as she hastily pulled clothes from her dresser. "Where are you going in such a hurry?"

"MacDonald is going to pick me up in fifteen minutes."

"Where are you going with him?" Walt scowled.

"He knows what KS Trust is and wants to show me." Danielle tossed the clothes she intended to wear on the bed.

"He wants to show you? What does that mean?"

"I have absolutely no idea, but I love a good mystery, and you need to get out of my room so I can get dressed!"

"HAVE YOU HAD BREAKFAST YET?" MacDonald asked when Danielle got into his car.

"No. I confess, I was still in bed when you called." Danielle buckled her seatbelt.

"It'll take us about twenty minutes to get where we're going. How about we stop at a drive-through and pick up a couple breakfast burritos? We can eat them on the way."

"You buying?"

"Sure." MacDonald put the car in gear.

"It's Saturday, why aren't you home with your boys?"

"They spent last night at my sister's. After he called this morn-

ing, I called my sister and asked her to keep them a little longer."
MacDonald drove the car down the street, away from Marlow
House.

"Who is he exactly?"

"The attorney for the Gusarov estate. Did you know, last night
Gloria Comings faxed the estate's attorney an affidavit, swearing
Isabella's will—the one Stoddard put into probate—wasn't a
forgery, that Isabella had indeed changed her will, removing Earthbound Spirits."

"I bet they're pissed." Danielle chuckled.

"It looks like there will be an investigation of Earthbound
Spirits."

"So this means KS Trust, whatever it is, will get the entire
shebang?"

"Looks that way."

"So are you going to tell me, or just make me wait? What is
KS Trust?"

"Vanya Gusarov, Stoddard's father, set up the trust before he
died. According to the attorney, it was never Vanya's intent for the
trust to inherit Dignity Care and Life. He assumed his company
would be passed down to his grandchildren and great-grandchildren
—Isabella's and Stoddard's children."

"But Isabella died and Stoddard had no children," Danielle said
with a sigh.

"Exactly."

"So what is KS Trust?"

"Wait until we get where we're going. I don't know the entire
story yet."

Danielle frowned at MacDonald, yet didn't press the issue.
Instead, she asked, "I wonder what's going to happen to the
company now. You don't think Christiansen will be able to keep his
job, do you? I know he hasn't been convicted of anything yet,
but still."

"According to the attorney, no. From what I understand, DCL's
board of directors has already called for an emergency meeting. It's
a pretty safe bet Christiansen and Haston will be removed from
their positions."

MacDonald turned into a fast-food restaurant drive-through and
ordered two breakfast burritos and two cups of coffee. They were
back on the road again within fifteen minutes.

"You never said where we're going." Danielle opened MacDonald's burrito and handed it to him with a napkin.

"Just outside of town. Some property held by KS Trust."

Twenty minutes later, they turned down a street several blocks from the ocean and came to a small beach cottage surrounded by wrought-iron fencing. MacDonald pulled alongside the curb and parked the car.

"Here we are." He turned the ignition off and opened the door.

"Where are we exactly?" Danielle got out of the car.

"Let's go see."

Together they walked toward the locked gate leading to the cottage. MacDonald rang the bell.

"Yes?" came a voice from the speaker a few moments later.

"Chief MacDonald from Frederickport. You are expecting me."

"Just a moment, please," came the response.

A few minutes later the door to the house opened. To Danielle's surprise, Will Wayne walked outside.

"Will?" Danielle said in surprise when he came to the gate and unlocked it.

"Morning, Danielle, Chief MacDonald." Will opened the gate.

"I don't understand?" Danielle looked from the chief to Will.

"I didn't know until this morning," MacDonald said.

"Know what?" Danielle frowned.

"Come in the house. I'll explain there," Will said.

Danielle and the chief followed him into the house. There was no one sitting in the small tidy living room. Will led them to the doorway to the kitchen, yet stopped before walking in the room. Instead, he pointed inside. A woman, her long red hair liberally streaked with gray, sat at the kitchen table, eating breakfast while a nurse sat across from her, drinking a cup of coffee. The nurse looked up to the new arrivals and nodded, but didn't invite them in.

Will nodded to the nurse and then turned from the doorway, shutting the door before leading Danielle and MacDonald back to the living room.

"If you haven't figured it out yet, that's Karen, Isabella's mother, my ex-wife."

"I don't understand." Danielle looked back to the close door.

Will motioned to the living room sofa and chair, inviting Danielle and MacDonald to sit down. After they did, he resumed talking.

"I found out about Karen just a few weeks ago. In the beginning, I kept track of Karen and Isabella through my former employer, and after he died, I used the Internet to keep track of Isabella. She had a Facebook page, and that helped.

"I finally mustered my courage to return to Frederickport and meet my daughter, and then I learned I was too late. She was dead. I couldn't get much information online regarding the circumstances of her death, so I hired a private investigator to look into Isabella and her life. I also wanted to know if Stoddard had anything to do with Isabella's death, so I had him investigated. The private investigator discovered the Gusarov secret."

"Karen," Danielle murmured.

"Yes. Karen has been alive all these years and kept here. I didn't even attempt to contact Stoddard and ask him if I could see her. After all, he and his family did everything in their power to keep us apart, and from what I learned from the private detective, I'm fairly certain Isabella had no idea her mother was still alive."

"She was so close," MacDonald said.

"I know." Will shook his head. "I introduced myself to her nurses and explained who I was. After Stoddard died, they were more willing to let me see her. They knew Stoddard's wife knew nothing about her sister-in-law and figured there was no one in the family to visit her anymore. Although, Stoddard only came a couple times a year."

"What's wrong with her?" Danielle asked.

"She came down with early onset Alzheimer's after Isabella was born."

"She must have been so young," Danielle said.

"She was in her twenties when she first showed signs. Which is rare, but it does happen."

"I don't understand why they hid her away," Danielle said.

"This type of Alzheimer's is highly hereditary. There was a good chance Isabella, Stoddard or Stoddard's children might some day come down with it. That wasn't something the old man wanted the world to know."

"So they hid her from everyone," Danielle said.

"When you say it's highly hereditary—did anyone else in the family have it?" MacDonald asked.

"I suspect her mother did. When I was with Karen, I think I only saw my mother-in-law maybe three times. Karen told me her mother was a recluse. Back then, I thought her mom was a closet alcoholic, because the few times I saw her she seemed, well, out of it."

"According to the attorney, Vanya Gusarov set up KS Trust to take care of Karen's financial needs after his death. When she's gone, whatever is left goes to charity," MacDonald told them.

"Does she remember you?" Danielle asked Will.

With a sad smile, Will said, "Me? No. But Bobby, yes. She says he's coming back for her and the baby."

"What are your plans?" MacDonald asked Will.

"Initially, I planned to return to Phoenix. But I realize I can't. Not now. I need to make sure Karen is taken care of. Maybe Stoddard only stopped by twice a year, but at least it was someone from the family looking in on her. Fortunately, from what I've seen so far, the staff they hired to take care of her seems genuinely fond of her. I haven't noticed any signs of abuse or neglect."

"So you're sticking around?" Danielle asked.

"Yeah, I think so. Might be a nice change, living by the beach again, and I can keep an eye on things. I'm having my attorneys look into the possibility of getting me appointed as Karen's guardian or whatever they call it. Considering I have my own money, and I'm not after hers, and I'm the closest thing she has to a relative—she was the mother of my child—I'm hoping the courts will consider my petition. I have no desire to interfere with DCL or the charities that will ultimately inherit her estate; I just want to make sure Karen spends her remaining years as comfortable as possible."

FORTY

"What are you doing here?" Joe asked Danielle when he found her coming out of Chief MacDonald's office.

"Checking on my iPhone. It was taken into evidence after Smith attacked us."

"What have you been using for a phone?"

"I bought another one the next day."

"Those aren't cheap."

"No problem. I'm rich, remember." Danielle grinned. "Anyway, I was meaning to upgrade my phone. Figured I'd donate my old one. But it looks like I won't be getting it back anytime soon."

"Sorry about that. Hey, are you in a hurry? How about I buy you a cup of coffee." Joe nodded to the break room.

Danielle smiled. "Sure. I could always use a little extra caffeine."

"I don't suppose you heard about Samantha yet?" Joe asked as he led Danielle into the break room and showed her to a table.

"Lily's nurse? Did you guys find her?" Danielle sat down and watched as Joe poured them each a cup of coffee.

"Yeah. She admitted to taking the phone, but swears she had no idea what it was going to be used for or who had her take it."

"Are you saying some stranger just called her up and asked her to take the phone, and she did it?"

"Not exactly." Joe sat down at the table with Danielle. "Apparently, Samantha lost her last job after some pharmaceuticals went missing. There wasn't a police report; it was all handled in-house. After she was assigned to Lily's case, she received a call from a blackmailer. He threatened to go to her current employer and let them know why she really lost her last job."

"He told her to steal my phone in exchange for keeping quiet?"

"At first, he just wanted her to spy on you and Lily, let him know who was staying at Marlow House. But then he told her to take your phone and had her drop it off about a block away in some bushes. He also instructed her to keep Will away from the house the afternoon Smith showed up."

"I assume the blackmailer was Christiansen or Haston, if it was a he."

"Probably. Samantha claims she freaked after we brought her in to be interviewed. She was afraid they might kill her next, so she just took off."

"I thought she didn't know who the blackmailer was."

"I don't think she did. But she had a good idea it was someone connected to her old employer—the one who fired her."

"Who was that?"

"She was a nurse for one of the assisted care facilities owned by Dignity Care and Life."

"Ahh…that explains it. Yet it's quite a coincidence, her getting assigned to Lily's case."

"It wasn't a coincidence, according to Haston."

Danielle arched her brows. "He still talking?"

"I think he's embraced the motto, confession is good for the soul. But yeah. He admitted to pulling strings to get her assigned to Lily's case."

"I'm still trying to figure out how Darlene pulled it all off. Shooting her husband; stashing the extra Flex; meeting up with Brian."

"According to Haston, Darlene switched cars with him and Chuck right after she shot Stoddard. They were in the T-Bird. After they switched cars, Darlene went to find Brian. She knew he ate breakfast at the diner every morning. They took the Flex to Darlene's rental, planting the gun in your car on their way. They had another car waiting in the garage."

"Weren't they afraid someone would notice them switching cars? Both of those vehicles sort of stand out," Danielle asked.

"They made their switch on Beach Drive. Only a couple houses on that street, and on the stretch of road where they made the exchange, there aren't any houses, just vacant lots."

"I'm curious; did Haston make any kind of a plea deal before he started talking?"

"Nope. Waived his rights to an attorney. Christiansen, on the other hand, won't say boo without his lawyer's okay."

"If that's the case, then I guess he didn't make a plea deal. Two murders, Stoddard and Darlene, not to mention the attempt on our lives. Isn't Haston talking himself into a date with a needle?"

"I guess that's up to the courts." Joe shrugged. "Of course, Haston didn't actually kill anyone. Oh, he was an accomplice to murder, but Darlene is the one who shot Stoddard, and Chuck killed Darlene."

"Crazy." Danielle shook her head. She thought about Darlene—who would have ever imagined she was such a talented actress, capable of pulling off something like this? If it hadn't been for Joe, Danielle might very well be on trial for Stoddard's murder. Thinking about the lengths the woman went to, Danielle remembered Darlene's blue eyes. Stoddard mentioned his killer's eyes were brown. *I bet she wore brown contact lenses.*

"Danielle, Joe…" Brian greeted them. He didn't enter the room immediately, but stood at the doorway, as if contemplating if he should come in or not.

Danielle looked up from her coffee. "Morning, Officer Henderson."

"I thought you weren't coming in today," Joe asked Brian.

"I wasn't going to." Reluctantly, Brian walked all the way into the room. He went to the cupboard and grabbed a mug.

Joe turned his attention back to Danielle. "So what are you up to today?"

"I was going to go see what I can find in the way of Halloween decorations."

"Halloween?" Brian frowned. He sat down at the table with his coffee. "It's just October first. Isn't it a little early for decorations?"

"Halloween will be here before we know it. Lily and I are going to decorate Marlow House all spooky. It'll be fun."

"Marlow House would make the perfect haunted house," Brian grumbled. Joe laughed in response.

"Gee, why do you say that?" Danielle asked sweetly.

"You have to admit, some strange things seem to happen there.

THE GHOST WHO WANTED REVENGE

Sometimes I have to wonder if the place is haunted." Brian sipped his coffee.

"Don't tell me you believe in ghosts?" Danielle asked.

Joe glanced over to Danielle and noticed her mischievous grin.

"Don't be hard on Brian," Joe said seriously. "Of course he doesn't believe in ghosts. Just with all the crazy things that have happened lately, sometimes our imaginations run wild. I know mine has."

Danielle looked at Joe, her head tilting slightly to one side. "So you don't believe in ghosts?"

Joe laughed. "Yeah, right. I don't think so. No such thing as ghosts."

"So how do you think Christiansen's gun ended up on the roof?" Danielle asked.

"Well, I certainly don't think a ghost put it up there," Joe said with a chuckle. "Christiansen obviously saw the officers and panicked, threw the gun."

"Hmmm...I suppose that could happen," Danielle muttered.

"As for Marlow House being haunted, we already have one haunted house in Frederickport. We don't need two. Exceeds our quota." Joe grinned.

"We do?" Danielle glanced from Joe to Brian. Brian shrugged in response.

"The Presley house," Joe said.

"The Presley house?" Danielle frowned. "I don't know where that is."

"It's a couple blocks from yours," Brian explained. "It's been vacant for years."

"And people say it's haunted?" Danielle asked.

"Only on Halloween." Brian sipped his coffee.

"Oh, you're saying it's fixed up as a haunted house every Halloween," Danielle asked with a grin.

"No." Joe shook his head. "Some people really believe it's haunted. But they say the ghost only comes out on Halloween."

"Whose ghost is it?" Danielle asked.

"Heck if I know." Joe shrugged. "It's just a silly legend. Like I said, there are no such things as ghosts."

"Well, you know..." Danielle looked down in her cup and gently swirled the coffee around. "When I was a kid, I told my parents I could see ghosts. Of course, I'm sure you already know that."

"You were a kid." Joe patted her hand. "Kids have active imaginations."

She turned to Brian. "So is Joe right, you don't really believe in ghosts?"

About to take another sip of coffee, Brian paused and looked up into Danielle's eyes. Their gazes locked as they silently studied each other.

Finally, Brian spoke. "I really don't know what I believe anymore."

IAN TOOK Lily and Danielle to dinner at Pearl Cove that evening to celebrate the arrest of Stoddard's killers. When they returned home, Ian stayed up with Lily as the two waited for the nurse to show up for Lily's evening IV. Danielle excused herself and went up to bed. She was exhausted.

Since coming home from dinner, Danielle hadn't seen Walt. She suspected he was up in the attic with Sadie, but was too tired to investigate. Instead, she climbed into bed and fell fast asleep.

HER BED SEEMED to be moving—swaying gently from side to side. Licking her lips, she tasted salt. Breathing deeply, she could smell the ocean.

"Are you going to open your eyes or not?" Walt asked impatiently.

Danielle opened her eyes and looked around. She sat in a sailboat with Walt in the middle of a calm sea. The shore was nowhere in sight.

"Where are we?" she asked, looking down. Running her hands over her lap—over the skirt of her white lace dress—she smiled. The feminine dress reminded her of something worn in the late 1800s. Reaching up, she touched her head. She wore a straw hat, and her dark hair fell over her shoulders in curls.

"Isn't that obvious? We're sailing." Walt smiled.

Danielle noticed he wasn't wearing a suit, as was his normal attire. Instead, he dressed casually, in white linen slacks and a white linen shirt, its top few buttons undone. He also wore a straw hat.

"I've never been sailing." Danielle looked around eagerly.

"I used to go all the time when I was…well…when I was."

"I didn't know that."

"There is a lot about me you don't know, Danielle," Walt said seriously, handing her a glass of wine.

"So what is the special occasion?" She sipped the wine.

"I figured you needed some quiet time. You've been through a lot these last few months. And I couldn't think of a more peaceful place than this."

"I suppose you could have just let me sleep." Danielle grinned.

"You are sleeping," he reminded her.

"You know what I mean." Danielle sipped her wine.

"Would you rather I leave you to your own dreams?"

"My own dreams?" Danielle smiled softly and lifted her glass in a toast. "This is my own dream. One of my best."

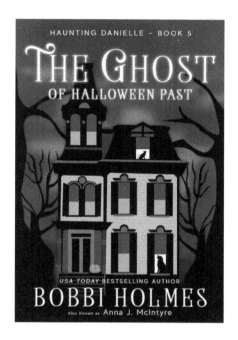

RETURN TO MARLOW HOUSE IN

THE GHOST OF HALLOWEEN PAST

HAUNTING DANIELLE, BOOK 5

Spending Halloween in a haunted house is nothing out of the ordinary for Danielle and Lily. After all, Marlow House Bed & Breakfast has its own full-time ghost. But there is another haunted house in Frederickport, Oregon. Its ghost only shows up on Halloween. Why just once a year? And how is this frightening spirit connected to all that's happened to Danielle since she arrived in town?

As Danielle tries to sort through the Halloween haunting, Sadie the golden retriever has her own issues—a mysterious black cat who seems even more adept than Sadie at communicating with spirits.

NON-FICTION BY

BOBBI ANN JOHNSON HOLMES

Havasu Palms, A Hostile Takeover
Where the Road Ends, Recipes & Remembrances
Motherhood, a book of poetry
The Story of the Christmas Village

BOOKS BY ANNA J. MCINTYRE

COULSON FAMILY SAGA

Coulson's Wife
Coulson's Crucible
Coulson's Lessons
Coulson's Secret
Coulson's Reckoning

UNLOCKED 🔒 HEARTS

Sundered Hearts
After Sundown
While Snowbound
Sugar Rush

CPSIA information can be obtained
at www.ICGtesting.com
Printed in the USA
LVHW040731130621
690102LV00002B/402